THE ALPHA'S SON

THE ALPHA'S SON

Penny Jessup

Tiny Ghost Press

*actual size

Cover Art by: Kayleigh Fine
Title Font: Paula Painmar

For my mate. Every day is a festival with you...xxx

May the Moon Gods light the path between souls...

BONEHEAD

"Hold the door!" I yell, but this couple is too busy making out to notice me.

The doors of the 7 are closing fast and I need to be on that train. I'm running late, of course.

"Hey!" I shout... Still nothing.

With less than a second to spare I jump through the shrinking gap, slipping inside right at the last moment. The subway train lurches forward before I've even found my balance.

"Thanks," I mutter, but the couple doesn't hear me.

They're preoccupied, going at it like they're the only people in the world. Like, full-on lip-smacking, nausea-inducing tonsil hockey.

Gross.

From their scents I know they're human, but seriously, they're making out like a pair of freshly mated werewolves.

Like, totally get a room!

It's only two stops from Grand Central to Times Square, but after an hour on a stuffy train from Stony Point, the last thing I want is to watch two hipsters eat each other's faces off. And to top it all off I'm super late to meet Katie.

I lean against a subway map, tapping my foot and

trying to distract myself by scrolling my fave TikToker's feed. But it's no use. I can hear their tongues slapping over my headphones.

And I thought wolves were mate-obsessed.

These humans would give an Elite Pack wolf couple a run for their money.

I know it's a cliché. *I'm not like the other werewolves.*

But for me, sketching boulders in Central Park is way more appealing than picking out wedding china.

If only every other wolf in my pack felt the same way. If only these lovebirds did.

We pull into Forty-Second and Bryant Park and I stare at the couple, hoping this is their stop.

Passengers of the love train, this service terminates here!

They're too neck-deep to even look up.

The train takes off again, rolling out of the station, and I glance at the time.

Crap. I was supposed to meet Katie on the red steps in Times Square at two. I'm nearly a whole hour late and my excuse is totally lame. *Why can I never wake up before midday on the weekend?*

Mom always says I'm going to sleep my life away. I always tell her if that means I don't have to bother finding a mate I don't care.

By the time we pull in at Forty-Second and Times Square, I'm bouncing out of my sneakers, ready to get off this stinking train.

The doors slide open, and I take off like lightning. *Get me away from that ridiculous PDA!*

I dodge and weave through the crowds on the platform, then bound up the steps two at a time, heading for the exit.

This isn't the first time I've overslept and kept Katie waiting. We've been besties since we were pups, so she's pretty used to the mess that is my life. But she's also my favorite person in the universe and I hate letting her down.

The blazing summer sun hits my face when I finally

emerge at street level. Outside the station, the streets of Manhattan are packed, as usual. For a second I'm overwhelmed by the sounds of the traffic and the smells of the pretzel wagons.

Heightened wolf senses can be a blessing. Like when you're trying to have some alone time in your room, but it's laundry day and Mom is on the way to empty your hamper. You can usually make out the sound of her approaching with enough time to slam your laptop shut and clutch onto a pillow. Usually.

But sometimes, especially in the city, the world can seem like a lot. Want to know what three-day-old hot-dog water smells like? Ask a New York wolf.

I pause for a second to readjust.

I close my eyes and take a deep breath. Eventually, the honking of car horns, the sirens, the constant chatter from all around become a dull hum in the back of my mind.

Finally, I feel ready. I open my eyes.

I squint through the glare and take off down Forty-Third Street. If I'm fast I'm only a minute away.

My phone is buzzing in my pocket so I try to pull it out without losing any pace. Katie has sent me a string of texts.

Where are you?

Did you oversleep again???

Maaaaaaaaaaaaaaaaaax?????

I continue running, trying to type a panicked reply when—

"Oomph!"

I hit what feels like a brick wall and stumble backward. My feet catch on each other and, in spectacular fashion, I trip, toppling toward the pavement. My phone slips from my hand and shatters right as my ass hits the ground.

Pain radiates through my hips and spine as I squint up at the thing I ran into...only it's not a thing. It's a person. A guy.

"Watch where you're going, bonehead."

3

"I'm... I'm sorry," I say, grimacing.

The sun is backlighting the guy, which makes it hard to see his face. But he's tall, wearing a black blazer with a white T-shirt underneath, black skinny jeans, and combat boots. He doesn't sound that much older than me.

"You should be more careful."

"I said sorry."

This dude is starting to annoy me. He doesn't even offer to help as I collect the pieces of my smashed-up phone. The least he could do is apologize too.

"Here," the guy says and sticks out his hand to help me up.

I give him a dirty side-eye but accept his offer.

The moment we touch, time slows down, seconds stretch into eternities. Birds hang frozen in midair. The pedestrian-clogged sidewalks are a blur.

The guy pulls me to my feet like I weigh practically nothing. I stand face-to-face with him, and his features come into view. My breath catches in my throat.

His eyes are piercing emerald green, offset by dark, angular brows. His face is narrow and symmetrical, and black hair swoops across his forehead, framing his devastatingly handsome features. He has cheekbones that could cut steel and his lips are the perfect shade of peach...

He looks like a damn Abercrombie model.

And his scent... His scent hits me like a tidal wave.

My olfactory senses are overwhelmed by his intoxicating mix of mint, lemon, and something else... Is that cherry blossom?

The backs of my knees are tingling, my legs wobbling like pudding in a cup. I've never felt this way before. What is this? This feeling...what is it?

Is it because of...of *him*?

"You okay, bonehead?"

Suddenly, the world snaps back into real time. People push past us, the traffic roars like the ocean, the sun is bright and blaring.

And this dick just called me a bonehead! For the

second time!

"Don't call me *bonehead*."

"Why not...bonehead?"

"You broke my phone!"

"You ran into me."

"Doesn't seem like I did too much damage. I'm the one who ended up on my ass."

Whoever this jerk thinks he is, it doesn't give him the right to speak to anyone like that—no matter how clumsy they are.

He looks like he's about to say something else when he's distracted by a gust of wind blowing up through the grates from the subway.

A dark, questioning look colors his expression.

For a moment we stand silently and he stares daggers in my direction. And then without saying another word he steps past me, as if I'm not even there, and continues walking.

"Hey, you jerk! You can't just walk away! What about my phone?"

"Whatever," he says, without turning back.

"Hey wait!"

He doesn't wait and he doesn't respond either.

He keeps walking.

When he finally disappears into the crowd, it dawns on me.

His scent... That weird feeling. Something else... Was he...a werewolf?

"Ouch." A broken piece of glass pricks the skin on my palm—I was clenching my fist harder than I thought—and my smashed-up phone reminds me...

"Katie!"

The longer I stand here the later I become.

Down the street, I can't even see the ridiculously good-looking—possibly a werewolf—but totally a jerk anymore.

I turn and start running again.

Who was that guy? Why does he think he can act like such an asshole!?

And why has he made me feel all...tingly?

THE TROUBLE WITH MATES

"There you are!" Katie says when she spots me huffing as I make my way up the red stairs.

I can tell my cheeks are flushed—maybe from the running, but maybe from my encounter with an annoyingly good-looking jerk—and I'm super out of breath.

My bestie, on the other hand, is radiant. The wind catches in her corn-blonde hair as she turns and smiles. Her pale face breaks into a broad grin when she sees me.

At least she doesn't look angry.

"Took you long enough," she says when I reach her.

I bend over my knees, spluttering. "Sorry...I'm...always late..."

"It's fine," she says, grinning cheekily.

"No really," I say, finally able to speak like a normal person. "I'm such a lame-ass. I shouldn't have kept you waiting."

"I haven't been waiting. I knew you'd be late so I purposefully told you to show up an hour earlier than I did."

My jaw drops open. "That's so sneaky!"

"You call it sneaky, I call it clever."

I didn't think Katie could be this devious.

"Come on."

At about an eleven on the smug meter, Katie links her arm through mine and leads me back down the steps.

"How's the new house?" I ask.

Up until two months ago, Katie lived down the street from me and my parents. After her parents got divorced, she and her mother moved to a new place in Queens.

"It's nearly ready for visitors," she says.

Katie's mom could only afford a fixer-upper and she asked Katie not to invite friends over before it was fixed up.

"Good, I'm dying to see it."

"You're just dying for some of my mom's spaghetti and meatballs."

"That too!"

We laugh and make our way west toward Shake Shack, our favorite restaurant in Midtown. And downtown. And, well...anywhere.

"I sent you a bunch of texts before you got here," Katie says. "Why weren't you texting me back?"

"Oh, my Moon Gods! I almost forgot to say...this obnoxiously rude guy bumped into me and I dropped my phone."

"What happened?"

"It completely smashed!"

"Not with the phone, with the guy." She slaps my arm.

For some reason, my cheeks start burning up.

Why does my heart start hammering like an overly caffeinated woodpecker when I think about him?

"He was just some dude with bad manners," I grunt. *Bad manners and amazing hair.*

We arrive at the restaurant and join the line to order. Katie and I have been coming here since we were kids, and we always get the same thing.

It's a ShackMeister with a banana milkshake for me and a Shroom Burger with a chocolate shake for Katie. Both with fries, obviously.

"How much time have we got?" I ask, sliding into a

plastic green seat. "If that guy hadn't wrecked my phone I could check for myself."

"We've still got hours before the show. Don't worry I won't let you be late to see Aisha Miller."

Today is a big day for Katie and me. We have tickets to see our favorite contemporary ballet dancer, starring in a new piece by this big-deal choreographer from Paris.

"We better not be," I say. "I still haven't finished paying my parents back for the tickets."

"Neither."

Katie takes a long sip of her shake. She and I took ballet classes together when we were five but I kept tripping over my own feet and had to quit. She stuck with it a lot longer than I did. I still enjoy ballet, just as a spectator.

"I'll never get over how a wolf from the Elite Pack somehow became one of the best dancers in New York," Katie says.

"I know. I wonder how the alpha feels about that."

It's a rarity for a wolf from a pack to have a career that isn't directly tied back to the pack in some way.

Aisha is different. She got out. That's part of why I idolize her so much.

"I don't care what the alpha thinks," Katie says, wiping the corner of her mouth with a napkin. "I'm just glad we're *finally* going to see her in person."

"Same! Seriously, I was starting to get scared we'd be in a home for elderly wolves before we got to see her."

After we scarf down our burgers and shakes, we head to Central Park. By the time we've wandered off the main path and under a cluster of oak trees the summer heat has me sweating and my shirt is sticking to my back in an unpleasant way.

"That looks like a nice shady spot?" I say, pointing to a patch of grass.

We sit and I pull out my sketch pad from my backpack. Surveying the area for a suitable subject, I pick an interesting cloud formation and begin tracing the outline while Katie rests her head in my lap.

"Are you excited?" she asks.

"About what?"

"About the blue moon that's coming up in a few weeks," she says as if it should have been obvious.

"Ugh, my mother hasn't stopped talking about it."

"Have you received your invitation for the festival yet?"

"Not yet," I say. "Thank the Moon Gods."

Suddenly, Katie sits up and glares at me. "Don't be such a lame-ass."

I stop drawing. "I can't help it if I'm just not that interested."

"The Blue Moon Festival is a big deal," she says. "It only comes around every two or three years."

The Blue Moon Festival is this bizarre tradition our pack has. Every blue moon, the unmated wolves from the pack go to the woods to find their soulmates.

It's mega lame.

"Just think, in a few weeks we could have found our mates!" Katie says, her eyes so wide and optimistic she looks like an anime character.

"Don't even joke about that."

"It's a sacred ritual, you shouldn't be so blasé."

"It isn't sacred," I say, rolling my eyes. "It's scientific. The full moon makes our wolf hormones go crazy. The blue moon is an extra full moon in the space of a month. So of course, we all go extra berserk. The festival is just a summer camp for randy wolves."

"You don't believe that," Katie says.

"It's all about probability. With all those amped-up wolves in one place, of course some people will find their mates."

"The Blue Moon Festival is an important milestone in a young wolf's life."

I scoff and lean back on my elbows. "You sound like a school counselor."

"I don't care. The festival is important." Katie crosses her arms and makes a point of not looking at me.

"I'm sorry," I say. "I don't mean to be a dick. I know it means a lot to you."

She pulls at the grass. "I'm just excited about us going

to our first festival together. You know, it's not like you can avoid it forever."

As much as I hate to admit it, Katie's right. Every wolf in our pack who is over sixteen and unmated is supposed to receive an invitation to the festival. Attendance isn't compulsory but it is expected. With a mate-crazy best friend and lovesick parents who've devoted their lives to the pack, I don't have much of a say in the matter.

"You've had your invitation then?" I ask.

"Not yet," she says, tossing a few blades into the air. "They better not have forgotten us. My mother would have words for Alpha Jericho."

I can't help but laugh at the thought of Katie's mom going toe to toe with our alpha. It would be like a Chihuahua taking on a pit bull.

"I bet she would."

"Wouldn't it be weird if we ended up being mates?" Katie says, laughing awkwardly.

"Yeah, really weird. We've been friends forever."

"Yeah...weird..." Katie trails off.

"Hey." I nudge her foot with my elbow. "Don't worry. You're going to get your invitation."

"Sure," she says.

"They can lose mine in the mail though."

"You really don't care about finding a mate?"

Katie doesn't usually press this hard. She knows this is my least favorite topic of conversation. So why is she acting super weird today?

"Do you think Aisha Miller became the best dancer on the planet by obsessing about finding a mate?" I ask.

Katie shrugs.

"I want to be like her one day. I want to draw and travel. Not be tied down."

"Who says you can't have a mate and do all that?"

"My parents got mated at their first festival; they've never even left New York. Seriously, the only thing more terrifying to me than spiders would be following in their footsteps. And you know how much I hate spiders."

"You *really* hate spiders."

Katie's shoulders have slumped forward and her optimistic expression has disappeared. I hate myself for making her feel like shit. Especially when we're on the cusp of having the best night of our lives. So I sit up and take her hand.

"I know all this mate stuff means a lot to you. I promise when we get our invitations we're going to go to that dumb festival together and we're going to have an amazing time."

"You promise?" she asks.

"Pinkie swear."

She smiles widely and takes a deep breath.

"I bet you won't think it's dumb when we're an hour into the Mating Run and you're surrounded by a bunch of sexy, naked she-wolves."

"Ha! Whatever!"

She shoves me playfully and I topple over onto my side. Katie plops down beside me and we both lie there giggling until it's time to leave.

It takes us about twenty minutes to walk into Midtown. The theater is in this sleek modern dance center just off Broadway.

The foyer is swarming with too-cool, artsy New York types. Everywhere I look there's a black turtleneck, a bold lip, and a severe haircut.

Katie collects our tickets at the box office, and I grab us a couple of sodas from the bar. We don't have long until the show is supposed to start so once we have everything we head inside.

The auditorium fills up quickly.

"It's time," Katie says, nudging me.

We exchange manic, excited grins. It takes all of my willpower not to squeal like a schoolgirl.

Then just before the show is about to start, a strange sensation washes over me. My body tenses and a low growl rolls in my throat.

Among the other smells wafting through the theater, I catch a whiff of a scent I recognize.

Mint, citrus, and...cherry blossom.

I look up to one of the private boxes and see...him!

The potential werewolf I bumped into earlier is being shown to his seat.

The asshole who called me *bonehead* and didn't care that I'd fallen on my ass, who made me feel like there was a herd of butterflies freaking out in my stomach...

...is here in the theater, in a private freaking box no less!

Who is he?

The lights dim slowly. The show is about to start but I can't take my eyes off him.

Just as the curtain rises, he turns, as if he could sense me watching him. Our eyes meet in the darkness.

The jerk is staring straight at me!

AT THE BALLET

I'm locked in a staring contest with the jerk in the private box.

He's staring at me like I'm a mangy cat that's crawled in off the street.

Why is he looking at me like that? All angry brows and confusion.

Excuse me for breathing!

I want to tear my eyes away but for some reason, I can't. My palms grow clammy. My heart thuds in my chest.

And then the music starts.

Lights rise on the stage and for a second I'm distracted. I glance at the dancers emerging from the wings and twisting about in the space, moving with strength and speed.

When I look back the boy is gone. He and his stern expression are nowhere to be seen. All that's left in the private box is a vacant seat.

"What are you staring at?" Katie whispers. "It's started. Oh, look! There she is!"

Aisha Miller has made her entrance and is gracefully moving toward center stage. The audience lets out a collective gasp as she performs a spectacular leap and lands without so much as a dull thud. It's impossible not to watch her in awe.

Her dark hair is tied back but, unlike the other dancers with their tight ballet buns, Aisha's cascades down her exposed back in an exquisitely curly ponytail.

She is wearing a pink dance costume, with wispy trails of sheer fabric flowing to her feet. The color contrasts perfectly with her copper skin. Her arms are slender, and her legs look strong.

As the music crescendos she spins on one leg, and I'm completely mesmerized. The way she moves. So in sync with the music. It's enough to make you forget where you are, to forget everything.

The other dancers swarm around her but I barely notice them. It's all about Aisha.

"She's gorgeous," Katie whispers and I nod.

There's no denying she's a star. But even more than that she represents something to me that I didn't know was possible.

Most wolves think the arts are a human thing. Not something to take seriously and not something that can become a proper career. But Aisha is living, breathing proof that you don't have to be like the rest of the pack. You can be different.

"This is the best thing I've ever seen," I whisper back in Katie's ear.

The rest of the show passes like a dream. Aisha's power and presence only grow throughout the evening.

Concert over, the cast takes their bows. I spring to my feet, clapping my hands like a nutcase, hollering like I'm at a BTS concert.

Aisha is the last to bow. She comes forward from the back of the stage as the other dancers separate to let her through. She curtsies and blows kisses as the audience cheers.

I notice Aisha glance to her left. Up to the empty box where the jerk was sitting earlier. A flash of disappointment crosses her face when she finds no one there.

Does she know that guy? Why would he just leave if she

was expecting him to be there?

A bald guy in the front row hands Aisha a massive bouquet of flowers, and she gets down on her knees to give him an equally massive kiss on the cheek. Is that her boyfriend? I try to sniff out his scent but can't.

Weird. I'm usually pretty good at picking up other wolves.

Eventually, the curtain is lowered and the house lights are raised. I turn to Katie, who is properly crying, and give her a big hug. Tonight is a night we will remember for a long, long time.

And for me, it's not just because of the ballet.

When I finally get home, I'm exhausted. Thankfully, my dad picked me up from the station and drove me the rest of the way.

The TV is on in the living room, and I float in like I'm drifting on a cloud.

"How was the ballet?" Mom asks without looking away from some show about dog grooming.

"Incredible."

"A letter came for you."

"Uh-huh..."

I barely register what she's just said, I'm in such a happy, delirious state that I continue wafting through the house, up the stairs, and into my room.

I flop back onto my bed and fall right to sleep.

When I wake up, I'm struck with an intense urge to do some drawing. So, I quickly jump in the shower, then brush my teeth. Dad has made a big deal about fang health since I was a pup.

With a towel wrapped around my waist and my toothbrush sticking out of my mouth, I stand in front of the mirror and take a good look at myself.

I'm pale, skinny, and a little short for my age. About average for a human but most sixteen-year-old wolves have muscles growing on top of their muscles by now. My hair is a sandy blond mess that I can never seem to tame. My eyes are wide and brown and there's a mole on my left cheek right under my eye.

Suddenly, the image of that guy staring at me flashes into my brain, like he's glaring at me through the mirror, looking at me with his mean, judgmental face.

"I'm not a bonehead," I mumble, spitting toothpaste and making little dots on the mirror. "What an asshole!"

When I'm finally dressed I grab my backpack and a fresh pencil and head downstairs.

"I made toast," Mom says as I pass through the kitchen—snatching a piece of cold, burnt bread, and sticking it in my mouth—before heading out the back door.

"What about your letter?!" she calls but the door is already swinging shut behind me.

Our house isn't big but it backs onto a large piece of woodland. Wolves this close to the city usually live near some kind of big green space so that we can run when the moon is fuller and we have extra wolfy energy.

I'm thankful for the woods. Being a teen means overactive hormones and being a wolf means sometimes needing to shift to let out all those pent-up emotions. I'm also big into drawing nature and I get a lot of my inspiration from this forest.

Today, though, I'm inspired by one thing only and that is Aisha Miller.

I can't get her dance moves out of my head.

I head down to the river and find a big rock to sit on. I come to this spot a lot. It's so quiet. All you can hear is the wind in the trees and the water splashing on the rocks.

I take out my pad and a pencil and I start to sketch. At first I try to draw Aisha mid-pirouette but a fish darting about in the river distracts me. For a second I study the water. There's a similarity between the way Aisha moves and the way the water spirals, so I add it into my drawing, mixing the swirl of the current with the curving of her limbs, using the wisps of plant life beneath the surface to represent her flowing outfit.

An hour or so must pass but I keep turning the page and starting new sketches, finding new details in the stream to focus on.

At some point, I completely lose myself in my process and when I shake myself back to reality I look down at my pad and I'm shocked to see what I've drawn there.

It's as if he's floating in the river... I've somehow drawn a perfect likeness of the guy from the city. His stern eyes stare back at me from the page, full of disdain. My mind must have wandered, but why was it wandering to him?

I slam the book shut, shove it in my bag, and make a mental note to toss him in the recycling.

Why is he haunting my inner thoughts like this?

I wanted to draw nature and think about Aisha's dancing, not *him*. I want to forget ever having run into him.

With a huff, I swing my bag over my shoulder, I'm not doing any more drawing today and anyway, it's time to head home. My stomach is starting to grumble.

It's a Sunday and that usually means Dad will be making steak sandwiches. His steak is kind of famous among the neighborhood wolves.

When I get back to the yard I smirk to see I was right. Dad is standing at the barbecue in an apron. He sees me coming and smiles, waving his tongs at me.

I raise my eyebrows and wave back.

The back door slams behind me, and I drop my bag and head into the living room.

"Hey, stop avoiding me," Mom says, coming down the stairs, holding that envelope. "Did you see Dad's making steak sandwiches? Yummo!"

I chuckle. My mom is a big goof but I love her for it.

"Here," she says, slapping the envelope onto my chest. "This came for you. I think you'll want to open it."

I take the envelope from her and she swans off toward the kitchen. When she mentioned the letter before I didn't pay much attention, but now that I'm holding it my stomach is suddenly all the way in my throat.

My address is written in elaborate cursive, with golden ink, and on the back, the letter is stamped with the royal seal of the alpha.

I know what this is.

I swallow once, gulping, and then tear open the letter.

For the attention of Sir Maximilian Xavier Remus,

You are cordially invited to attend the BLUE MOON FESTIVAL, to be held this August from the 4th and continuing for four nights.

The FESTIVAL is a sacred rite of passage for all unmated wolves in our illustrious pack and we are delighted to once again host the event at the Pack Retreat upstate in Rochester, New York.

As usual, the blue moon will be at its fullest on the third night of the festival at which point you will be requested to take part in the traditional Mating Run. This is an excellent chance for you to find your mate and contribute to the propagation of our kind.

We look forward to having you there and wish you the best of luck with finding your mate.

May the Moon Gods light the path between souls.

On behalf of Alpha Jericho,
Sincerest regards from the Pack Secretary,
Tobias Volk

"So, is it your festival invitation?" Mom says, poking her head back through the doorway.

"Yep," I say, sighing.

"I knew it!" Mom's eyes light up and I cringe as she squeals. "Aren't you excited?"

"Uh-huh," I lie.

"Wait till I tell your father! Marvin!"

Mom runs off to tell Dad, and I stare at the invitation in my hands.

This retreat could define the rest of my life and that prospect terrifies me. But I guess there's no avoiding it now.

The scent of Dad's steak sandwiches wafts in through the windows. It should set my mouth watering but, instead, I think I'm going to hurl.

THE FESTIVAL BEGINS

"You two must be excited," Mom says in a high-pitched voice, peering at Katie and me in the rearview mirror.

It feels like we've been driving for days, when in fact it has only been a few hours. Katie stayed over last night so that we could make an early start.

From my house to the Pack Retreat upstate it takes about four and a half hours. That's four and a half hours of my life I've had to spend with Mom acting like a giddy preteen, and four and a half hours I'll never get back.

Outside the window all I can see is forest. Trees whip by as we speed toward the festival.

"We are, Mrs. Remus," Katie says, elbowing my ribs.

"I remember my first festival," Mom says. "I found the whole thing quite overwhelming at the time. And I had a terrible problem with leeches. I remember we all came back from a hike and I was covered in the slimy little suckers!"

"Mom, gross."

"Then I met your father and he showed me how to use salt to get them off and, well, things only got more wild from there..."

"Double gross!"

My parents have always been completely head-over-heels, sappily, gushingly in love. Mom in particular can never pass up an opportunity to embarrass me with her not-safe-for-children mushiness.

"Don't be such a prude," she says, swiping an arm behind her and gently slapping my knee. "The festival is the chance for you kids to find your mates under the best circumstances. The blue moon in a few days gets rid of so much hassle. All that sniffing and dancing around each other. There's no need for that with the blue moon. You'll know right away."

I roll my eyes and continue staring at the passing woodland, wishing we could just turn back.

"And who knows," Mom continues. "You might find your mate right under your nose."

I glance sideways at her reflection in the mirror and catch her looking from me to Katie, smiling suggestively. She's always thought the two of us might end up being mates. Not that I would mind being mated to Katie, she is my best friend after all. But I've just never thought about her in a romantic sense. She's been my adventure buddy since we were little kids and my fiercest ally as an abnormal teenager. We have an amazing time together and I love her, just...more like a sister.

Finally, Mom notices my pointed stare, begging her to stop. She giggles then looks back at the road.

"How did Mr. Remus make you feel when you first met?" Katie asks. Why is she encouraging this?

"Are you asking how I knew he was my mate?" Mom asks.

"I"—Katie falters, her pale cheeks turning pink—"I guess."

My mom tilts her head to the side and thinks about the question, drumming her fingers on the steering wheel.

"Well...it's a bit like skydiving, like you're falling but you're not afraid."

"Mom, neither of us have been skydiving," I say.

She laughs. "No, I guess you haven't. In that case...it's a bit like the feeling you get when you're hungry, only you don't know what you want. You keep looking in the refrigerator and nothing feels like it's going to hit the spot. Then you remember the jar of pickles at the back of the top shelf in the pantry and suddenly you know for sure. Pickles! That's what I want. That's the snack for me."

Mom goes quiet, and there's a strange, happy-yet-faraway look in her eyes.

I glance at Katie and even she is getting a little weirded out by my mom's trancelike state.

"You okay, Mom?"

She blinks a couple of times and suddenly she's back in the car. She readjusts the steering wheel and laughs a little at herself.

"Sorry, I forgot what I was doing there for a second."

"Well, keep your eyes on the road, please," I say. "We'd like to make it to the festival in one piece."

I stare back out the window as we take a left down a long tree-lined street. We must be getting close.

I gulp and take a breath. My mom nearly drove us off the road thinking about mates. It's obvious this whole situation is dangerous.

After about twenty minutes a row of tall, skinny flags appear, lining the path, fluttering in the breeze. They have the pack's insignia printed in the middle and alternate colors from green to yellow to purple. The colors of the Elite Pack.

Eventually, the path leads to an open field, where hundreds of cars are parked. Mom pulls into an empty spot and we get out, grab our bags from the trunk, and strap them on our backs.

"Well, this is where I have to leave you," Mom says, looking like she's about to cry. "The retreat is just up there past those trees, you'll see it when you reach the top of that rise. Good luck, kids!"

Houston, we have liftoff! Mom starts crying as she pulls us both in for a massive hug.

"You're going to have such a nice time."

When we can finally pry ourselves away from my overzealous mother, she takes my face in her hands and kisses my cheek.

"I love you, kiddo. I hope the next few days make you happy."

I roll my eyes but even I can't help getting a little choked up. I'm not completely heartless.

"Love you too, Mom."

After a few too many goodbyes and one last panicked search for a potentially forgotten toothbrush, Katie and I leave my mother and make our way to the top of the hill.

"Gosh, there's so many people here," Katie says, looking astounded at all the cars and the other wolves all struggling with giant packs.

"Who knows, our mates could be out there."

"Ha, yeah," I say.

We reach the trees my mother mentioned. Below us on the opposite side of the hill sits the retreat. It's mega.

At the base of the hill is a giant cabin; it's woodsy and rustic but is probably the size of freaking Madison Square Garden. Behind the main cabin there are at least a hundred smaller cabins, and behind them is a green grass field the size of a football stadium. To the right of the retreat is the shore of the lake and a boat shed. Deep blue-green water reflects the trees and mountains that surround it. Lining the perimeter of the camp is the edge of a forest, which stretches for as far as I can see, rising into the foot of the mountains.

For a moment Katie and I stand there, awestruck.

"This is wild," she says.

I'm truly gobsmacked. After all the years of hearing about the retreat, I'd assumed it was some run-down, *Friday the 13th* campsite but this is...next level.

"Shall we?" Katie says and I nod again.

We take off running down the hill.

When we reach a gravel-covered area out front of the main cabin I'm suddenly overwhelmed by just how many other wolves there are.

"Everyone is so...so..." Katie stammers, unable to finish her sentence.

"Hot," I say, knowing exactly what she was going to say. Wolves are usually pretty gifted in the looks department, what with being all preternaturally strong and all. But seeing this collection of hotties en masse is kind of...intimidating.

The girls look like models who've stumbled out of the pages of a sportswear catalog and the guys all look like celebrity personal trainers.

With all these beefcakes around, the chance of someone wanting to be my mate is negligible. Maybe I can get through the weekend swimming, eating s'mores, and not having to worry about my eternal fate.

"Have you guys got your invitations?" a squeaky voice behind us asks.

Katie and I turn to find a short dark-haired girl holding a clipboard and staring at us with a toothy grin that's so wide I'm worried she's about to strain a muscle.

"Hi," I say.

"May I see your invitations?" she asks again.

"Oh yeah, sure."

I shoved my invitation somewhere in my pack on the way out of the house and I've completely forgotten where I put it. Flustered, I toss my bag onto the gravel and start searching all the outside pockets before digging into the main compartment.

"Here," Katie says, having produced her still-crisp invitation from a plastic wallet she's attached to the zipper of her pack. "Katie Andrews."

Katie sticks out her hand and the girl with the clipboard reciprocates.

"Eleanor Peng," she says, shaking Katie's hand too vigorously. "Pleasure to meet you. I'm one of the festival volunteers and I'm in charge of distributing cabin assignments to new arrivals. Aren't you just pumped for the festival? I know I am!"

Eleanor laughs awkwardly as I continue to search in my pack.

"We're both really excited," Katie says, placating the crazed camp attendant.

"And imagine who you could end up being mated to!"

"It could be literally anyone," Katie says, doing her best

to play along, although even she's struggling to match Eleanor's enthusiasm.

"Yes but this year it could be someone particularly special." Eleanor leans toward Katie with a conspiratorial glint in her eye. "This year will be the first time Jasper Apollo will be here."

I look up from my frantic searching.

Jasper Apollo. I know the name. Of course I do. Jasper is the son of Jericho, our alpha. He's next in line to lead the pack.

For some reason the sound of his name sends a strange warm sensation to my toes and the tips of my fingers.

"Just think," Eleanor continues. "You could arrive here today a complete nobody and wind up mated to the alpha's son!"

She bursts into her distinctive awkward cackle again and I'm shaken from my reverie. I go back to searching my bag.

Finally, I find my crumpled-up invitation and hand it to Eleanor.

"Fantastic," she says, having a meltdown behind her eyes.

"Sorry, it...got squashed."

"No matter," she says, before unleashing another hyena-like outburst. She glances from the invitations to her clipboard and back again.

"Katie you're in cabin B14 and Max you'll be in cabin C27."

"Oh, I thought we'd be in the same cabin," Katie says, disappointed.

"The cabins are separated by gender I'm afraid," Eleanor says.

"Very binary," I mumble so only Katie can hear.

"With all the extra energy from the blue moon," Eleanor continues, oblivious, "we don't want to encourage any wolves to jump the gun before the Mating Run."

"Oh, no of course not," Katie says, ignoring me.

Eleanor hands Katie back her invitation, and she accepts it, blushing a little.

"Well, have an amazing festival. There will be drinks at the Alpha's Lodge at six, followed by dinner and a welcome soiree. That gives you a couple hours to get settled in. Me and the other volunteers will be here all festival in case you need anything."

Something tells me the other volunteers probably aren't taking this quite as seriously as Eleanor.

"May the Moon Gods light the path between souls!"

Eleanor waves manically before crossing the courtyard to accost another set of new arrivals.

I smile at Katie who shrugs at me and smiles in return.

"I guess we should find our bunks," I say. "Meet you back here in a couple of hours?"

"Oh, yeah, sure," Katie says.

It takes a few minutes of hopeless wandering before I find my home for the next few nights. My cabin is toward the back of the configuration and right next to the woods. Inside there are four sets of bunk beds. A couple already have bags on them, which I assume means they're taken. I head for the bunk closest to the window and toss my pack onto the top bed.

Hoisting myself up, I immediately notice the view outside the window. The woods and the lake are framed perfectly by the cracked window frame, with the mountains in the distance behind them. It's breathtaking. I'm suddenly really glad I brought my sketch pad with me. If nothing else I can probably get some great drawings out of this weekend.

A couple of bros enter the cabin laughing and slapping each other on the back.

"Hey man! Name's Todd," one says. "Looks like we're going to be roomies!"

I roll over and sit up. Todd is a big, big guy with pale skin, orange freckles, and cropped ginger hair. He's muscly but in that soft kind of way.

"Hi," I say, in a higher pitch than I intend.

"This dweeb here is Simon," Todd says, whacking his friend on the back.

"What's up?" Simon says. Todd's friend is almost his polar opposite. He's still got muscles but he's much leaner, with black hair and umber skin.

"Hope you don't mind snorers," Todd says, laughing at his friend's expense.

"You dick, I don't snore," Simon retorts. "Hey, I call top bunk!"

"No way man, I called it in the car!"

"Doesn't count unless you're in the room, my man."

Instantly they forget I'm here, as they start wrestling, trying to claim the top bunk opposite mine.

I lie back and sigh. "It's only four nights."

But I wish I didn't have to share a cabin with a bunch of bros. I wish I could just be in a cabin with Katie and no one else. And I wish there wasn't all this pressure to find a mate. Everyone seems so excited to be here. And with the news that Jasper Apollo is coming, I'm sure that excitement will be dialed up to an eleven.

I dig into my pack and pull out my sketchbook before hopping down off my bunk. I desperately need some air and I don't think Beavis and Butt-Head will even register me leaving.

I head from the cabin straight into the woods.

"You just have to make it through four nights."

THE ALPHA'S SON ARRIVES

"Ouch!"

I slap at another mosquito flying around my head and end up whacking myself in the neck.

There are like, a million of the little bloodsuckers out in the woods. I've only been walking for ten minutes and I'm already dotted with bites.

The woods themselves are lush and green. The ceiling-like tree canopy provides a shady, damp environment for moss and fungi to thrive. Big, gnarly roots rise from the soil, curling back around on themselves like giant snakes. The trees are as tall as skyscrapers, with vines draped around them like lights on a Christmas tree. The landscape is peppered with boulders more and more as I head toward the base of the mountains.

I have a bit of time before I'm supposed to meet Katie, and I'd much rather spend it out here drawing than back in my cabin with my wrestling roommates.

Up ahead is a boulder tall enough and dry enough to sit on. I have to scramble a little to reach the top, but once I'm there I try to get comfy. With my trusty pencil in hand,

I start to sketch the landscape.

A breeze drifts through the forest, rustling the leaves and mixing with the buzz of insects and the chirping of birds. I let myself get lost in my drawing. And then...

SNAP!

A loud crack, like a branch being stepped on, startles me. I spin to see where the sound came from but turn too quickly and lose my balance. Before I know it I'm falling backward.

With a strange panicked noise, I squelch-land in a puddle of mud. I lie there and wish the earth would swallow me whole.

Then I hear laughter.

"So graceful, bonehead," a voice says—a voice that sends shivers of anger rippling through my veins.

I look up and find his stupid face staring down at me. The jerk from the city. Is he here for the festival?

So he's a wolf after all! I knew it! That's why he sent my senses tingling.

I stand and do my best to wipe some of the mud off my chin.

"You don't have to be a dick, you know," I say. "You could have helped me up instead of laughing."

The jerk stops chuckling. "Watching you struggle is much more enjoyable."

What an asshole!

"You know I only fell because you surprised me. What are you doing sneaking about out here anyway? Shouldn't you be mingling with all the other brain-dead campers?"

"I could ask you the same thing."

"I needed some air," I say, wiping more of the mud off my face. "And privacy. What's your excuse? Are you some kind of asshole stalker?"

The jerk raises an eyebrow.

"I was just minding my own business, when you started flailing about like a ridiculous chicken."

Again, he snickers and my face starts to burn.

"Stop laughing!"

"I'm sorry," he says, about as genuinely as a gas station greeting card. "It's just...you looked really funny and"—he sniffs the air and scrunches up his face—"you totally stink."

"What?! I..." I sniff at my clothes and realize he's right. The mud pit I fell into was more than rank. And I'm coated in the sludge.

"This is your fault!" I shout.

"You'll never find a mate smelling like that," he says. "There are showers back by the cabins. You should probably think about taking one."

"You're such an asshole!"

"Whatever," he says, shrugging. "See you around, bonehead."

Without another thought he saunters away, leaving me dripping mud onto my trainers.

"You still owe me a phone!"

"May the Moon Gods light the path between souls," he calls out sarcastically, without turning back.

What a completely colossal asshole! There is nothing else for me to do except grab my sketchbook—which has survived with only a couple mud splodges splashed on the cover—and trudge back to the cabin.

Trekking from my cabin to the shower block feels like an eternal hike. I'm greeted with more than a few strange looks. What a great first impression.

At least the jerk made one good point. No wolf in their right mind would want to be my mate. Maybe it's not how he meant it, but I find that thought pretty darn comforting.

I'm running late to meet Katie—of course—by the time I've managed to wash the mud out of every nook and crevice on my body and cleaned up my clothes the best I can.

With my unruly hair refusing to settle in any style I ask of it, I hurry to meet her.

Katie's alone outside the main cabin, bathed in twilight when I get there, looking delicate and radiant in a lilac dress. I can't remember ever having seen her look so pretty before. There's even a matching flower in her hair. Next to Katie I look like a toddler who's been allowed to dress themself for the first time.

"Sorry I'm late," I say, breathlessly. "You...look amazing."

"Thanks," she says, blushing and biting her bottom lip.

"I bet you could find your mate tonight looking like that."

"Don't be a moron," she says, giving my shoulder a playful shove. "You ready to go in?"

"Ready as I'll ever be."

She links her arm through mine and we make our way inside.

The Alpha's Hall is grander than I imagined it would be. As long and wide as an Olympic swimming pool, and lit by a massive chandelier made from at least fifty sets of deer antlers. Wooden columns line the room, supporting a second-level balcony that runs around the perimeter. Paintings, at least twice my height, hang on every log-lined wall. And at the far end, two large staircases descend from the balcony.

To the right of the entrance, a string quartet is playing elegant welcoming music; wait staff in white shirts and waistcoats wander through the sea of wolves offering trays of canapés and glasses of champagne—or sparkling cider for those of us not old enough to drink.

The room is full of werewolves all dressed to impress. Girls in colorful cocktail dresses and guys in suit jackets and crisp white shirts.

I tug at my gray button-down, which I've paired with a pair of light-blue skinny jeans and white sneakers.

"See those lugheads over there?" I point to Todd and Simon, who I've spotted across the room.

"The ones seeing who can eat the most tiny sausages in one go?" Katie asks.

"Those are my roommates."

"Gee, I'm sorry," she says, laughing. "They're sort of cute

though, don't you think?"

"Sure, if you're into the walking dead."

We wander farther into the room and I grab us a couple of mini quiches from a passing server.

"Oh my Moon Gods! These are delicious!" I exclaim, spitting crumbs.

Every new tray of hor'doeuvres that passes, I grab as many tiny, delicious snacks as I can and shove them in my mouth.

"At least the food is great!" I try to say, but Katie is unable to decipher my words through all the chewing.

I keep my eye out for the jerk in case I need to make a swift left turn but he's nowhere to be seen. Maybe he's not much of a joiner. That would explain the solitary walk in the woods.

"Hi, guys! Enjoying the meet and greet?" Katie and I are suddenly confronted by peppy Eleanor, looking very formal in a black dress with a white Wednesday Addams-style collar.

"Yes, thank you, Eleanor," Katie says, ever the diplomat.

"I heard the alpha's son is supposed to turn up at any moment now," she says, looking like she's about to burst from excitement.

"Really?" Katie says with the highest eyebrows I've ever seen. "That's great."

"My father works for his father," Eleanor continues, beginning to ramble. "Well, actually it's more like they work together, my father's kind of important."

"Oh, is he Beta Castillo?" Katie asks. "I'm sorry I can't remember your last name."

"Oh, haha no!"

"Is he a gamma wolf then? On the security council?" I ask, swallowing a mouthful of deviled egg.

"No, he doesn't have a rank. But he's one of the alpha's closest advisers, actually, they're more like friends. Best friends. They go way back."

"That's great," Katie says, clearly running out of things to say to this manic cheerleader.

"Anyway, have a good night!" Eleanor says, beaming.

"You too," Katie says.

Eleanor spins around and heads off to harangue some other unsuspecting partygoers.

"She's a lot," I say.

"She's probably just nervous," Katie says.

I'm always in awe of how understanding my best friend can be. Unlike me, who's more likely to judge a book by its overly peppy cover.

"Oh hey, I forgot to say you'll never guess who I ran into earlier..."

I'm about to tell Katie about my recent run-in with the jerk from the city when the music stops. The room falls quiet and the doors on the second floor open.

Three people step out onto the balcony but it's hard to see their faces from where we're standing.

"That's Jasper Apollo!" I hear Eleanor whispering excitedly to a boy nearby.

All eyes are on the heir as he and his accompanying guests make their way to the top of the staircase.

They stand at the top of the stairs and take in the crowd beneath them.

My eyes go wide. My mouth falls open and my stomach drops.

I can't believe what I'm seeing. It can't be true, it just can't...

Standing above me, in a sleek black suit, is Jasper Apollo, only that's not how I know him...

To me, he's the jerk from the city. The guy who broke my phone, laughed at me when I fell in the mud, and won't stop calling me *bonehead*.

The jerk who's been tormenting me is Jasper Apollo...

...the alpha's son!

BEER PONG

He's the alpha's son!?

I stare at him in disbelief. So that's why he always acts so superior. Still, being the pack's heir doesn't give him the right to be such a jerk!

Everyone else is staring at him as well. But unlike me, they all have wonder twinkling in their eyes.

His black hair is swept across his ridiculously symmetrical face, and he wears a stoic, humble expression. Okay, stranger. Where's the condescending smirk?

His suit is impeccably tailored, sitting squarely on his shoulders with shiny satin lapels. A slim-fitting black button-down is tucked into his pants, which he fills out perfectly, and the look is topped off with stylish patent leather shoes. He looks every bit a prince. Not at all like the jerk I know.

"Ladies and Gentlewolves," the man to his left says, projecting his voice across the hall, "may I present the alpha's heir, Jasper Apollo!"

The room erupts in applause. I'm the only one who doesn't seem to be going crazy for this guy.

Jasper—because I guess that's his stupid name—holds his arm out and the girl to his right slips hers through it.

I've barely noticed her as I've stood like a stunned meerkat. She has dark, wavy brown hair that falls over her exposed, muscular shoulders. She's wearing a pastel-green dress, which contrasts nicely with her bronzed, terra-cotta skin. She's beautiful but the thing that catches my attention is how strong she looks. The muscle definition in her arms is ridiculous. The girl works out!

The two of them walk slowly down the stairs as the music starts again. People begin to move around the room once more but there's a new energy in the crowd, like a collective held breath. Everyone is aware they're in the presence of royalty.

I grab Katie and pull her to the side.

"That's him!" I say.

"Who? What?" she asks, looking around, super confused.

"The alpha's son, Jasper Apollo."

"I know—they just announced him," she says, staring at me like I've grown a second set of limbs.

"No..." I shake my head and try to refocus. "Jasper is the guy who knocked me on my ass in Times Square."

"Ohhhhh," she says, catching on. "That's him?!"

"Yes!"

"And there's more..."

"Oh my Moon Gods..."

"I ran into him in the forest this afternoon and he was a complete jerk. I called him an asshole stalker."

"What were you doing in the woods?"

"What? Drawing. That's not important. The point is he hates me. The alpha's son hates me!"

"Okay," Katie says, placing her hands on her hips, puckering her lips like she's trying to solve a difficult math problem. "What should we do?"

"I just... We have to avoid him at all costs!"

"Yes, you're right. Oh, look..."

Katie points behind me and I turn to see the hall starting to empty. The crowd is heading through a large set of double doors into another room.

"Dinner is being served!" Eleanor says, popping up out

of nowhere. "Are you two coming? Remember, no funny business before the Mating Run."

"We're...we'll be there in a second, thanks," I say.

Eleanor runs off and I look back to Katie with a panicked, pleading expression.

"It's fine," she says, sounding exactly as if it is not, in fact, fine. "Let's just go to dinner. There's so many people here there's every chance he won't even notice you."

"Is he still looking?"

I glance up from behind Katie, where I've been trying to hide for the entire dinner.

We're sitting at a table about halfway up the room. It's not quite as wide as the Alpha's Hall but just as long, with two smaller chandeliers hanging above us. The festivalgoers have all been assigned seats at circular tables draped with white tablecloths that probably cost more than my entire yearly allowance. A rectangular table is positioned at the end of the room, its diners facing the rest of us. This is where Jasper is sitting, dead center. The girl who entered with him is to his right, and a selection of wolves—wealthy kids or the kids of wolves in power, I assume—sit on either side.

Our plan to go about dinner and hope for the best hasn't worked quite the way we thought it would. I'd just taken my first bite out of a juicy-looking chicken thigh when I felt his cold stare land on me. He hasn't looked away since.

"What's he doing?" I whisper from my hiding spot.

Katie attempts her best nonchalant over-the-shoulder sneak peek.

"Max he's...he's not looking."

"What?" I sit up and risk a peek for myself.

Jasper isn't looking anymore. He's staring at his food, looking like it just insulted his mother. I don't want to risk him catching me staring so turn my attention back to the succulent piece of meat on my plate.

Barely a moment passes and I can't help myself.

I want to see what he's up to, so without turning my head I glance in his direction. He's saying something in the ear of his date. She nods solemnly and they both stand. He drops his napkin on his half-finished meal, nods to the guy on his left, and they exit the banquet hall.

"Huh." He didn't even finish his meal.

"Great, can we just eat now?" Katie asks.

"Yeah, I guess."

I should finish the drumstick on my plate, but instead I stay staring at his empty seat.

Why would he just leave?

After dinner, we all head outside to the grassy patch between the Alpha's Lodge and the cabins. A bonfire is blazing in the middle of a circle of log benches.

The charming, sedative string quartet has been done away with, replaced by speakers blaring some seriously cheesy pop bangers.

Someone passes holding a red cup and then suddenly it's like everyone has one. People are drinking and dancing and starting to let loose. You can tell it's about to be a blue moon from the amount of people who are already crying or making out.

"Here roomie," Todd says, splashing me as he shoves a red cup into my hand.

"Oh no thanks, I'm not old enough…"

"S'no problemo, bro. Neither are we. Just don't tell anyone." My roomie is already slurring. "I got your cute friend one too."

He stumbles a little as he tries to hand Katie the cup in his other hand.

"Whoa, cool it, bud. I've got the little lady taken care of," Simon says, sidling in and getting a cup in Katie's hand before his friend can manage it.

"You guys wanna come party? We're gonna play beer pong over by the pay phones."

Katie and I look at each other before smiling and shrugging.

"Let's party!" I say.

It turns out I'm really good at beer pong. Or really bad. I'm not sure. Either way, I drink a lot of beer and within the space of less than an hour, the world has become a big, fun, blur.

I'm not even hating hanging out with Todd and Simon. Yeah, they're total cavemen but they're pretty fun and they're really good at partying. Katie seems to be getting on with them both as well.

If the festival is just four nights of this it might be all right!

"Scooooooore!" Simon yells after sinking yet another Ping-Pong ball into one of my cups. "Drink, drink, drink!"

I grab the cup and pour the stale, room-temp beer down my throat, spilling about half of it on myself in the process.

From the corner of my eye, I spot a girl in a green dress and I spin around—nearly losing my balance. Is that the girl who was with Jasper earlier?

She crosses past the doors of the lodge, heading for the bonfire. Without thinking, I start to follow her, leaving the boys and Katie and beer pong behind.

"Hey, where you going, dude? We haven't finished!" Todd calls out.

I ignore him—suddenly, on a mission. It is the girl from earlier, and wherever that girl is going there's a chance Jasper will be there. My drunk self wants to give that jerk a piece of my mind.

The Moon Gods must be on my side because sure enough, I find the girl in the green dress, standing a ways from the bonfire in the shadows, speaking to the alpha's son.

I watch them for a moment, swaying from foot to foot. From where I'm standing it looks like they're having some kind of disagreement. With blurry vision, it's hard to make out exactly what they're talking about but it looks like the girl is encouraging Jasper to join the party and he's resisting.

"Good luck, girlfriend," I slur to no one in particular. "He's a big, antisocial jerkwad."

And that's enough to get me riled up. Before I know it I'm stomping over.

Jasper spots me first and holds up a finger to the girl as if to say, Hold that thought.

"Can we help you?" he asks, without a shred of recognition, like he doesn't even know who I am.

"Ohhhhh, so now that we all know who you are you're too good to call me *bonehead*?"

"Olivia, can you excuse us?" he asks his friend in green.

"No way, chico," she says, raising an eyebrow, looking wildly amused. "I'm staying for this."

"Don't pretend like you don't know me!" I say, pointing and nearly losing my balance. "You know meeeee. I'm the bonehead! Remember!?"

"You're the what?" Olivia asks.

"You're drunk," Jasper says, reaching out to grab my arm.

I'm not sure if he's trying to keep me upright or pull me aside to stop me from making a scene but either way I'm not having any of it.

"No, you don't get to touch me!" I say pulling away and stumbling backward. "You don't get to treat people like this just because you're a...a...handsome prince or whatever."

"Handsome?" Olivia says, chuckling. "Jasper, do you know this guy?"

"Yes," he growls. "*Someone* was too busy looking at their phone to see where they were going and crashed into me in the city a few weeks back."

"Right," Olivia says, catching on, sort of.

"Yeah, and you...you...hurt my butt!"

Olivia bursts out laughing. Jasper looks mortified and then really, really mad.

"You did what, Jasper?" she asks, giggling.

"That's enough," he snaps at me. "You need to go back to your cabin."

He tries to touch me again and I pull my arm away super overdramatically. The force sends me stumbling backward, and finally, I trip and topple into the grass. It's the third time I've fallen on my ass in front of the alpha's son, but who's counting, right?

I'm so drunk and embarrassed I don't even try to get up. I want to lie there and die.

"Poor kid," Olivia says.

Jasper doesn't say anything but I feel a pair of strong hands lifting me up.

I want to protest and tell him to get his hands off me but it's all finally too much. I pass out in Jasper's arms.

CAPTURE THE FLAG

"Max, are you awake? You're going to be late..."

Katie's voice drags me back to consciousness. I blink my eyes as I wake from the deepest slumber.

My mouth is dry and chalky and my head is throbbing. The sun is so bright it's like I'm staring straight into a floodlight.

I don't think I've ever been that drunk before. Who knows where I ended up crashing?

To my surprise, I'm in my bunk, wearing the same clothes I was in last night, except for my shoes.

"Morning," Katie says, standing on her tiptoes and peering over the edge of the bunk. "You've missed breakfast. But I brought you coffee and a pastry."

"Thanks," I say, sitting up, rubbing my head.

Katie hands me the coffee and I take a sip. It tastes good. White with about five sugars, just the way I like it. She hands me the pastry but I'm not sure I can stomach it right away.

"What happened last night?"

"I'm not sure, we were both pretty wasted, I think, and you wandered off. Looks like you managed to get yourself back to your cabin in one piece though."

I try to remember what happened but it's a complete blur. Then I remember something...a glimpse of his face and...

"Oh no, I think I did something bad."

"Like how bad?" she asks.

"Like I should probably walk into the forest and never be seen again."

Katie twists her mouth into an awkward smile.

"I'm sure it's just the hangover talking..."

"No, I—"

I go to tell Katie all about what happened with Jasper, but she cuts me off.

"Wait, you'll have to tell me on the way to the meeting point. Everyone's already heading off for a big game of capture the flag."

I curl my lip. The idea of running around in the hot sun with a bunch of sweaty wolves is enough to make anyone want to hurl, let alone a teenager suffering from the worst hangover of their life.

"That sounds like a nightmare."

"It's mandatory," Katie says, without a shred of irony. "It's supposed to be like a get-to-know-you thing, to help break the ice before the Mating Run."

"Can I just pretend I don't feel well?"

"I told Eleanor I'd make sure you were there. She looked like she was about to burst a blood vessel when you weren't at breakfast."

I drop my head and glare at Katie. This was a complete and utter betrayal.

"Come on, it'll be fun," she says, gently tugging me from the bunk.

Begrudgingly, I swing my legs over the side. I notice my shoes have been neatly placed at the end of the bed. Who put them there? I definitely wouldn't have been so careful in my drunken state.

"Oof, you should definitely get changed and maybe brush your teeth," Katie says, waving a hand under her nose. "You smell like beer."

I give myself a little sniff and she's right. I reek!

After a super quick shower, we left the campsite and followed a trail into the forest.

"So, the last thing you remember is Jasper picking you up off the ground," Katie says.

We're following marker signs pointing in the direction of the "meeting point."

"Basically," I say.

My warm, thumping blood is drawing—apparently— all the insects of the forest to me. I have to keep swatting them away as we walk.

"Do you think he's the one who put you to bed?"

I nearly burst out laughing thinking about Jasper carefully taking off my shoes and tucking me in. He's been nothing but a dick to me since we ran into each other— there's more chance he would have tossed me straight into the bonfire.

But then I stop and think... If it wasn't him then who was it?

I snort, laughing. "No, that can't be what happened. There's no way that jerk would do anything so nice."

By the time the other campers come into view, I'm sweating and puffing. I am so out of shape.

The trees spread out, circling around the mass of activewear-clad wolves, to form a clearing.

Everyone goes quiet as they watch Jasper and Olivia make their way to the top of a rocky outcrop.

Olivia has her game face on. She's wearing gray leggings with a graphic design featuring pale-yellow color blocks, and a matching long-sleeve top. She looks ready to win gold at the Olympics.

Jasper on the other hand has the same unreadable expression he wore when he arrived last night. Just like Olivia, he's wearing running tights, only his are black, ending just above his ankles. He's got a black muscle shirt on and his arms are well and truly out.

I can't help but gawk at his wildly defined muscles. I bet

I could work out for a thousand years and still not have the same definition he does. It's suddenly hard for me to swallow.

The heat must really be getting to me.

"Wolves!" Olivia says, projecting her voice so that we can hear her right at the back. She sounds like Beyoncé commanding her pride in *The Lion King*. "This morning you will be tested. It's hot and the terrain is unforgiving. In order to win you will need to be at the top of your game. Your speed, strength, and agility will be on display for everyone to see and judge!"

"I thought we were playing capture the flag?" I panic-whisper in Katie's ear.

"That's what they said at breakfast," she whispers back. "Maybe it's like a wolf version."

"The rules are as follows," Olivia continues. "You will be split into two teams. Jasper and I will be team captains. The green team will be with me, and purple with Jasper."

I don't know which would be worse: having to be on Jasper's team or having to play against him.

"There is no shifting allowed. You are to remain in your human form for the duration of the game. If you are tagged you must leave the field and report back here. Eleanor has generously offered to remain at this meeting point with water and snacks for anyone who is disqualified from the game."

I notice Eleanor standing at the base of the outcrop, holding a bag full of granola bars, looking extremely pleased with herself.

"The game is over when one team successfully captures the other team's flag and returns it to their home base. There is no safe zone. You can be tagged out at any location in the playing field."

"What are the boundaries?" some guy toward the front asks.

Olivia grins and raises an eyebrow. She lifts both of her hands in the air and gestures to the trees.

"You're looking at them."

A symphony of *whoas* and *huhs* echoes across the

group.

"The entire forest is at play," Olivia finishes up. "The game begins when you hear this sound."

She produces a thin shiny whistle hanging on a chain around her neck and blows.

Birds evacuate the trees at the reverberating, high-pitched squeal. My head throbs mercilessly.

"Is everything clear?" she asks, handing the whistle off to Eleanor, who I'm sure knows exactly when and how to blow the damn thing.

Everyone nods, grinning sportingly at their neighbors.

"Good!" Olivia says. "All of those with an odd-numbered cabin, you're on my team; evens, you're with Jasper."

A murmur passes through the crowd as everyone tries to remember their cabin number.

"Right," Jasper calls out, stepping forward. "Purple team with me, we're heading east."

He springs off the back of the outcrop and begins marching east. All the people with even-numbered cabins follow their great leader.

"The rest of you with me," Olivia says, heading in the opposite direction.

Katie and I turn to look at each other.

"Bummer, we're on different teams," she says.

"Yep, I'll probably get out pretty quick if you get bored and want to just hang out here."

Katie puts her hands on her hips and raises her brows at me. "You should at least try and have fun."

"Fine!" I moan. "Catch you later."

We head off with our designated teams.

My team marches west on a constant incline until I think my legs might fall off. At least I've sweated out most of my hangover by the time we reach home base.

Huddled behind some well-placed boulders, Olivia addresses the team once more. She starts rattling off some game plan which I'm sure is incredibly smart and very strategic but that I don't manage to take in one single sentence of.

And before I know it she claps and says, "Right,

everyone knows what they're doing?"

Uh, sure.

"Hands in then."

Everyone on the team, including me, puts their hand into the large circle we've formed, and on *three* we all do a war cry and throw our hands in the air. Then the whistle blows.

The team disperses in an instant, emptying the immediate vicinity.

"Well, what's wrong, chico?! Don't just stand there!" Olivia shouts at me, jogging off into the trees.

I spin around once, pick a direction, and run.

I'm suddenly completely alone in the forest—these pack wolves sure know how to hide. I spot a tree that's fallen on its side, mangled roots sticking up in the air, and notice there's a hole in the ground where it used to stand. The perfect hiding spot. I jump and scramble my way down then get cozy in the soil.

I'll wait here until this whole ordeal is over.

An indeterminable amount of time passes uneventfully. I sit beneath the tree roots and let the cool earth soothe my hangover. About an hour into the game, a couple of my teammates run by, doing their best to stay low and out of sight. They don't notice me.

Another peaceful hour or so goes by and I wonder if the game has already finished and everyone has gone home without me.

Then the cries start. Voices call out in the distance. I can't tell exactly where they're coming from.

Then I hear footsteps. Someone is running in this direction. They're moving fast...really fast. The earth is vibrating under me.

I poke my head out of my hidey-hole to have a look around.

Like a cheetah bursting through the jungle, Jasper emerges, racing through the trees. He leaps a root and sidesteps a boulder. To avoid a small stream he grabs hold of a low-hanging branch and swings across, like a goddamn modern-day Tarzan.

His face is stern and determined. His muscles are tight and his movements precise. He's a wolf on a mission. And then I realize...

He's holding our flag. The purple fabric is fluttering about in the wind.

I think he spots me but it doesn't deter him from his course; he plows onward with the grace and speed of a gazelle.

"What are you doing, bonehead? Chase him!"

Olivia is hot on Jasper's heels, charging through the forest about ten seconds behind.

She passes me and I stand frozen. Surely, she doesn't think I can catch him. Olivia clearly has the better odds.

Only, she's not paying attention to where she's putting her feet. Her left toe catches on an upended root and she goes flying forward, toppling over. I leap out of my hole and run over to her. She's clutching her ankle, wincing in pain; she looks up at me with dark, rageful eyes.

"What are you staring at!? Go get him!"

I nod and before I know it I'm taking off after Jasper.

Instantly, my lungs start to burn and the muscles in my legs seize up, but I keep running. I push harder with every step and I don't even know why. I guess I don't want Olivia to lose the game because I distracted her. Or maybe I just don't want Jasper to win.

Somehow, I instinctively know which way to go. I can sense him ahead of me. Every so often I catch a whiff of his scent. *Cherry blossoms...* And every time I do I push myself to go harder.

The sun flashes across my face as I sprint, and somehow I think I'm catching up. Jasper must have realized Olivia is no longer behind him and slowed a little. Or maybe I'm faster than I think. Either way, Jasper's scent becomes stronger—he's just up ahead.

More like a rhino than a cheetah, I stampede through the underbrush. I burst through some branches and find myself in a clearing. Jasper is on the other side about to disappear but he stops and turns. I skid to a halt as well.

He looks at me with confusion, as if I was the last person he expected to see. Then he raises a brow like he's impressed. But the next second, that determined, steely look is back and he's off again.

There's no air left in my lungs, my heart is about to explode, my feet are screaming in pain. There are scratches on my arms from where they've caught on branches. And I'm drenched in sweat. But I have to win. It's life-and-death. Losing is no longer an option.

Somehow I manage to catch up to Jasper.

I'm so close, I reach out a hand to touch him, and...he speeds up.

I push even harder, harder than I knew I could, and I manage to bring myself level again. Jasper looks back and gestures at me with his head but I don't know what he's trying to say.

And then suddenly he jumps, lifting off the ground at least twenty feet high. Why has he done that? It's only going to slow him down. But then I see why.

I'm racing toward a massive freaking hole in the ground. A long valley tears through the landscape. The sound of turbulent, rushing water rises from the gap in the earth.

Jasper lands gracefully on the other side.

There's no way I'll make that jump!

But I'm going too fast, I don't know if I can slow down in time. I do my best to dig my heels in and stop but I'm too close. I reach the edge of the cliff and the ground beneath me disappears.

THE NEW ARRIVAL

There is no ground beneath me, just rushing water and jagged rocks.

I scream as I begin to plummet, but suddenly I'm jerked backward.

Someone has hold of my shirt collar and is pulling me back. They hoist me onto the soil and I tumble into them before flopping to the ground.

Olivia looks down at me, panting for breath. She must have caught up with us just in time to stop me falling to my doom.

"Thanks," I say, huffing.

"That was close, chico."

We both look across the ravine. Jasper is there, watching us. I could have died and he knows it. Does he look sort of relieved?

There's not enough time for me to figure out the answer to my question. Jasper lifts an eyebrow cockily before sprinting into the woods like a majestic stag.

I take Olivia's hand and she pulls me up.

"You nearly had him, bonehead," she says, patting me on the back. "You're full of surprises."

"Ha, yeah..."

I still have no idea how I, the boy who's managed to get

out of every PE class since middle school, nearly caught up with Jasper. He's literally a genetic masterpiece. His dad is the alpha, the strongest wolf in the pack. He's a purebred and I'm just a geek from the suburbs. But I was keeping up with him. How?

"Must be a blue moon miracle," Olivia says.

In the distance, we hear cheers of victory echoing through the forest.

So, we lost the game. At least now we can stop running around and nearly dying, right?

Olivia and I head back to the meeting point. I ponder what she said about the blue moon and wonder about the impending lunar phenomenon. Maybe it can boost a wolf's speed as well as their libido. Or maybe I just really didn't want Jasper to win.

Olivia is still limping a little from when she tripped.

"Is your ankle all right?"

"I'll live," she says and accelerates.

As soon as we're back at the meeting point I find Katie.

"Congratulations," I say.

"You look kind of rough," she says, appraising the dirt stains on my shirt, the graze on my leg, and the more-ruffled-than-usual state of my hair. "You must have gotten involved after all."

"Meh, I mostly just hid in the bushes."

"Did you have fun?"

"Let's just say I gave Jasper a run for his money."

"No way," Katie says. Her mouth drops wide enough for a whale to come swimming out.

"But I wasn't fast enough."

"Oh well, maybe you'll get another chance to catch him in some other game."

"Maybe," I laugh.

We join the other sweat-drenched wolves heading back to camp.

As we emerge from the forest I immediately spot a black town car parked out front of the Alpha's Lodge. Standing by the rear end of the car is a Louis Vuitton suitcase.

"Who does all of that belong to?" I ask, but Katie has no response. She's as shocked as I am.

A second later a driver comes out to collect the suitcase followed by a statuesque dark-copper-skinned girl with long flowing waves of hair like a waterfall. She's wearing a turtleneck sweater in cream and white skinny jeans. From this distance, it's hard to make out her face behind her large, ostentatious sunglasses.

"Is that...?" Katie trails off midquestion.

"What? Who is it?" I ask.

"Don't you recognize her?"

I turn back, squinting to see better, as the movie-star-level-gorgeous girl whips off her sunglasses while shaking her hair out in slow motion.

I gasp. "That's Aisha Miller!"

The other campers continue to flow past us, like a river around a boulder. But we can't move. Our favorite werewolf dancer superstar is here!

"Of course she has the sense to turn up *after* capture the flag," I say.

Aisha discusses something with her driver before he nods politely and takes her suitcase through the doors of the main cabin. I don't even blink twice about the fact that she's staying in the Alpha's Lodge. Because...of course, she is!

Then she turns to face us...us! And she waves...

Oh my Moon Gods! Is she waving at me?

Tentatively, I raise my hand and wave back, just as someone knocks into my shoulder, throwing me off-balance.

When I look back, Aisha's no longer looking in this direction. I'm suddenly sure she was never looking in this direction. Because Jasper is jogging over to her, returning her wave.

Like a barely competent fifth grader, I put two and two together. Aisha is staying in the main cabin, where Jasper is staying. Jasper was at the ballet in the city. She even looked for him when she was taking her bow. They know each other.

How could someone so graceful, someone who can bring hundreds of people so much happiness, be friends with someone so devoid of emotion?

"Wow, they look pretty close," Katie says as Jasper wraps his arm around Aisha and walks her into his father's lodge.

My sudden excitement turns to bitter-ass disappointment. I would love to say hi and tell her how great I think she is. But there's no way I can do that if she's with that jerk. I can picture his condescending smirk. I bet he'd think it was pathetic and look down his perfectly straight, completely proportionate nose at me.

Some of the festival volunteers have set up barbecues down by the canoe shed. Cleaned up and starving, we find our way down to the water. My mouth starts watering as the aroma of barbecued pork wafts under my nose. My eyes nearly jump out of my head at the sight of four whole hogs being spit-roasted.

It's a sunny day and the surface of the water is calm. The lake itself is wider than I first thought, disappearing behind the trees as it bends.

Katie and I make a direct line for the food. A couple of picnic tables are laid out with plates and cutlery and, of course, potato salad. A queue has already formed where one of the volunteers is serving up succulent pork, so I grab a plate and ignore the creamy spuds.

I join the back of the line and my stomach growls like a wolf who's found its mate.

"That smells so good," a smooth voice behind me says.

"Tell me about it," I say, glancing over my shoulder and freezing.

The owner of that voice is Aisha Miller. The prima ballerina is standing behind me in line for barbecue!

"I'm so hungry I could probably eat the whole hog," she says, laughing.

I struggle to form words. Whatever I'm trying to say comes out as weird gurgling noises.

"You...you're...I...uuunnnhhh..."

"You okay?" she asks.

"I..."

"Are you always this articulate?"

"He's just really hungry," Katie says, popping up next to me and saving my, literal, life. "He nearly outran Jasper this morning and hasn't quite recovered."

"Wow," Aisha says. "That's impressive. You must be fast."

"I'm so fast," I say, and instantly want to slap myself in the face.

"That's great. I'm Aisha by the way. How are you two enjoying the festival so far?"

"Oh, we know who you are," Katie says. "We're actually big fans."

"Is that right?"

"Yeah, really big, right Max?"

Katie elbows me in the ribs, hard, jolting me back to life.

"YES!" I shock everyone—even myself—with how loud that comes out. "Sorry, yes. We're big fans. We just saw you in New York a month ago."

"He does speak," Aisha says, smiling.

"Sorry," I say. "You just surprised me. My name is Max and this is my best friend Katie."

"It's nice to meet both of you." Aisha glances up, looking impatient. "Man, these guys are slow. I'm going to shift and kill someone if I don't get fed soon."

Eventually, we all get some meat on our plates and Aisha asks if we want to eat with her.

"I always get overwhelmed at these things, there's too many wolves hungry to find a soulmate," she says as we find a spot to sit on a lush, grassy knoll.

"You've been to a festival before?" Katie asks.

"Yeah, just one. About three years ago when I was sixteen."

"You didn't find your mate?" Katie's eyes are swimming with romantic daydreams, and little love hearts float around her head.

"No, but that's fine. I'm already mated."

Aisha can tell we're shocked by the way we both stop shoveling food into our mouths.

"To dance," she says, laughing. We both roll our heads back in recognition. "I'm committed to ballet, I don't have time for some wannabe alpha thinking he can claim me as his mate."

"Maybe you'll find one this year," Katie says, never one to give up on love.

Aisha shrugs. "Maybe."

"Katie is really into all that mate stuff. She's super excited about the Mating Run," I say.

"That's great," Aisha says. "I hope that works out for you."

She touches Katie's arm, showing her sincerity, and then turns to me with a raised brow.

"And what about you? You're not excited about the Mating Run?"

"Me?" I ask, suddenly flustered. "I haven't really thought about it."

"Max is an artist like you," Katie pipes in. "He's more focused on his art than this festival."

I shoot Katie a look and she shakes her head like she doesn't understand. It's not that I want Aisha to think I'm all mate-thirsty. I just don't want her to think I'm a complete party pooper.

"What kind of art do you do?" Aisha asks.

"Drawings," I say. "Mostly landscapes."

"Well, I'd love to see them sometime."

My cheeks heat up as I remember all those sketches I did at the river. The ones where I drew Aisha dancing and...the one of Jasper's face.

"So are you friends with Jasper?" Katie asks.

"Oh yeah, we went to boarding school together," Aisha

says, shrugging like it's nothing.

"It's his first festival isn't it?"

"Yeah, Jasp is younger than me by, like, six months; he was still fifteen when the last festival happened."

I have to stop myself from giggling at her nickname for him. *Jasp!* I never imagined he would be the type for cutesy epithets.

"Do you think you two might be...?" Katie asks, unsubtly bringing the subject back to mates.

Aisha guffaws. "Me and Jasper? No way, girlfriend! He's like my brother. We go back too far for that."

"You never know what the Moon Gods have in store," Katie says.

I don't know why but I'm relieved finding out there's nothing romantic going on between Jasper and Aisha. Maybe there's a chance Aisha and I could wind up being mates. I don't feel a strong pull to her besides thinking she's an amazing dancer, but we are getting along.

"Speak of the devil," she says, interrupting my train of thought.

I look up and see Jasper approaching. He's wearing black jeans which taper in at his ankle, new trainers, and a perfectly crisp white T-shirt.

"Hey dude," Aisha says, waving him over. "I was just talking to these cool kids."

Jasper tilts his head so that he can see us over his sunglasses.

"Kids, sure," he says, huffing.

That jerk! Now he wants to embarrass me in front of Aisha!

"Be nice, Jasp. Did you know Max here was an artist?"

"Can't say I did."

"Come on, join us," Aisha says.

I'm in love with how chill she is around him. She talks to him like he's just another wolf.

"I have some pork I couldn't finish if you want?" I say, holding out my plate.

I notice Aisha trying not to laugh and I wonder why on earth I just said that. Or why I was suddenly feeling generous. I totally wanted to finish my plate of food and it's not like I want him to sit with us. Do I?

Jasper looks at the plate of food like it's a rotting corpse. "I'm vegetarian," he says.

"Oh."

"Right, everybody! It's time for canoeing!" Eleanor's chirpy, high-pitched voice interrupts the conversation.

The rest of the campgoers chuck their dirty paper plates in the bin and head over to the boat shed to get a canoe.

"That sounds fun!" Aisha says. Jasper doesn't look so impressed though. "Don't mind him, he's just really bad at rowing."

I have to stop myself from exploding with laughter. Even Katie can't help but giggle behind her hand.

"Two people per canoe!" Eleanor declares. "Only two people per canoe. Find a canoe buddy and get paddling!"

"Hey Aisha," I say. "You fancy being my canoe buddy?"

I'm shocked that those words came out of my mouth, and from the way Katie is looking at me, so is she.

"You two don't want to go together?" Aisha says, looking as awkward as I feel.

I go to start speaking, to say that yes, of course I will go with Katie. But she stands and stomps off before I have a chance.

Instantly, I feel awful. I've just completely snubbed my best friend, and I've done it in front of everyone.

"That was really shitty of me," I say, very aware of Jasper standing off to my side, looking down on me like I'm a pathetic ant at a picnic.

"I'm not much for canoeing anyway," Aisha says. "Why don't you run and try and fix things with Katie?"

"Good idea," I say.

I hop up and jog over to where people are already launching their boats into the water.

"Katie! Katie! I'm sorry," I say as I catch up to her. "I shouldn't have left you hanging like that. Can we still canoe together?"

Katie turns and the look on her face is a message. She

is not ready to forgive and forget. Her lips are pressed together and her glare is stonier than the mountains in the distance.

"Don't worry about it, Max, I found someone else to go with."

Eleanor exits the canoe shed holding a fiberglass boat.

"Coming partner?" she asks Katie.

My best friend glares at me for a moment longer before replying, "Yes." She helps Eleanor launch the boat into the water.

The shore is quiet now and I feel as if everyone has managed to find someone to canoe with except me.

I turn around. Jasper and Aisha are still back at the picnic site. I think they see me looking but I'm too embarrassed to go over and speak to them. I don't want Aisha to think I'm coming back to ask her again and I don't want Jasper to see me when I'm feeling shitty and lonely.

Aisha is speaking to Jasper, gesturing in my direction, but I don't want to seem like I'm prying so I turn back around. I'll just sit here by the lake and watch the others out on their boats, and when Katie gets back I'll do my best to apologize. Hopefully, I can make it up to her.

There's a sudden noise from inside the shed and I'm bowled over to turn and find Jasper carrying a canoe toward the shore.

"I'll go with you, come on," he says.

"Why?" I ask, making no attempt to hide my surprise.

"Because it's part of my duty to make sure everyone participates in the festival. And because Aisha is making me."

I turn my head over my shoulder—Aisha flicks her hands toward the water, encouraging us both to get going.

"Are you coming or not?"

Jasper is looking at me like I'm the biggest imposition in the world.

Spending time out on the water with him is not my idea of a good time either. But my only other option is storming off like a big sulky baby in front of Aisha and my future alpha.

"Fine. As long as you don't call me *bonehead*."

I get up and head to the boat. Together we push it out onto the water and jump in just as we leave the shore.

I grab my oar from inside the hull and grip it tightly.

I can't believe I'm about to spend my afternoon in a tiny boat with Jasper, who's been antagonizing me since before we arrived at this stupid festival. Maybe it's what I deserve after the way I dropped Katie.

One thing is for sure: spending this much time with Jasper will be punishment.

SPLASH!

Jasper sits in the head of the boat, silently dipping his oar into the water, propelling us forward. His body doesn't move except for his arms, he doesn't look around at the scenery or me. And he doesn't speak.

I do my best to paddle on the other side of the boat, trying to keep us from going in circles, but I think my rowing technique may leave a lot to be desired. And my upper body strength for that matter.

The other canoe teams are ahead of us, most having disappeared around the bend already.

My shoulder begins to ache and I moan slightly as I dip in my oar, struggling to pull it through the water.

"Change," Jasper says, breaking our silent standoff.

He lifts his oar and switches sides. Fumbling, I hurry to do the same before we start spinning endlessly. I feel better in my new position.

Did he make the transition for my benefit? I doubt it.

As we glide along I start to feel calmer, like I left all my anxiety about Katie and Aisha back at shore. The wind gently caresses my face and we make our way around the bend.

After another fifteen minutes or so Jasper calls out again: "Change."

I do as my leader commands.

Finally, the silence becomes too much for me. I can stare quietly at amazing landscapes with the best of them, but I can't pretend like we aren't out here together, as if we aren't the only two people in this boat.

"Are you really"—I say, my voice catching a little in my throat—"vegetarian?"

I notice Jasper's posture shift like a bird ruffling its feathers.

"Yes."

"Oh, that's interesting."

For most wolves it's a given that you eat meat. Hell, we crave the stuff. To be a vegetarian werewolf is almost unheard of and very difficult. It takes a lot of supplementary proteins to stave off the meat cravings. And a lot of discipline. That kind of willpower has always evaded me.

"How...how long have you been vegetarian?"

"Since I was twelve."

"Wow, that's young. What made you decide to stop eating meat?"

Again, Jasper's feathers ruffle.

"My mother was vegetarian."

"Right."

Everyone in the pack knows Jasper's mom, Alpha Jericho's mate and our former luna, died in a car crash six years ago. As a pack, we all felt the alpha's grief. It took a long time for things to feel normal after that.

"She was the daughter of Shinji Tanaka, right? The alpha of the biggest pack in Tokyo?"

It's hard to tell from the back but I think Jasper clenches his jaw.

"Yes."

"I heard his pack was even bigger than ours. Have you ever been to Japan?"

Jasper lifts his oar out of the water and places it in his lap, huffing. Have I offended him? It was probably not such a great idea to start talking about his mother and her family. But I was only trying to make conversation.

"Sorry, I shouldn't have—"

"You ask too many questions," Jasper says in a whisper so low and gravelly it's almost impossible to hear him.

"Right, yeah, people do say that about me. I'll...stop. Sorry."

I resign myself to rowing quietly and keeping my mouth shut until we're back at the shore and I can find Katie to apologize.

The forest drifts by on either side. Gray, pebble-covered shores disappear in the shadows between green pines. I wish I'd brought my sketchbook out for the trip. Although I'd be too scared to ask Jasper if we could stop anyhow.

"I haven't," Jasper says out of nowhere a minute later. "Been to Japan—I haven't."

"Oh."

I stare at the back of his head and continue paddling.

We row for another twenty minutes or so—enough time that my arms are seizing up—before we see the other canoe teams making their return to camp. I hope Jasper will see them and decide it's time for us to turn back as well. I've done more physical activity today than I have in the last sixteen years. But we pass the others and canoe onward for at least another ten minutes.

Finally, we come to a shallow area. The water underneath us is so clear and still that I can see the rocks on the lake bed and even spot a fish swimming past.

Jasper sighs. "We should head back."

He sticks his oar straight down, catching on a rock as I continue rowing, turning us a full 180 degrees. Now facing the direction of home, we begin our return.

The sun is starting to sink toward the horizon and everything has a fuzzy afternoon glow about it. The way back doesn't feel like it takes as long as the way out, but my arms are about ready to fall off by the time the camp comes into view.

In my relief I stretch my legs and accidentally kick the spare life vest that's lying in the bottom of the boat. A mega creepy-looking spider scuttles out, making me gasp. Its long black legs are spindly and I freeze in terror.

Spiders are my worst fear.

This terrifying specimen is hurrying toward my foot.

"Ja-Ja-Jasper..." I stammer.

He exhales audibly like he's expecting another dumb question.

"Jasper, there's a...a...a..."

"What is it?" he says, turning to face me. His sudden movement spooks the spider, which jumps from the bottom of the canoe right onto my leg.

Instantly I'm on my feet trying to shake the bitey demon off. Jasper is shouting something about calming down but I'm panicking, I can feel its needly legs on my skin.

The boat is rocking like crazy and I've lost track of where the spider is on my body. I try to spin to see where it is and upset our balance. The canoe slips out from under my feet, flipping over, sending me and Jasper splashing into the water.

Fully submerged, I kick and thrash about trying to find the surface.

A hand reaches down and grasps me by my collar, hauling me up and out of the water.

Jasper hoists me into the fresh air and I gasp frantically trying to get as much air in my lungs as possible. Only when I feel like I can breathe again do I notice that Jasper isn't panicking at all. He's not even treading water. He's standing calmly, with water lapping at his chest.

I let my feet sink and find that I can stand too.

I risk a glance at Jasper and am met with the coldest, most unimpressed expression I've ever seen. The future alpha is soaking wet. Droplets are trickling from his hair, dripping down his face. My lips twist into an apologetic kind of grimace.

"So tedious," he says.

Turning away from me, he takes hold of our capsized canoe and begins to walk it back in the direction of the boat shed On the grass, a crowd of people is watching us. Most of them look concerned for their future alpha. Aisha and Katie are laughing so hard they might wet themselves.

I shiver in the chilly mountain water and follow Jasper toward shore.

"I think you've been punished enough," Katie says, walking toward the Alpha's Lodge with her arm linked through mine. "That water is runoff from the mountains. It must have been freezing."

"It was, believe me," I say.

After making my big splash I headed straight for the showers, where I let scalding-hot water shock life back into my body. And when I was done it was time for dinner.

"I'm still sorry," I say, thinking I haven't apologized enough to Katie.

"Look, you were excited by the shiny new plaything. I get it."

"And then you got stuck with Miss Overachiever as a boat buddy."

"We actually had a pretty nice time. Eleanor is cool when she's not forcing us to wear name badges. We should hang out with her more."

"Well, I'm glad you've made a new friend."

"Two new friends actually..."

We head in through the back entrance, directly into the banquet hall. The tables are laid with fresh centerpieces.

"Who's the other new friend?" I ask.

"While you were dunking Jasper, I got talking with Aisha. I hate to say it but she's even cooler in person than onstage."

"I wouldn't go that far..." I say, but we both know I'm only covering my ass.

"Come on, you think she's amazing." Katie bumps me sideways. "You can say it. I mean it's not like you're going to end up mated or anything."

Both of us go quiet. We're still pondering the implications of what Katie just said when Aisha herself wanders over. Both of us snap to attention like obedient puppies.

"Hey, guys!"

"Hi!" we say in perfect unison.

"Ready for dinner?"

"Yeah, we should probably find our seats," I say, trying to play it as cool as possible.

"Oh, no need," Aisha says, a wicked grin on her lips. "I pulled some strings and you guys are going to sit with me tonight."

"Oh, that would be amazing!" Katie says. "Which is your table?"

"That one..." Katie points to the long table at the head of the room.

"That's the alpha's table?" I say. "Only important wolves sit there."

"I'm friends with Jasper and now you guys are my friends...so I guess you're important."

"I don't think Jasper will be cool with me—"

"Don't worry about Jasper," she says, taking Katie's hand and pulling her toward our new seats. "He's a big softy really."

We take our seats and I wait with an anxious ball of moths in my stomach until Jasper finally arrives. He enters the hall from a private doorway off to the side, accompanied by Olivia.

I try to take comfort in the fact that even though we're at the same table, I'm still separated from him by Katie, Aisha, and Olivia. Three women stand between me and the jerk who I threw overboard this afternoon.

Jasper—having not looked up once since entering the hall—reaches the table, twitching his nose like he's caught the scent of something repulsive. He flicks his head in my direction. Then just as quickly, he returns his gaze to the floor. He helps Olivia to her seat, then takes his own, never letting his gaze waver from his cutlery.

My fingers are trembling slightly and my stomach is wobbly like cranberry sauce from a tin.

Before dinner is served one of the older volunteers stands. His pale face is blotchy, his caramel hair curls into a bird's-nest-type arrangement on his head, and he has a crescent moon tattoo under his left eye.

"That's Marcel," Aisha whispers, leaning into Katie. "He's the son of the High Priest. He's about to bless this year's festival."

The lights are dimmed as Marcel begins to sing in a haunting baritone voice.

Katie leans over with a look of amazement on her face. "The language he's singing in... I think it's Lupine."

"Whoa! I didn't think anyone knew how to speak it."

Lupine is the language our oldest ancestors spoke back in ancient times. I thought it was a lost language but apparently, it's not so lost.

Marcel reaches some lofty notes, and as his prayer reaches its crescendo, the dull buzz of electric shutters joins in.

"Guys, look up," Aisha says, smiling.

We turn our attention to the ceiling as two large panels slide back, revealing a window. The night sky opens up above us, like a curtain of glitter.

And the moon...

To say it's beaming would be an understatement. One night away from the peak of its cycle, the moon is huge. Silver light illuminates the banquet hall, casting a shimmery glow onto the faces of every wolf in the room.

"Do you know what he's saying?" Katie asks Aisha, about Marcel's undecipherable prayer.

"He's asking the Moon Gods to look down on the faces of the unmated gathered here tonight and to bless them with a connection, a path between souls"

Of course.

I tilt my head as far back as it will go and take in the luminescent wonder floating above. I close my eyes and it's almost as if I can feel it, the wisps of moonlight reaching down to kiss my cheeks and my forehead.

Without meaning to, I turn my head to the side and open my eyes.

Unlike everyone else, staring moonstruck to the heavens, Jasper's head is bowed, his face covered in shadow. His whole body is tense.

Why is he acting so weird?

The prayer ends and the lights are brought back up. I snap my gaze to the ceiling.

Marcel closes out his prayer by saying, "May the Moon Gods light the path between souls."

Every voice in the room responds in kind. "May the Moon Gods light the path between souls."

My mouth makes the shape of the words but no sound comes out.

BLUE MOON, I SAW YOU STANDING ALONE...

The light of the moon shines through my cabin window that night, keeping me awake. I try everything I can to get comfortable. I roll onto my side so I'm not facing the light. I pull my sheets up over my head. But nothing works.

I'm completely wired. Have been since dinner. Every nerve ending in my body is on high alert.

Is it the blue moon? Is my body messed up because of luna energy?

I roll onto my back and it's like the moon is pressing down on my chest, crushing me.

My school counselor told me I had anxiety one time when I was freaking about this history test I thought I was going to fail. This is like anxiety times ten.

The other guys in my cabin are all snoring soundly, which only adds to my frustration.

I roll back toward the window and stare at the moon.

Why do I feel like she's calling me, compelling me to do something? *Well, what? What do you want me to do?*

I sigh and sit up. I'm being ridiculous.

Down by the foot of the bed my sketchbook is sticking

out of my bag. Maybe drawing the moon will help focus some of this nervous energy.

I slip out of my bunk, pull my hoodie over my tank top and lace up my trainers. I grab my sketchbook and pencil and leave the cabin.

Heading off into the darkness of the forest, I know the moon will lead me where I need to go.

It's quiet out in the woods but not eerily so. The buzz of cicadas and the trilling of bullfrogs keep me company as I walk. The shadows are deep but there is enough moonlight that I find my footing easily.

In a short while, I emerge from the trees into a small clearing. The moon shines down in full view.

It's breathtaking. I take a deep breath and soak it in.

"Shouldn't you be sleeping?"

I jump at the sound of his voice. *Jasper.*

He's sitting cross-legged on top of a boulder to my right, his hands resting on his knees and his palms turned upward.

What is he doing out here?

"I couldn't sleep..." I say. "The moon is too bright."

Jasper sighs and looks up.

"Too bright," he whispers to himself. "Too bright and too big—and about to fall on top of us."

Has he forgotten I'm still standing here?

"It's really striking," I say, stepping farther into the clearing. "Incredibly beautiful."

"I think it's hideous," Jasper spits through clenched teeth.

I'm shocked. The moon is sacred to wolves. Our spirits are guided by her light, our moods governed by her pull. We're like the tide ebbing and flowing at her whim. It's bad manners to talk shit about her. To some, it's completely heretical.

But I'm curious. I've never met a wolf who wasn't kind of obsessed with the moon.

"You think it's ugly?" I ask, a little hesitant.

"Ugly, oppressive, you name it," he scoffs. "I find it suffocating. Every night, no matter where you go it's there, like a spotlight. No matter what, you're always being watched. It's intolerable."

"Oh."

I can't say I relate, but I guess the alpha's heir would be under a lot of scrutiny. A lot of people would expect a lot from you. That's *a lot* of pressure.

"I'm sorry," he says. "I know I shouldn't speak like that. I don't mean to offend."

I'm taken aback. Did he just apologize?!

"It's okay," I say, wandering even closer. "I think that's the most words you've ever spoken to me."

He laughs a little, making me grin in turn.

"Besides, this blue moon thing is making everyone act weird."

Jasper chuckles even more.

"I didn't even really want to come to the festival, to be honest."

"Oh yeah." Jasper lifts an eyebrow in my direction. "Why not?"

"I guess...it all just seemed a bit much."

I can feel my cheeks warming and I start to freak out a little. Why am I blushing? Why does talking about mates with Jasper make me feel strange? Why am I telling half-truths?

"Sure," he says coolly. "It is a lot."

I look up and Jasper's watching me with this understanding grin. Did we just find some common ground? Is that even possible?

"I mean, I can hardly complain. It must be a lot more for you, right? Everyone is crazy excited that you're here and wondering who you're going to wind up mated to. That must be difficult."

"I suppose," he says, his eyes glazing over pensively. Then his face turns cold, his eyes settle on one spot, and his jaw tenses. "But it's my duty. To my family and my pack."

"Riiiiight," I say, nodding, pretending I can even start to comprehend what his life must be like. I've managed to move closer to the boulder; I shift my weight and rest my shoulder against it. "I'm sorry."

"Why are you sorry?"

"It just sounds like there's a lot on your plate."

"Yeah, and I have no appetite."

"If it's any consolation my mom thinks me and my best friend are going to be mates. She can't wait for us to start pumping out grandpups."

Now Jasper laughs properly. He almost topples backward off his rocky perch, but he gracefully catches himself before he does.

"So, bonehead," he says once he's settled again, "why are you out here in the woods in the middle of the night?"

"Oh, well I..." After our conversation about how Jasper hates the moon, I don't really want to tell him I came out here to draw it. "I couldn't sleep so I thought I could do some sketches."

"Aisha said you were an artist."

He remembers.

"She said you're a nice kid." *Wait, does this mean they've...talked about me?* "And she thinks I've been too hard on you."

Wha-a-a-a-at???

I can't believe what I'm hearing. I must have caught Jasper with his guard down.

"You were probably just stressed..." I say, trying to act cool as a cucumber.

"Can I see some of your work?"

I step away from the boulder, my eyes bulging out of my head. I'm not usually that shy about sharing my work. But for some reason, Jasper wanting to look at my sketches is freaking me the fudge out. What if he thinks they're stupid? What if he thinks I'm terrible?

Why do I care?

"Come on, I'm sure they're fine," he says, whisking the sketch pad out of my slippery fingers and opening it up on his lap.

My body goes into shutdown mode as Jasper flips through the pages.

I watch like a deer in headlights as he spends a decent

amount of time on each page, studying the pictures, appreciating them.

"Wow, bonehead," he says after a while, "these are pretty good. You're talented."

"Um, thanks," I mumble. The flush in my cheeks has become red-hot flames of embarrassment.

"Oh hey, is that Aisha?"

Jasper's question makes my stomach drop out of my ass. He's reached the drawings of Aisha in the lake, which means he's only a few pages from finding the picture of his face!

If he sees that picture he's going to think I'm obsessed or something.

"Oh, yeah, you can probably stop now, those are just, like, preliminary sketches, they're not finished, or even very good."

Jasper glances sideways at me. "You're acting weird."

"Weird?! I'm not acting weird. You're acting weird!"

I'm acting completely deranged. *Way to prove his point, moron.*

"You should show Aisha these. She'd love them."

There's a 0 percent chance of me doing that.

Jasper turns the page and becomes very still. Silence hangs in the air between us like a cloud. I can't tell for sure but I assume he's reached the drawing of him. His eyes scan the page, taking in his own features, the ones I drew.

He doesn't say anything. And he doesn't react in any discernible way. He just stares at the picture for a long, long time, before quietly shutting the book.

I wait anxiously for him to call me a psycho or a stalker—hell, I'd even take *bonehead* right now. But he doesn't call me names. He just holds the book out for me to take.

"You're a talented artist, Max."

My heart is all the way in my throat. Up until now, I wasn't even sure he knew my actual name. It was certainly the last thing I expected to come out of his mouth. But here he is, looking into my eyes, saying it.

I wish he'd say it again.

"You okay?" he asks.

"Uh, yeah." I reach up to take back my sketchbook and as I do our fingers brush together.

It's like breathing for the first time. My mouth drops open as this easy, electric feeling begins at the point of contact and moves through me like a wave, flooding my senses. I feel weightless and filled with light. I feel relief and comfort and fulfillment in a way I've never experienced.

I think I'm about to faint when Jasper pulls his hand away sharply.

That feeling disappears instantly and the forest is suddenly a little more shadow-filled than before.

I shiver and wrap my arms around myself. *What was that?*

"You should probably get some sleep," Jasper says.

The chill, friendly way in which he spoke to me just a moment ago is gone. Here is the cool, stoic, unfeeling Jasper I'm used to.

"Right," I say, suddenly wishing I was under the covers back in my cabin. "Big day tomorrow."

He scoffs and rolls his eyes. "Of course."

"What?"

"You're really just like everyone else aren't you? Obsessed with finding a mate."

I have no idea where this is coming from, but hell if I'm going to let him speak to me like that.

"I told you the only person who cares about mates is my pup-obsessed mother. Don't you listen?"

"Oh, so this whole thing is a joke to you?"

Jasper stares at me with piercing, spiteful eyes and, without thinking, my feet begin stepping backward. Automatically, I retreat toward the forest.

"No, it's not a joke, but I thought you said—"

"This is a big deal," he says, pushing off from the rock and landing gracefully, like a ninja. "You have no idea how big."

"I get it, it's a lot of pressure but—"

"How could you understand?" Jasper turns his face to

me and his eyes are cold, uncaring. "You're just some dumb kid."

My jaw starts quivering but there's no way I'm going to start crying in front of him. As much as my body is trying to make me, it's not going to happen.

"And you're just the alpha's dumb son. You're not even the alpha, but you're acting like the fate of the whole pack is on your shoulders. You're not so special, you know!"

Jasper's entire body becomes rigid and his look of apathy turns to pure, ice-cold disdain.

"Go back to bed, Max."

"Don't tell me what to do!"

"I said LEAVE!"

Jasper's growl is fierce and resonant. I'm pushed back by the sheer force of the sound.

His face softens; he can tell that he's just frightened the Skittles out of me. But I barely register the change. I'm already turning, already running back into the forest.

I run back through the darkness until I reach the cabin and dive under my covers. I'm shaking as I clutch the thin blanket to my chest.

Why does he think it's okay to talk to people like that?

And why has he upset me so much?

My life would be way simpler if I'd never run into him. I try to breathe and stop myself from shaking. I just want the festival to be over already. I just want to go home, so I can forget all about this stupid place. And I can forget all about Jasper Apollo!

BREAKFAST WITH ELEANOR

I'm glad to find Katie at breakfast. She isn't sitting at the fancy people's table. Instead, she's sitting at one of the round tables at the far end of the room with Eleanor, Simon, and Todd. Jasper is nowhere to be seen.

Unlike lunch and dinner, breakfast is the only meal that isn't served to everyone at the same time. Campers are welcome to stroll into the dining hall anytime between 7 a.m. and 10 a.m., to fill up on pancakes, waffles, eggs, fruit, and cereal.

At the buffet table off to the side, I pile up a short stack, throw on some berries, cover the pancakes in a mountain of crispy bacon, and pour on copious amounts of maple syrup. I take my overladen plate and join Katie.

"Morning," she says cheerily.

"Hi," I say, nodding to the entire group.

"Whassup, man?" Todd asks, shoveling scrambled eggs into his mouth.

"Not much," I reply, sitting.

"Eleanor was just telling me about the Mating Run," Katie says.

Apparently, she and Eleanor have become tight in the space of a couple of days. A pang of jealousy twists my heart.

"Wow," I say, tucking in.

"I was just saying based on the statistics there's a 70 percent chance of finding one's mate on the run," Eleanor says. Someone's had too many cups of coffee this morning.

An inexplicable shudder runs down my back. "That's high."

"If every unmated wolf is here and they all run, how come that number isn't even higher?" Katie asks, resting on her elbows.

She pushes her empty bowl away. Wow, she's already finished her usual—muesli and fruit—so she was either hanging around waiting for me or she was really into this convo.

"Not every unmated wolf is here," Eleanor responds like a living, breathing encyclopedia. "Every unmated wolf is invited to the festival, but attendance isn't mandatory. Some people can't afford it, or they're out of state. Some just don't feel ready to take part."

So how come I wasn't given a choice? I quietly curse my parents for assuming I would *want* to be here.

I guess I didn't exactly protest. Katie was excited about doing our first festival together. I figured it wouldn't be so bad as long as we were hanging out.

Jasper is starting to make me wish I'd opted out.

"Right," Katie says, nodding like she's just learned the location of Atlantis. "But everyone who does attend will find their mate if they're also here, right?"

"Not necessarily," Eleanor goes on. "Firstly, not everyone who is here is going on the run. It's expected but again, it isn't compulsory. And secondly, the bond between mates isn't always obvious. Even with the pumped-up energy from the blue moon, sometimes the connection isn't apparent right away."

"But don't we all just run around sniffing each other?" I ask. "I don't see how two mates could wind up missing each other."

"It's a bit more complicated than that," Eleanor says, desperate to explain further. "The Mating Run takes place in the woods, and there are no instructions other than shifting and running. The Alpha's Retreat sits on approximately fifty square miles of undeveloped land. If you and your mate start the run heading in opposite directions there is little chance you'll sense your bond. The blue moon is intense but not that intense."

Eleanor has cracked herself up, laughing at the "joke" she's made.

"Gosh," Katie says, getting that faraway, wistful look she gets when we listen to Taylor Swift or we've just demolished a tub of Ben & Jerry's Phish Food. "I hope that doesn't happen to me."

Her eyes flicker swiftly in my direction.

"That's why you need a plan," Eleanor says matter-of-factly. "I plan to loop around the camp in continuous concentric circles, covering the most amount of land in the least amount of time. Guaranteed to increase the likelihood of crossing paths with every attendee by 50 percent."

"That's clever," Katie says.

I scoff at my pancakes. "That's insane."

"Don't be a dick," Katie says, nudging me, making me miss my mouth with my fork.

I look over and Eleanor has gone quiet, staring down at her unfinished hash browns.

"Sorry," I say, suddenly feeling awful. "That just sounds like a lot of effort."

Eleanor perks up, shaking out her straight, black hair and correcting her posture.

"It might seem extreme, but I'll be that much closer to finding my mate."

"I guess I just thought mates were like, meant to be and all that. So, like, if it's meant to happen it'll happen. You won't need to force it."

Eleanor looks darkly at her unfinished breakfast once more.

"I guess it just means more to some people than others," she says, barely audibly.

"You got that right."

I turn my attention back to the increasingly soggy short stack in front of me, but I can feel Katie's penetrating stare.

"I...have to go," Eleanor says, picking up her plate and pushing her chair back. "I have volunteer duties."

"No wait, stay," Katie says, sympathy making her voice go all high-pitched. "Please, Max was just being a jerk because he's not keen on finding his mate yet."

Yet?! More like ever!

As if she can read my thoughts, Katie turns to me, staring like she's about to shift and bite my face off.

"Um sorry, Eleanor. I didn't mean to be rude, I just didn't sleep well."

"I really should be going anyway, there's a lot I still need to do to get ready for tonight."

With her eyes on the floor, Eleanor shuffles off to her duties.

Katie slaps my arm. "Why did you have to upset her like that?"

"I'm sorry, I haven't had any coffee yet."

"You've been weird ever since we got here," she says, lowering her voice so the bro twins can't hear us. "I know this isn't your dream scenario but can you stop ruining it for other people?"

"I haven't been ruining this for other people. The only reason I came here was because you wanted to do it and I've gone along with everything we've had to do without complaining once."

"You think this is what not complaining sounds like?" she hisses, and I stop to think for a second.

Maybe I haven't been ruining the festival for everybody, but I haven't been making it fun for Katie either.

I open up my mouth to begin apologizing, but she's on a roll now. "You may think finding your soulmate is a big joke but to some of us it's serious."

"I never said it wasn't serious," I mutter.

"No, you just made it clear that you don't give a shit about it!" Katie's voice has risen from a stage whisper to the cusp of shouting. Her face is red and she looks like her hair is almost about to fly off to release the buildup of steam from her brain.

Todd and Simon have stopped flicking Tater Tots at each other with their forks and are staring at us.

"Katie, calm down..."

I've chosen the exact wrong thing to say to an uncalm person, but Katie isn't the type to flip her lid. She stops looking at me and turns her attention to the middle of the table. Her chest rises and falls with intentionally deep breaths. Her face is redder than before, the flush in her cheeks rising in splotches. Tears are welling in her unmoving eyes.

"Look, I'm sorry, okay? I had a weird night and I'm not on form..."

"You had a weird night," she says, shaking her head slightly. "What's your excuse for yesterday then?"

"Yesterday?"

"When you dropped me for Aisha without a second thought."

"I apologized for that. I was just excited to meet her."

Katie huffs and finally turns to face me. Her furious expression drops away and I see the sadness that's been fueling her anger rising to the surface.

"Is that all?" she asks, her voice cracking.

"What do you mean?"

"Tonight when we take part in the Mating Run, who would you rather discover is your mate? Her or me?"

My pancakes churn in my stomach as Katie's question reverberates in my ears.

"Her or me?"

The honest-to-the-Moon-Gods truth is I've never really thought about who my mate might be. I guess I've never thought about Katie in that way. We've been friends forever. We know each other better than we know ourselves. I've never even considered it.

Clearly, she has.

When it comes to Aisha, the thought might have crossed my mind. But just for a second, like watching from the platform as an express train speeds through the station.

Aisha is cool and good at ballet; if I had to wind up with a stranger for a mate, I'd want it to be her. But I wouldn't hate it if Katie and I turned out to be mates either. It would just be weird because she's family.

Katie stares at me demandingly as I think this over, and somewhere in my expression the truth—that while I don't particularly *want* to wind up mated to either of them, I've never even considered it an option with Katie—must shine through.

"I see," she says as the light in her eyes, the warmth that's always made me feel at home, disappears.

"Katie..."

"Don't," she says, pulling her hand away as I go to touch her. "Maybe I'm the idiot for wanting something from someone who has no clue. Or maybe you are." She looks me dead in the eye. "Because at least I'm not pining over some prima ballerina who is so far out of my league she's not even playing the same sport."

"What are you talking about?"

"Everyone knows that Aisha is going to end up mating with Jasper. It's obvious."

"What?"

This new information seems to have come out of nowhere. Even though I know Katie is lashing out, trying to make me feel as bad as she does, something inside me lurches forward, an aching feeling I can't explain.

"Aisha is going to be mated to Jasper and you'll just have to deal with whichever unlucky girl gets stuck with you."

"No, she isn't!" The words flow out of me like an evil spirit, a demon I can't control.

I slap a hand over my mouth but it's too late. The nasty sprite is out.

"So it's true?" Katie says. "You'd rather end up with her, a stranger, than with me?"

I have no idea how breakfast with Eleanor has turned into the biggest fight Katie and I have ever had. But here we are.

"That's not what I meant..." I say, but Katie's fragile facade is already cracking.

I've seen her like this before. When our ballet teacher shouted at her for not bending her knees enough. When her first boyfriend, Eric Peterson, broke up with her in seventh grade. Her lips start quivering, a funny wrinkled pattern appears on her chin, and her eyes turn pink.

My best friend is about to cry and it's my fault.

"Katie—"

"Stop..."

With a speedy determination, Katie begins marching toward the door. I don't even understand how I've managed to upset her so badly. I have no idea why the idea of Aisha and Jasper winding up together set me off. Honestly, I couldn't care less. So why did I snap?

I look across the table at Simon and Todd, who are staring like I've just crashed my car and it's leaking oil.

"Go after her, dude!" Simon says.

In a second I'm on my feet, chasing Katie out onto the gravel forecourt.

By the time I make it outside, Katie is already at the edge of the forest and showing no signs of slowing down.

"Katie!"

I manage to catch up to her and go to take her arm but she pulls away from me.

"Leave me alone!" she yells before stomping off through the underbrush.

Out of breath and thinking it might be best to give her some space, I let her go.

Whenever we've fought before it's always been about silly trivial things—a broken toy, an unshared muffin—but this feels different. Less of a tremor and more of a city-leveling earthquake.

Katie doesn't look back as she disappears amongst the foliage.

I just hope we're able to rebuild.

SWIMMING WITH WOLVES

Deflated after my fight with Katie, I walk zombielike back into the dining hall and sit at my half-finished stack of pancakes.

Todd and Simon are on their way out, offering a "sorry bud" and a "too bad, bro" as they pass.

I slump into my chair and turn up my lips at the pile of food in front of me. It looks like a gross pile of mush to me now, so I push the plate as far away from me as I can.

"Morning, dude," I hear Aisha say. She's approaching the table carrying a full plate of waffles. "How's it hanging?"

She stops in her tracks when she sees my expression.

"Oh, not good, hey?"

She slips into the chair next to me—*Katie's chair*—and puts a reassuring hand on my knee.

"What's going on?" she asks.

"Katie and I had a fight."

"Riiight." She nods like a therapist. "Do you want to tell me what it was about?"

The irony that our fight was sort of about Aisha and now she's the one trying to comfort me is not lost.

But it wasn't really about Aisha, I realize. She's more like a symptom. The truth of the cause sits in my gut like a lump of stone.

"Mates," I mumble.

"I see," Aisha says, crossing her legs, making herself comfortable. "Does she want to be your mate?"

"I think so."

Finally, it's all become clear to me. The reason Katie reacted the way she did yesterday when I asked Aisha to go canoeing. The reason she was so excited for us both to go to our first festival *together*. I've been so ignorant, so willfully blind. But I guess I just didn't want the friendship to change...or end.

I'm worried it has.

"And you don't feel the same?" Aisha asks slowly.

I shake my head.

She sighs caringly. "It's tricky business this mating stuff. And the blue moon messing with everyone's hormones doesn't help much either."

"You got that right."

She grins when I'm finally able to make comprehensible words.

"There he is!"

But her joy is somewhat premature. I feel awful. Not only have I been ignoring the clear signs Katie has been giving me, I've also been so insensitive to her feelings that she's had to run away from me, into the *literal* unknown. I slump back into my chair and wonder if I'm about to cry too.

Aisha appraises me, puckering her lips and squinting.

"I know what will cheer you up," she says.

Fifteen minutes later we're standing in our bathing suits at the edge of the lake.

"I'm not sure this is a good idea," I say. "The water was freezing when I fell in yesterday."

It's a gloriously sunny day, the sky is a bright cartoon blue, the few puffy clouds look like cotton candy, the trees are emerald, and the water does look delightfully refreshing.

But the icy sting of my unexpected dip is fresh in my mind.

"The water is warmer here," Aisha says. "It's more stagnant."

Great...?

The swimming area is a designated section of the shoreline a short distance behind the cabins. There are wolves splashing about in the shallows and a few farther out. Some are swinging from a hanging tire and launching themselves into the water.

It can't be that cold if they're all swimming in it.

"What better way to wash your blues away," Aisha says in a singsong voice.

I stand frozen glancing along the shoreline.

Colorful beach towels dot the pebbly shore like rectangular flowers. The sweet pine scent of the air fills my nostrils and helps begin to clear my mind.

Maybe she's right.

"If a quick dip can't shake that gloom off your shoulders I don't know what will." Aisha smiles and begins walking toward the water.

She's wearing a black bikini; her athletic body is shining in the sunlight. Compared to her I feel like a marshmallow, soft and pale.

"First one to the platform is an omega," she calls over her shoulder, picking up speed.

Out in the middle of the lake is a wooden platform with an algae-covered ladder attached to the side.

Aisha is already halfway down the shore. I refuse to be left behind, even though the thought of swimming out in that icy water is giving me severe brain freeze. I take off after her.

We splash our way into the shallows, the water shocking my body awake. When the cold, breath-stealing liquid is up to my waist I take a giant gulp of air and brace myself. I dive under headfirst and come up gasping. The water is so cold it's hard to breathe.

It's definitely the same temperature as yesterday!

Aisha is already making strokes toward the platform, cutting through the surface of the water like a samurai sword. I kick my feet and try to remember my freestyle technique from when I took swimming lessons in elementary school.

It's hard to gain any speed or catch my breath, but eventually I find my rhythm. I stroke as hard as I can, kicking frantically, and I make it out to the platform.

Aisha, who beat me by a mile, takes my hand and helps me up the slimy ladder. Cold water runs off me, dripping from my swimming shorts.

We take a seat on the decking, looking back at the other wolves still splashing about, and let the sun warm our skin. We're farther out than I thought. I feel like we're so far away that we could growl our loudest growls and no one would hear us.

"Feel better?" Aisha asks.

"My head does feel clearer," I respond, and it's the truth.

Our little swim has helped me feel less like the world is collapsing. I know Katie and I are going to be fine. We're best friends and we always will be. One stupid fight at a stupid festival can't shake that.

"See, a little exercise will always shake the blues away."

"Totally."

"You wanna talk about what happened?"

Aisha looks at me like she's ready to listen. I'm amazed. We only met yesterday and I basically fangirled majorly. I wouldn't have been surprised if Aisha thought I was a complete wacko. But her big, princess eyes are full of genuine concern and I feel as if she wants to help.

"I guess I just always thought of Katie more like a friend...a *best* friend."

"Well, that's okay. If that's how you feel."

"But I should have been able to see that she felt a different kind of way. Or I should have made her feel like she could tell me."

"Sure, but it can be hard talking about feelings. Even to the people you love the most. Hell, sometimes that's harder."

"It's just...well, she's so obsessed with mates."

"Of course she is, she's a teenage wolf."

"I don't think just because you're a wolf you have to buy into the whole mate-bond thing."

"Yeah, well, what else would you expect from her? That's what we're all taught to be obsessed with. Look around, man. Everyone here is just hoping to find their person."

"Sure."

Everyone on the beach is smiling, laughing, but then I notice something else as well. There's a strange scent on the wind. A mixture of sweat, salty and sharp, and something sweeter, something like wildflowers, tangy and enticing. *Wolf pheromones.* Everyone back on the beach, and probably all the wolves at camp, are low-level emitting their scent, designed to attract the opposite sex.

"I guess I'm not like everyone else," I say, sighing and resting my chin on my knees.

"Maybe this isn't all your fault then," Aisha says, bumping shoulders with me. "If Katie knows you as well as you know her, maybe she should have known what matters to you and not pushed the whole mate thing."

"Maybe."

Aisha has a point, kind of. But it's not enough that I don't still feel like trash.

Waves lap at the edge of our platform, sending water slopping onto the decking. The coolness against my feet and my butt is a nice relief from the hot sun beating down on my back. Aisha stretches out her legs, crossing one ankle over the other, and leans back on her hands.

"So you're really not into the whole mates thing then?" she asks, side-eyeing me.

"Nah," I say and lean back so that our shoulders are next to each other. "I just don't get it. I'm only sixteen. There's stuff I want to do before I settle down forever."

"Makes sense," she says, nodding appreciatively.

"What about you?" I ask. "Excited to find your mate?"

"I told you I'm already mated to dance."

"But what about tonight? You might find some guy

during the Mating Run."

"Not if I don't plan on running," she says.

Eleanor said that the run wasn't compulsory. That wolves could opt out if they wanted. I assumed most people came here for the sole reason of joining the run. I guess Aisha isn't like most people either.

"You're not going to do the Mating Run?"

"Nope," she says.

"Why not?"

Aisha tilts her head, squinting at me through the glare. "Don't tell anybody this, okay?"

I nod eagerly.

"I don't want to find a mate, because I already found a boyfriend. A *human* boyfriend."

"What...?" My mouth hangs open.

"Does that freak you out?" she asks. "I know a lot of people think mixing the species is weird or gross, or some kind of betrayal or whatever..."

"No! Not at all! I think that's cool."

My parents raised me to believe that everyone was equal. My mom is always going on and on about how there are too many male alphas running the packs, and my dad always advocates for human rights amongst his colleagues.

"Sorry, I didn't mean to sound shocked. I've just never met anyone who's dating a human before."

"It's not very common."

"Or maybe I just haven't met many people."

I smile and Aisha smiles back. I'm glad she felt comfortable enough to tell me her secret. Maybe it's just a side effect of our private island in the stream, but I still feel privileged to have been let inside her life like this.

"What's he like?" I ask.

"His name is Troy and he goes to Columbia, to study molecular biology or something sciencey. We met a couple years ago in New York and since then he's come to every single performance I've done."

I have a momentary flashback to the night at the ballet when I first saw Aisha dance. I remember a guy in the front row handing her flowers. Maybe that was Troy.

"He sounds sweet," I say.

"He's the best."

A cool wind blows across my shoulders as I take a breath and lean farther back.

"The rest of the camp is going to be disappointed."

"Why do you say that?"

"Everyone thinks you're going to end up being mates with Jasper."

Aisha sits up in a rush, laughter bursting out of her like a comedy volcano erupting.

"Me...and...Jasper...? That's crazy!"

I start to giggle and then laugh and then both of us are cackling like we've completely lost the plot.

As we start to calm down, a cloud crosses the sky, blocking the sun.

"So you don't think you and Jasper would be a good match then?" I ask, starting to shiver a little.

"Nah, we're a bit like you and Katie. Just good friends. Besides, I don't know if you've noticed but he's a little uptight."

"Oh my Moon Gods, I know! I pity the poor wolf he does end up with."

Aisha chuckles but stops herself. "We shouldn't be too hard on him."

"Why not?"

"Jasper is the future alpha of our whole pack. The biggest pack on the East Coast. There's a lot of pressure on him. And his father...woo! He's a tough cookie."

"You mean Alpha Jericho? You must know him, right?"

"Yeah, I've met him a few times. But he doesn't stick around if you know what I mean. Not much of a talker. What I do know is he has high expectations for Jasper and he does not like being disappointed."

Jasper always seems so confident and unshakable. He always seems so judgmental and stern. But I never really stopped to think what made him that way.

"Speak of the devil," Aisha says, peering across the water. "The sequel."

Back on the shore, Jasper has arrived at the beach. He and Olivia are wandering down the pebbles. An unswallowable lump lodges itself in my throat as I watch him. He's wearing a pair of black swim shorts, some black slip-on shoes, and wayfarer sunglasses. His tanned chest seems broader than it does when he's wearing clothes, and each of his abs might as well have its own postal code, they're that defined.

What if he spots me and Aisha out here? Will he swim out to meet us?

The thought of him seeing me in all my pasty, marshmallowy glory makes me want to dive to the bottom of the lake and stay there.

"You see something you like?" Aisha asks, and I turn to find her leering at me suggestively.

I nearly topple right off the platform.

"Wha...? No...I—"

"Hey, calm down. I was only kidding."

"Yeah, well, I was only distracted because he makes me so furious," I lie. "I honestly don't know how you can stand to be his friend."

"Like I said, don't be too hard on Jasper. He's got a lot going on."

Just like clockwork a man and a woman dressed in camouflage pants and khaki-green T-shirts come jogging down the beach toward Jasper. I watch as they get his attention and proceed to have a very quiet, very urgent discussion. In a split second Jasper's voice booms across the lake.

"Everyone out of the water! Emergency meeting in the amphitheater in ten minutes! This is not a drill. Everyone out of the water now!"

I glance to Aisha as panic floods my limbs.

"This isn't good," she says, already on her feet and reaching down to help me up.

The sun has completely disappeared behind a bank of clouds and the wind has begun to pick up. Wolves are fleeing the water like a scene from *Jaws*. I brace myself as I dive back into the lake. I'm too scared to notice the cold.

GOING ROGUE

Aisha assures me everything will be fine before scurrying off to check in with Jasper. I hurry to my cabin to dress—even in an emergency I'd rather put on a shirt than stand around half naked.

On my way to the amphitheater I run into Simon and Todd, and we find our way there together.

The theater is built into a hillside a little ways from camp. Banks of seats curve in shrinking semicircles, leading down to a stage area.

In less than ten minutes everyone has gathered in the amphitheater. Some of the wolves from the lake are still in their trunks, towels draped over their sunburnt shoulders. Others have come back from hiking in their walking boots, with sweat-stained T-shirts.

I keep my eye out for Katie but I can't see her anywhere.

A blanket of low-level panic rests over the crowd.

From our spot at the back I notice more of the wolves in army gear posted at stations about twenty feet apart; they've formed a perimeter around the seating.

"Hey, what's with the Rambo wannabes?" I ask quietly, leaning closer to Todd.

"Pack guards on security detail," he says. "They usually stay out of the way so they don't bring down the mood."

"I heard they have their own cabin somewhere on the outskirts of the property," Simon adds, just as a hush settles over the crowd.

Jasper, who also had the sense to get dressed, and is now wearing a black T-shirt with black running pants—always black!—steps into the center of the platform below.

"Thank you for gathering here so quickly. I won't waste your time; we have just had reports that a rogue has been spotted on the property."

A rogue?!

Agitated whispers and rising voices join to meet the growing wind.

We've all learned about rogues from our parents. They're wolves who've abandoned their packs or been excommunicated. The separation of a wolf from its pack is such a traumatizing event that these wolves become crazed and violent. Rogues are hungry for blood, with an insatiable appetite for violence.

All of us gathered in one place like this is—well, it's like setting up a wolf buffet.

"Our security team is doing everything they can to confirm these sightings and apprehend the rogue before any damage can be done. But for them to do their jobs I need your cooperation. So until further notice, I'm asking you all to return to your cabins. Lock the doors from the inside and wait until you receive further instructions."

"What about the run?!" a lone voice calls out from the crowd.

I can't believe our lives may be in danger and some demented, lovesick moron is concerned about going for a run in the dark.

"Until we know it is safe I cannot see how we can continue with the evening's planned activities."

An angry murmur rises from all around. Jasper takes a step back, he looks nervous. Aisha was right. He's only a kid, just two years older than me, and here he is dealing with honest-to-the-Moon-Gods life-and-death situations while trying to quell the overactive hormones of a bunch of randy, don't-know-what's-good-for-them wolves.

"Please," he calls, trying to be heard over the increasing ruckus, "return to your cabins. We are doing our best to sort this out as quickly as possible. If we can neutralize the threat we will reevaluate the situation, but please, I'm asking for your help."

Just when I think Jasper is about to lose control, the crowd begins to move off. I guess not being mauled to death is more important than running around looking for a snuggle buddy. Everyone rises and heads toward the cabins.

"Come on, bro," Todd says, gesturing for me to follow. He and Simon have already begun heading back.

But as the crowd flows past me I realize someone is missing. Someone who wandered off into the forest earlier today. Someone who left because I upset her.

My whole body runs cold, dread seizes my heart like a skeleton hand.

Todd and Simon are staring at me like my skin has turned purple.

"Come on, man," Simon says. "What's the holdup?"

"Katie is still out there," I say.

The clouds burst as a sky-cracking bolt of lightning illuminates the forest. Not too far away, thunder crashes, shaking the ground.

Todd and Simon called after me as I sprinted away from the cabins and into the woods. *Let them shout,* I thought. I'd rather they think I was crazy than for anything bad to happen to Katie.

I know it's not the smartest move—running off without telling anyone where I'm going. But there wasn't time before my instincts took over, lifting my feet and pointing me in the direction I last saw Katie heading this morning.

Even under the dense foliage of the forest canopy, rain still manages to spatter the ground. It's thick, heavy rain, the kind that makes you wonder if the clouds have been saving themselves for a special occasion.

Running comes easy to me again, just like it did during capture the flag. I hurtle through the woods at a speed I didn't even know I was capable of, leaping uprooted branches with ease. I thank the blue moon or whatever strange circumstance has gifted me this new athletic ability. Last time I thought it was my determination to beat Jasper that spurred me on, maybe this time it's my desperation to find Katie before...before...

I can't even think about finishing that thought. Yes, there is a killer rogue out here. And yes, Katie has been out here all alone for several hours, but that doesn't mean... It doesn't mean anything bad has happened.

I wipe a drop of rain—or maybe sweat—from my forehead and keep running. The rain grows heavier as I move farther into the dank, dark heart of the woods. I keep my senses as alert as possible, sniffing for even a whiff of Katie's scent.

Mud flies up from underneath me as I dig in and stop suddenly. My eyes have caught on something. A flash of pink in my periphery. I try to think back to this morning. Was Katie wearing pink? *Think, Max! You need to think!* Why am I so unobservant?

But then it comes to me. Yes! She was wearing pink. A ribbon, to tie back her hair. I spin and run to where I've spotted her ribbon. But I arrive deflated. It's her ribbon all right. Only it isn't attached to her. The thin piece of fabric is hanging from a branch.

It's not bad news, I try to convince myself. It could have snagged on this tree and come undone. What it does mean is I'm on the right track. Katie came this way.

I lift my nose in the air and try to sniff her out, but all I get is an overwhelming stench of soil and rotting foliage. I have to keep running.

Making out the blurred line of a path in the mud I pick up my pace and follow it. The rain has turned into an all-out maelstrom. Heavy droplets smack into my face, soaking my clothes and blurring my vision.

I spot the ravine from yesterday and think about

slowing down but I can't, Katie needs me. Without hesitating, I prepare myself to make the jump, and just as I'm about to take off I hear my name.

"Max!"

Skidding to a stop, I turn to find Katie standing behind me with all her limbs attached, completely alive and untouched by the rogue.

"What are you doing out here? You're soaked!"

Tears spring to my eyes but are quickly washed away by the continuing downpour. I run over to Katie, who is standing beneath a rocky outcrop shielding herself from the rain.

"You're okay," I gasp, taking her in my arms and pulling her into me. The feeling of her on my chest, the tangible, solid force of her, sends shivers of relief through me.

"I'm fine," she says, a little confused. "I'm wet now thanks to you, but I'm fine. I was about to hike back to camp when it started raining so I thought I'd just wait it out."

I look into her crystal-clear eyes and touch her face. She looks at me like I'm being super weird.

"What's going on?" she asks. "Why are you acting like...like you've just seen a ghost?"

"Back at camp...we were swimming...and...emergency meeting...and..."

"What, Max? What's the emergency?" Katie's confused expression becomes one of concern, graduating into full-blown worry. "Why did you come out here to find me?"

"Jasper...called an emergency meeting," I say, still trying to catch my breath. "And there's a...on the loose...a...a..."

"A rogue?" Katie asks as the color drains from her cheeks.

She isn't looking at me anymore. She's looking over my shoulder.

"How did you know that?" I ask, terror creeping up the backs of my legs like a pair of lizards.

"Because...look..."

I turn around slowly but back up quickly when I see what Katie has been staring at. Standing on the other side of the ravine is the rogue. It's in its wolf form and probably the largest animal I've ever seen. Bigger than my dad even! His dark, matted fur is sticking up in clumps, interspersed with patches of raw, scab-ridden skin. His ribs are visible and his eyes sunken into his skull. Rain is pouring over his long, crooked muzzle, making the white scar on his cheek glisten; there's a sickly yellow tint to his eyes, and his fangs drip with thick, gooey saliva.

He stares at us from across the crevice, waiting for us to make a move before he pounces.

I reach behind me and find Katie's hand, we grip each other tightly.

The rogue is snarling, staring at us like a starving beast who's just spotted dinner. Lightning crashes overhead and he snaps his jaws.

"You have to go," I say before I even know what I'm doing.

"No, Max, we can fight him if we shift."

"That thing will tear us in half before we even manage the change."

Shifting is fast, considering the sheer amount of anatomy that needs to be rearranged. But in the few seconds it takes for us to go from humble, sweet-looking teenagers to ferocious wild animals, the monster across the ravine will have leaped over here and turned us into kibble.

"I'm not leaving you."

"Just do it," I say, hissing through clenched teeth. "I can outrun it."

"You can't," Katie says, fighting back tears.

"I can, this messed-up blue moon shit is giving me superspeed. Okay? I'm the freaking Flash. But you need to run back to camp and get help. Maybe I can keep ahead of him until someone comes."

"No, Max..."

My entire body is trembling with fear and adrenaline. I feel like my heart is about to explode, but it's my fault that Katie is out here. It's my fault that she's in this situation to begin with. And as scared as I am, I'm determined to get her out.

"When I say go, you run back to camp, got it?"

"What about the ravine? The jump! You'll never make it."

"Yes, I will." I squeeze her hand one last time. "Go!"

I pull away and dash for the ravine. The second I run the rogue leaps into the air with all the ferocious energy of a beast on a mission.

One quick glance behind me, to check that Katie is on her way to safety, then I pick up speed and sprint toward the crevice.

I push off with all my strength, leaping into the air. The rogue watches me as I crescent moon over the gorge, landing safely on the other side.

There's no time for me to savor my victory because the rogue is close, running at full pelt. I dash into the forest while he changes direction to follow. For every step I take I can hear his sick, wheezing pants, and for every sharp intake of air I take, I hear his feet pounding the soil.

For a while, I manage to keep a good distance between us, but the landscape becomes harder to traverse. Rocks jut out of the soil, roots curl around them like greedy fingers, moss and mud make secure footing hard to find. And finally, I tread in a rain-soaked puddle and feel my legs go out from underneath me.

I tumble forward, rolling across the uneven ground and coming to a halt.

I scramble backward, trying to get up on my feet, but it's no use. There's no time left.

The rogue growls, its pale, droopy tongue slopping lustfully about in its mouth, then it leaps at me.

Time slows down as I brace for impact, for the crushing weight of the rogue as he pins me to the ground.

I scream as he crashes down on top of me and his claws pierce my skin. He rears back then plunges his fangs into my shoulder.

OUT OF THE FRYING PAN

Hot searing pain tears into my shoulder.

I open my mouth to scream but can't find my voice.

I squeeze my eyes shut.

This is the end. This is the end.

A fifty-ton rogue is about to tear my throat out.

He clamps down on my shoulder even harder, and this time my scream is loud enough to wake the dead. I imagine flocks of birds fleeing the trees as I howl in agony.

Then just as suddenly, the pain is gone. The weight is lifted from me.

I take a deep breath as the realization dawns on me. The rogue is no longer chomping on my collarbone.

Tentatively I open my eyes and instantly begin to scrabble backward.

Across the path from me, the rogue is wrestling with another wolf. They're fighting, snapping at each other's necks, rolling over each other, trying to claim the higher ground.

It's hard to make out the other wolf in the melee. But he's large, muscular, with a night-black coat. He's fast too.

I back up against the trunk of a tree, unable to stand just yet, and watch as they fight. They're both fierce warriors, total beast masters! I wince as they ram into each other again and again.

Daggerlike claws rip through the air attempting to gouge out eyes, fangs are exposed and dig into flesh.

They're evenly matched, but the black wolf—whoever he is—is fighting with a steely determination the rogue can't contend with.

Finally, the black wolf strikes the rogue, sending it flying across the forest. It hits the ground hard and rolls to a stop. The black wolf takes a labored breath, but he isn't done. He leaps from where he stands and lands directly on top of the rogue, biting deep into its shoulder—the same spot the rogue bit me—and tearing its arm from its socket. I flinch at the snapping sound.

The rogue lies still, wheezing in pain and unable to stand, as the black wolf turns to me. Panic suddenly rises in my chest. My throat constricts like I have a nut allergy and just ate a Snickers bar.

I have no idea who this wolf is. No idea if he is a friend or a more terrifying foe than the last.

I press my back against the tree; there's no way for me to escape.

The wolf continues to approach, his lips curled back to expose his fangs, a low growl rumbling from his chest.

"Max!"

I turn to my left at the sound of Katie's voice. She's running toward me with her arms outstretched. Just behind her is Olivia, accompanied by two more wolves. Katie kneels beside me and pulls me into the best best-friend hug I could ask for.

"Ah!" I say when I remember my wound.

"Oh sorry," Katie says, sitting back. "Are you hurt?"

"It got my shoulder..."

Katie leans forward, pulling the collar of my T-shirt away and looking at what I assume is a perfect indent of the rogue's teeth.

"It only just broke the skin," she says. "You should be

healed in a few hours."

Thank the Moon Gods for speedy wolf healing.

"Who is...that?" I ask, looking back at the big black wolf who is no longer staring in my direction. Instead, he's barking and grunting in a circle with the other two wolves.

In a second the wolf pair spring off into the woods and disappear. Maybe checking the area for more rogues.

Olivia approaches the black wolf, swinging a backpack off one shoulder and passing it to the animal, who takes it in his jaw and saunters off behind some shrubbery.

Katie and I wait as the bone-crunching, muscle-fusing sounds of shifting ring out behind the bushes. Before I know it, Jasper is stepping out from behind a tree, wearing gym shorts and trainers.

"Him...?!"

Jasper?! Jasper was the wolf who rescued me?

He shoots me a dark, rage-filled look.

"It was lucky," Katie says. "I ran into Jasper and Olivia on my way back to camp and told them you were in trouble. Jasper shifted right on the spot and we struggled to keep up; he was running so fast."

My mind is doing backflips trying to put the pieces together. Jasper, the jerk, heard that I was in trouble and came running. He fought bitterly to save me. He tore that rogue's arm off!

I realize I'm staring—maybe because I'm shocked Jasper came to my rescue or maybe because he isn't wearing a shirt—and dart my gaze to the ground.

"What were you thinking?!" he yells, stomping in my direction.

"I...I..."

"You could have been killed!"

"It's my fault," Katie says. "I came out here this morning and Max came to get me."

"That's no excuse," Jasper rages, his face flushed, his eyes focused like he has Death Star-style lasers in them that he's powering up. "You should have told me! You should never have come out here alone!"

"Jasper, back off," Olivia says, holding out a T-shirt. "He's just a kid."

"He's not just a kid," Jasper says, snatching the shirt and pulling it over his head.

I'm a little sad to say goodbye to his abs, but I'm even more upset that he doesn't seem finished handing me my ass.

"I'm responsible for every member of this pack. Everyone at this festival is in *my* care. The least I expect is some respect in return. Do you know what would have happened if we hadn't found you when we did?"

I glance over at the now unconscious rogue just a few feet away and think about how close I came to being eaten alive. I owe Jasper my life, sure, but I'd rather be rogue kibble than have to listen to him chew me out any longer.

"I'm sorry," I say, clenching my teeth, trying to keep myself from crying. "I wanted to protect my friend."

"But who has to protect you?! Don't you get that? Your actions have consequences. You put Katie and yourself in real danger."

"I was just trying to—"

"Not everything is about you, Max!"

"What is that supposed to mean?" I shoot back. I may have messed up and gotten myself in trouble but, of course, Jasper has found a way to turn this situation around to insult me. To make me look like an asshole and not him.

"You know what? I was wrong," he says, placing his hands on his hips and looking at me sideways. "You are just a kid. An idiotic little kid who wanted to play hero and nearly got himself killed."

As angry as I am I can't stop the tears from falling. I lower my head so he can't see me cry.

"I said I was sorry," I mutter. Katie places a hand on my leg.

"Just...get back to camp. Olivia and I will clean up this mess."

He's talking about the one-armed rogue.

"Come on," Katie says, helping me up.

"What a jerk!" I say, wincing as Katie applies disinfectant to my shoulder.

Katie grabbed the first aid kit she said her mother made her pack, and we went to find a place to cool down. We're sitting behind the cabins, on a patch of grass with a view of the lake.

"Stay still," she chides.

"I just don't get why he thinks he can act so superior to everyone. He's not that special."

"I dunno," Katie laughs. "I saw him with his shirt off, he's pretty special."

"Stupid abs," I say under my breath, resenting my lack of abdominal definition and also wishing I could get the sight of them off my mind.

Still not sure what that's all about.

"He just acts like the whole world is on his shoulders when other people have problems too."

"All done," Katie says, balling up the used cotton pads.

I pull my shirt collar back over my shoulder.

"How bad is it?" I ask.

"It'll be fine before the bonfire."

I groan internally at the thought of the bonfire tonight. The big sacrificial pyre that signifies the start of the Mating Run.

I had hoped that with all the day's drama the run would be canceled, but word has already spread through camp that the run is going ahead.

I guess they figured out the rogue was alone and, now that it's captured, the camp is safe.

Is it tacky to wish I'd been injured just a little worse so I could get out of participating?

"You know if Jasper hadn't been so fast, your shoulder would look a lot worse."

"I guess," I say, and even I know how sulky I sound.

"In some ways, Jasper does have the world on his

shoulders," Katie says, packing up her first aid kit. "If you'd been hurt worse people would think it was his fault. It's nice, you know, that he cares so much."

I don't say anything. I know Katie's right, as per.

Jasper was hard on me—hell, he came down on me like Dorothy dropping her house on the wicked witch. But he was also right. I should have gone to him first. I acted rashly.

"I don't want to think about what might have happened if I hadn't run into them at all."

"Yeah, it was pretty lucky," I say.

Across the lake, the sun is just beginning to set. A grapefruit glow has just started to hit the tops of the trees and reflect on the water's surface.

Every minute we sit here is one minute closer to the rest of our lives.

"I'm sorry," I say, turning to her. "If I hadn't been acting like such a dick you would never have been in those woods in the first place."

"It's fine," she replies. "How could you have known today was the day a rogue would show up craving the taste of flesh?"

I chuckle but only for a moment.

"Seriously though, I'm sorry. I took you for granted and I shouldn't do that. I'm the luckiest wolf alive to have you as a friend...a best friend."

"Max, stop, you'll make me blush."

"No really, Katie. You're the only person I want to be sitting next to today, tomorrow, and every day in the future."

Katie wraps her arms around me.

"You big dummy," she says, and I can hear her smile. "All I want is for you to be happy. Besides, I know I've been acting kind of strange too."

"This blue moon is messing with us," I say, and Katie sighs.

"Yeah, but I think maybe it has something to do with my parents as well."

"What do you mean?"

"I guess after they split up I started questioning everything I thought I knew about mates. I didn't know you could even stop being mates with someone. Then Dad left and..."

Katie sniffs and I pull her closer to me.

"I just didn't know what to believe anymore. I guess I didn't want to lose you too."

"Hey," I say, leaning back so I can look into Katie's eyes. "That's never going to happen."

We squeeze each other like we're squeezing our favorite person in the world...because we are.

"I know we might have had our wires crossed the last few days," I say, "but if I do wind up finding my mate tonight, I hope it's you."

"No you don't," she says, laughing and wiping under her eyes. "But that's okay."

We turn to look up at the increasingly mauve sky.

"I guess we should go get ready," Katie says. "It'll be dark soon."

"Yep." We stand and wipe the dirt from our butts. "There's just one thing I need to do first..."

"What's that?" Katie asks.

"I need to apologize...to Jasper."

THE WEIGHT OF THE WORLD

Somehow, I've managed to get lost. The Alpha's Lodge is bigger than it seems—like once you're inside, time and space have no meaning.

Every corner I turn I feel like I'm getting more and more disoriented.

I'm not 100 percent sure if I'm allowed back here beyond the dining hall, but so far the only person I've crossed paths with is an older lady pushing a trolley stacked high with clean towels. She barely seemed to notice me as I passed. Teenagers probably all look the same to her anyway.

I turn another corner and stare down yet another long hallway. The floor is carpeted in a rich red-and-gold pattern, and the walls are papered in a canary-yellow print, with pictures hanging every few yards or so.

My ears perk up at the sound of someone's voice.

I sneak down the hall in the direction of the sound. As I grow nearer I begin to make out the odd word here and there and realize I recognize the speaker. It's Jasper. I'd know his annoyingly monotone voice anywhere.

I come to a door and stop.

Maybe this is a bad idea. What if he just gets angry?

I'm starting to think I should turn around when Jasper raises his voice.

"I told you, Alpha. I handled everything."

He must be on the phone with his dad. His dad, who he calls *Alpha*!

And I thought my family was weird.

"I already explained to you what happened..."

Jasper sounds frustrated, like he's about ready to go ballistic but he can't. *This is too good.* I lean my ear against the door to hear better.

"No one got hurt, Dad!"

Jasper just about loses his cool, but the room suddenly goes quiet. I hear Jasper take a few steps and wonder if I'm about to be sprung. I'm thinking about leaving as silently as possible when he speaks again.

"I don't know how the rogue managed to get past border security... They're your soldiers, why don't you ask them... I am taking this seriously, Alpha."

Man, I'm starting to feel sorry for the poor guy. His dad sounds like he's riding him pretty hard, and it's sort of my fault.

Jasper might have acted like a jerk. But I'm the reason he's getting his ass whooped by his dad.

"I promise you," Jasper says, "the problem has been dealt with. The rogue was apprehended and questioned and there is no evidence of any other unregistered wolves in the vicinity. He is being transported to the pack's holding facility right now... Yes, father, I mean, Alpha, the Mating Run will go ahead as planned. There won't be any more problems... I take full responsibility... I'm...I'm sorry, Alpha. I know you're counting on me."

There's so much anguish in Jasper's voice as he's forced to apologize. Part of me wants to burst into the room and tell him to stop. He doesn't need to be sorry. He rescued me, he fought to fend off my attacker. But most of me knows that I'm the last person Jasper will want to see.

"Hold on, Alpha, I think someone is outside..."

Oh, crap!

Jasper's footsteps grow louder as he approaches the door. If he catches me out here he'll think I was listening in to his private conversation, which I totally was. But I can't let him know that. I run back down the hall but there's no way I'll make it round the corner before he opens the door and spots me.

The door handle rattles and just as I think I'm about to be caught someone grabs my arm and pulls me into another room.

"Is someone there?" Jasper calls.

I look at Aisha, who has her finger pressed against her lips and a seriously confused expression on her face. We remain frozen until we hear the click of Jasper's door closing.

"Not yet," Aisha whispers in a hurry, preemptively stopping me from exploding.

She takes me by the hand and pulls me into her room, shutting the door behind her. I glance around at her fancy furniture and ridiculous four-poster bed. I feel like I'm in a first-class suite on the Titanic.

"Do you want to tell me what you were doing listening in on Jasper's private conversation?" Aisha asks.

Iceberg, right ahead!

"I just came to apologize for earlier, for running off and nearly getting mauled by that rogue."

Aisha pops a hip and studies my face.

"I heard about that," she says. "You're lucky Jasper is a good fighter."

"I know," I say. "That's why I wanted to...you know...tell him thanks and sorry for making his life such a nightmare."

"Well, okay," she says, softening. "I believe you. But you shouldn't have been eavesdropping."

"I know, I'm an asshole."

"Nah, you just don't know how to stay out of trouble, do you?"

Aisha smiles and gestures to one of the sofas; she sits and I do the same.

"Jasper's dad sounds like a real hard-ass."

"He's the alpha," she snaps.

I clutch onto a sofa cushion for comfort and she exhales.

"Sorry, it's this dumb blue moon. My emotions are all over the place."

"You're not the only one," I say.

"But you need to stop being so hard on Jasper and his daddy. It's a big deal leading a pack, making sure everyone is safe. Jericho is hard on Jasper because he needs to be."

"You're right, I guess. I can barely get up in the morning let alone fight off a rogue. I can't imagine taking care of a whole pack."

"Exactly."

"You care about him a lot don't you?"

Aisha smiles and it reminds me of the kind of smile I get when I think about Katie.

"He's my best friend."

"He can still be a jerk sometimes," I say, grinning my best mischievous grin.

Aisha grabs a cushion and tosses it at me. "Okay, bonehead..."

I deflect her projectile, laughing. "No, don't you start calling me that too!"

"Why not, booooonehead?" she teases, elongating the o sound for dramatic emphasis.

I huff and toss a cushion back at her. She dodges the attack, gracefully.

"Don't you have a Mating Run to get ready for?" she asks, sitting back up.

I look out the window, the sun has nearly set completely.

Soon they'll be lighting the bonfire and starting the ritual.

My body suddenly feels light, like I'm no longer holding up my own weight. But not because I feel relieved. There is a distinct chill running up and down my spine. Because I know the inevitable is upon me.

Once again, Aisha is right... Time's up. There's nothing between me and the night's events now. No more apologies, or rogue attacks, no more silly camp activities...

It's time for the event everyone has been waiting for. Everyone except me.

I set my jaw and nod.

"Good luck, Max. May the Moon Gods light the path between souls." I force a smile and stand, but Aisha takes my hand, holding me in place. "*If* that's what you want."

She gives me a pointed look and I nod. She understands my hesitance to take part in the ritual, but she also understands the pressures of being a wolf. Maybe that's why she's able to look past all of Jasper's faults and see the good in him.

Aisha walks me to an exit and hugs me before leaving me in the cool evening air.

In just a few short hours everything could be different. My path in life might be altered, set before me in a way I can't prepare for. I'm scared and anxious but there's no avoiding it. I need to meet fate head-on.

It's time...for the Mating Run.

THE MATING RUN

I pull on my red hoodie and jump the two steps from my cabin to the grass.

The sky is dark now and the stars have begun twinkling ominously like trickster pixies.

The moon is poking over the tops of the trees. The sight of it makes me gulp. The scent of smoke, wafting from the bonfire, is drifting through camp.

This is really happening.

I head in the direction of Katie's cabin with my hands stuffed in my hoodie pockets. Campers are buzzing past me, heading in the same direction.

Some people look excited, like they're at a midnight screening of a new *Avengers* movie, and are hurrying toward the gathering, while others are lingering around the cabins.

Everyone is kind of dressed up. Like they're going to senior prom or a wedding or something. I guess I missed the memo.

I pass Eleanor, who's decked out in a silver dress with sequins sparkling under the lights. Her jaw is tight and her hands are constantly switching from clenched to flexed.

Todd and Simon come barreling past, shoving each other and making jokes about who's going to find their mate first. Even my bro-y roommates have collared shirts on.

We're all about to wander into the woods and get naked but even so, I hunch my shoulders hoping no one will notice how underdressed I am.

Katie is waiting for me as I reach the end of the cabins. She looks super pretty in a teal dress that pulls in tight at her waist before pluming out and stopping just above her knees. She's curled her golden hair the way she does for school dances.

"You okay?" she asks.

"Totally," I lie. "Where's the fire?"

I'd assumed the bonfire would be in the same place it was the first night, but apparently not.

"Everyone is heading to the amphitheater," Katie says, linking her arm through mine. "This is less of a kegger and more of a sacred ritual situation."

I scoff and we join the hordes of horny wolves flowing past.

Torches are burning all around the amphitheater, casting a soft glow across the faces of all the excited, nervous, eager wolves filling the seats.

In the middle of the stage below the fire is raging.

Katie tugs my arm, gesturing with her head, telling me she wants to get closer to the front. We push our way through, trying not to step on anyone, and eventually, find a spot.

Jasper is standing off to the side, wearing another amazingly tailored black suit, and looking more stoic than ever. His nose twitches as I sit and, for a second, he glances in my direction.

I think he spots me, but his gaze doesn't linger.

Olivia is standing to his left, and in front of the fire is Marcel.

"Looks like we're in for another indecipherable pop hit," I whisper to Katie, and even though she's trying to act all serious, I see her grin a little.

By the time the moon has risen above the trees, everyone is gathered in the amphitheater.

Marcel opens his arms and the crowd goes silent. It's usually impossible to get this many wolves to stop barking, but tonight—crickets.

"Wolves!" Marcel booms. "Tonight we ask the Moon Gods to bless us and tonight, more than any other, we ask them to light the path between our souls. We are the chosen people of Selene, Nannar, Mani, Igaluk, and Tsukuyomi. The celestial beings who watch down on us from their Luna Palace, ensuring our fates and blessing us with the gift of mateship."

I wish they'd bless me with a concussion so I could sleep through this whole ordeal.

"We pray to them and ask for their blessings."

He closes his eyes and I roll mine when I realize what's happening. Marcel is about to sing. He opens his mouth and begins chanting in Lupine.

Everyone around me closes their eyes and lifts their heads.

I sigh and am about to join them when I notice Jasper hasn't shut his eyes yet either. In fact, they're wide open and pointed in my direction.

We lock stares and suddenly it feels as if the bonfire is burning ten times higher. The night closes in until I feel as if I'm sitting alone in the dark. There are no other wolves. There's just the fire, the moon, and...Jasper.

Marcel's voice floats away and becomes a distant hum, like a gentle birdsong.

My heart rate rises and my body vibrates. My teeth start chattering and I feel like I'm freezing, but at the same time it's way too hot.

Eventually, it all becomes too much and I slam my eyes shut.

The crackling of the fire is gone. And so is the prayer.

I open my eyes one at a time. Marcel is stepping back, letting Jasper take center stage.

"In a few minutes' time," Jasper says, "the Mating Run will begin."

Applause erupts, along with whoops and cries from the bleachers.

"We will head into the woods together. But once there you are encouraged to leave the group, separate from any friends you may have made while at the festival, and find your own path. Let the Moon Gods lead you in the right direction."

His voice is deep and captivating, but he keeps staring at this one spot in front of him, like he's finding it hard to remember all his words.

"When you have found a quiet place, we ask you to remove all clothing. As the grand marshal of this year's festival, I will shift and howl, signifying the start of the run. At that point, we would ask you all to change and partake in the hunt for companionship."

There's a lump lodged in my throat and no amount of swallowing is doing any good.

"Tonight is a special night in a young wolf's life," Jasper continues. "As a representative for my father, the alpha, I wish you all a successful Mating Run. I hope the Moon Gods see fit to pair each and every one of you with the perfect mate."

Jasper's stare falters for the first time in his entire speech and I swear for a fraction of a second he's about to look at me again.

But he takes a deep breath and lifts his gaze to somewhere over my head.

"There's nothing else for me to say except good luck, and may the Moon Gods light the path between souls."

The crowd goes wild. Jasper steps back and Olivia presses a reassuring hand onto his back. To a cacophony of wolves hollering and clapping, they leave the stage and Marcel steps forward one more time.

"Wolves, let the Mating Run begin!"

The crowd is immediately on its feet and suddenly, we're all walking away from the theater toward the edge of the forest.

People are already unbuttoning their shirts and letting their hair down as they disappear between the trees.

Katie and I stop and turn to each other. I take both of Katie's hands and squeeze them tight.

"Whatever happens tonight," she says, "you are the most important person in my life and I will always be your best friend."

"Katie," I say, worried that if I keep talking I'm going to burst into tears, "whatever happens...nothing is going to get between us."

I wrap my arms around her and pull her close to me.

"I hope you get everything you want and more," I say, pressing my face into her hair.

"Anyone would be lucky to have you as their mate," she replies.

When we pull apart both of us have glistening eyes.

"You have to go first," I say, stepping back and wiping my cheek.

Katie smiles and nods. She lifts a hand and presses it to my face.

"Just try to remember," she says, "there could be someone wonderful waiting for you in there. Don't let them slip by."

"Pinkie promise," I say. "Now go."

I give her a playful push in the direction of the tree line.

"Love you, squishface," she says.

"Love you too, bish."

I watch as Katie turns and walks confidently between two towering pines. There aren't many wolves left out here in the open. And it won't be long until Jasper's howl signals the start of the run.

If I don't go now I'll miss out on a private spot to get undressed. I take a big breath and try one last time to swallow the golf-ball-sized lump in my throat. Then I take my first step toward the forest.

Fate is waiting on the other side of those trees and I have no idea if I'm ready for it.

But I'm about to find out.

RUNNING INTO FATE

The forest is quiet and dark. I lose sight of everybody quickly and make my way deep into the maze of trees.

I'm able to catch glimpses of the moon, peeking between the leaves. She's watching.

My skin tingles the farther I go, and I sense that it's almost time. I need to find a spot to get undressed quickly. A spot I'll be able to remember in a few hours when it's time to get dressed again.

My breaths are starting to become quick and I know time is running out. I finally find a spot between a boulder and a tree where I won't feel too exposed.

I slide between them, kicking off my shoes and stumbling as I try to get my socks off without treading in the muddy soil. I ball up my socks and shove them in one of my sneakers.

Next, I unzip my hoodie and add it to the pile. Then I pull my T-shirt over my head and unbutton my jeans before whipping them off. Once I have all my clothes, except my underwear, in a neat stack, I take the plunge. I slip out of my tighty-whities, trying not to lose balance, and stick them somewhere in the middle of the pile.

Completely naked, I wrap my arms around myself and hop back and forth, from one foot to the other.

What am I even doing out here? This is more than ridiculous.

Suddenly, my ears prick up. The hairs on the back of my neck stand to attention.

A howl ripples through the forest.

In a second, another comes in response—then another and another.

The Mating Run has begun.

I close my eyes and feel the change start in the pit of my stomach. At first, it's like I've eaten some too-old cold cuts, but then the rumbling spreads through every vein and cell in my body. Muscles constrict painfully as they harden and grow. My bones rattle and vibrate before they crack and reform. Thick, soft, honey-colored fur grows from every pore on my body. My fingernails extend from their nail beds, lengthening into claws. My neck snaps backward as my jaws elongate; this part hurts so much I cry out. My fangs are the last thing to arrive, and then finally, fully shifted, I drop to all fours.

I shake out my fur and stand proudly as the wolf that I am.

Tonight, my senses are heightened even more than usual. The world is vibrating in waves and ripples around me. Sights, sounds, smells—everything is ultravivid.

I lift my muzzle to respond to the howls of my pack. My cry echoes through the trees.

Has anyone heard me?

It's been a while since I last shifted, and my wolf muscles have been itching for a good stretch. My natural instincts to hunt and run are kicking in. I'm salivating thinking about the night ahead. I'm free from society, chores, and homework. Tonight, the only things that matter are the moon and the forest. I'm crazy eager to run. So I do just that.

I take off into the forest and I feel like I can run faster than lightning. I thought the blue moon made me speedy when I was in my human form, but as my wolf, it's totally wild. I dart between trees attempting to break the sound barrier.

My limbs relax as my muscles warm up, and I know this is super corny, but I feel kind of excited, kind of alive. I feel...*wait—*

I dig in my claws and come to a stop. Something has caught my attention. A scent...an intoxicating, familiar scent. I lift my snout and take a determined whiff.

Mint, lemon, and...cherry blossom!

Without thinking, I run toward it.

I pant and run and pant and run. My wolf heart thunders in my chest.

Finally, I burst through a line of trees into a clearing. The moon shines down in full luminescent view.

I've been here before.

Just when I'm about to keep running, another wolf leaps from behind the trees.

A sleek, black wolf descends to the ground, making a crater in the soil as it lands.

And suddenly all of my senses are going haywire. My mind is completely clouded by the overwhelming scent of this wolf. The trees are spinning in circles around me.

The moon expands and it feels as if it could squash me like a bug.

My legs falter beneath me but I manage to hold myself upright.

What is happening?

What is this wolf doing to me?

I snarl and arch my back, telling the wolf to keep its distance.

The black wolf steps toward me and barks. The sound is like thunder ricocheting in my brain. On his command the world stops spinning, the moon returns to normal, and the forest is quiet once more.

All of my focus is trained, like a precision sniper, on the black wolf.

I take another breath and step forward.

Every bone in my body is aching to charge at him. I want to tackle him, rub myself up against his side, and let our scents mingle.

But I resist.

That would be...strange.

Clearly, the blue moon is messing with my senses. Why is this male wolf making my stomach do cartwheels?

The wolf huffs and shakes his muzzle. Moonlight reflects off his sleek, midnight-black coat. His green eyes glow against the dark sheen of his fur.

I tilt my head to the side and realize I've seen this wolf before. I know who this is.

Jasper...?!

He huffs and lifts his muzzle, but I'm not sure if he's telling me to come closer or stay away.

Does he recognize me too?

A low growl rises in my throat. My wolf instincts are telling me to protect myself until I can figure out what's going on.

Why have I ended up in a clearing with Jasper when I'm supposed to be finding my mate?

Why did his scent make me feel like I was at the top of a roller coaster about to drop?

Why is there an Olympic gymnast in my belly doing a tumbling routine?

Why do I feel like something's clicked? Like I've just slid the last piece of a puzzle into place?

My mother's words come back to me suddenly... *"Then you remember the jar of pickles at the back of the top shelf in the pantry and suddenly you know for sure... Pickles! That's what I want."*

I feel like I've found the pickles. *My* pickles.

Mom wasn't just talking about snack hunting, she was talking about how it feels when you find your...your mate!

But Jasper is a guy! And a complete asshat! He can't be...he can't...

My mind floods with images of Jasper. The way he's been glancing at me, the way I can't stop staring at his arms in that tank top, or his abs... The way we keep running into each other.

That first day in the city when he knocked me on my ass...even then I felt it. I felt it. I...

Oh no...nononononononono...

My eyes go wide and Jasper, noticing, tilts his head questioningly.

There's no way I can communicate what I'm thinking because it's too crazy, it's insane, it's impossible...

I'm Max Remus, the arty kid who loves New York and hates spiders. I eat too much pizza, watch too much TV, and I don't even like pickles that much!

But I can't deny the glaringly obvious truth that's standing in front of me. Jasper Apollo, the son of the alpha, is my...mate!

MEETING MY MATE

Jasper is my mate...

I can't believe what I'm thinking. I keep swirling those words around in my head, like those snobby guys do with wine, trying to make them make sense.

But it's too, too wild.

Not only is he, like, way out of my league—he's practically royalty and hotter than Noah Centineo—but Jasper and I haven't exactly been hitting it off. And besides all that he's a guy. He's a...guy!

I know this kind of thing is perfectly normal out in the human world. Most of the human kids at my school who are gay or bi have come out already and it's supercool. But in wolf culture it's not really a thing.

So I'd never thought that I could be... But I must be, because here I am, standing across from Jasper with a heart rate that would terrify any decent medical practitioner, and a belly full of butterflies.

We're staring at each other, neither one of us willing to move. But I can feel him. There's a connection between us now like radio waves. A pulsating current sparking and zapping, holding us in place.

Part of me wants to run back the way I came and dive under a bush. Whatever this means, it's going to make our lives wildly complicated.

Yet, no matter how daunting the idea of being Jasper's mate is, another part of me, the bigger part, wants to find out where this could lead.

One of my feet edges forward, skidding through the soil. Jasper huffs and lifts his head warily. But I'm moving now, the rope that's tied itself around my chest is pulling me forward and I'm giving in. I take a proper step in Jasper's direction.

I can barely breathe. Nerves and tingles are making my entire body shake like an overfilled smoothie blender. My jaw is clenched tight and I feel like any second I might explode into a billion microscopic pieces.

I take another step.

Jasper lowers his muzzle. The fur on his back is standing on end, like a punk rocker's mohawk.

He's shaking too.

I take another step, and as I do a breeze whispers through the clearing, sending a cloud of his scent right in my direction. It hits my nose like a delicious pillow and I rear back. Lights erupt and obscure my vision. There is no mistaking it—this boy is messing me up!

When I've recovered I take another step. I'm less than a foot away from him now and he still hasn't moved.

I lower my muzzle as a sign of submission, to show him I'm not a threat. To my surprise, his lips curl back, and he growls.

It's a warning, to keep my distance.

But we're mates. Aren't we supposed to be all over each other?

It's not that I'm suddenly sold on Jasper as a person, but if he's feeling anything like I'm feeling, I don't know how he's resisting.

I lower my head even farther and his growling stops.

That's right, buddy. I'm not going to hurt you.

Jasper's emerald eyes are unblinking. He's watching me like I'm a threat, which is hilarious considering how much bigger than me he is.

I edge a little closer until our faces are side by side. All of my instincts are telling me to push my face into his neck and bury myself in his fur.

If only I could touch him, if only I could...

I move my head and suddenly, a scream pierces the night air, breaking the tension. Instantly, both of us snap out of our hypnotic state.

The girl screams again and I feel like I've been dunked in ice water. *That's a human scream.*

Everyone should have been in their wolf form by now. Did someone not shift? Did some hiker get lost looking for her campsite? There's more than a hundred hormonal wolves prowling these woods. Whoever it is, they're in trouble.

"Heeeeeeelp!" she goes on screaming, and my ears twitch because I recognize the voice. It's *Katie*!!!

Jasper is faster than I am and he's already leaped beyond the tree line by the time I start running.

My heart is in my throat and there is more adrenaline pumping through my system than ever before. I'll be lucky if I make it to Katie before I pass out.

I catch up to Jasper, relying on that blue moon superspeed. We glance at each other, sharing a knowing look that whatever is happening up ahead, we have to take care of it before we can address our own situation. For some reason just knowing there is a situation makes my heart do a little backflip.

Katie's voice becomes louder as we approach, and the sound of wolves rises to meet it. Low, vicious growls are punctuated by snapping jaws and harsh barks.

Jasper and I burst through some low-hanging branches and find ourselves at the top of a slope above a stream.

I spot Katie at the bottom of the hill. She has her back pressed up against a tree and is holding her dress to her chest. Her face is blotchy and red and her eyes are puffed out from crying.

Between me and her are two wolves. One of them is lean and walnut brown, with a long pointy jaw and joints sharp enough to shuck oysters. The other is ginger and carries its larger-than-average frame on four sturdy legs. If I squint they almost look familiar.

The wolves are fighting, circling each other, trying to get to higher ground. The brown one jumps and latches onto the ginger wolf's neck, tackling him sideways. Locked together, they tumble down the slope toward Katie. The ginger one stops their momentum with its hind legs and tosses the brown wolf to the ground.

Katie is sobbing, crying out for them to stop.

In a second, the wolves are back snarling at each other.

Neither one is backing down. What happened to make these wolves want to take each other out so badly?

Jasper motions with his head for me to go to Katie, and before I know it he's leaped into the middle of the fight. I take that as my cue and circle around the three males, giving them a wide berth as I sneak down the hill.

Jasper growls—his commanding tone sends a shiver down my spine—and his agitated subjects back off.

I approach Katie, who recognizes me instantly and looks more than relieved to see me.

I nuzzle against her side and she places a hand on the back of my neck. Back up the hill, the walnut and the ginger wolf are still on opposite sides of Jasper, snarling.

Despite his alpha-like commands, these wolves aren't giving up.

When the walnut wolf goes to make another move, Jasper lunges at him. He recoils, whimpering. Jasper barks at him and finally the walnut wolf submits, lowering his head and backing up.

Jasper turns and sends another curt bark in the direction of the ginger wolf. He's less resistant and quickly bows his head. With another bark and a howl, Jasper instructs the fighters to take off in different directions. They're hesitant at first, both whining and unwilling to turn their backs on the other. But Jasper snaps his jaws one last time and instantly they turn on their heels.

He watches until they are gone and then he stares back at me. Our eyes meet and, with the commotion over, I remember exactly where we were before we heard Katie's scream.

What happens now? I don't want to leave Katie alone. She's clutching onto my fur and shivering. But there's so much that's unclear to me about Jasper, about Jasper and me...about everything...

"Max?" Katie asks, her voice quivering.

I glance at her briefly, and when I look back the end of Jasper's tail is disappearing into the forest. He's gone.

I huff and shuffle forward, my wolf instincts desperately telling me to run after him.

"Max, can we go back to the camp?" Katie asks.

I close my eyes.

I've just met my mate. But I have no idea what that even means. And on top of that the person I'm mated to turns out to be the one person I have no idea how to get along with.

Before I came here I didn't care about mates even a little bit, and now...now I want to run after mine and tackle him to the ground.

Katie sniffles and I turn around.

Jasper will have to wait because my friend needs me now.

I nod at the dress in her hands and turn around so she can get dressed. She ruffles the fur on my neck when she's done.

"Let's go find your clothes," she says.

She keeps her hand resting on me as we walk through the forest, back to the place where I started the Mating Run, where I first heard Jasper's howl.

The entire time we're walking, all I can think is that Jasper's out there somewhere. My ears stay alert in case I can make out the sound of his breath nearby

"Hey, Max," Katie says, scratching behind my ear. "Was that Jasper you showed up with?"

I huff and shake out my muzzle, grateful to be in my wolf form. I have no idea how I'm going to explain everything to Katie.

How have I ended up with Jasper as my mate? Will Jasper accept what has just happened? Will he accept me? Do I even want that?

My biggest fear about coming here has come true. Everything has changed. My world has shifted off its axis in a way I could never have imagined.

There are so many questions running through my mind.

But they are all going to have to wait until the morning.

The only thing I'm certain of now is that I'm in real need of a decent sleep.

MUD -WRESTLING

There's no way I'm getting any sleep. Not with the chorus of wolves howling outside my window.

I didn't really notice it until I tried to lie down, but the forest is truly alive with the mating calls of a few hundred horny campers.

I roll over, trying to shake the image of Jasper's wolf out of my head. The look in his eyes before he disappeared is burned into my brain.

I know I had to go back to camp with Katie. But why did he just run off? Why could he keep his paws off me?

Ugh, is that even what I want?

I slam my head against the pillow. I feel heavy and exhausted but also wired. Tingles are still flickering in my limbs.

With a sigh I throw my legs over the edge of the bunk and head out to see if Katie is having the same trouble.

"Katie," I whisper when I arrive outside her cabin.

"Max?" she replies blearily. She pokes her head out through the cabin door.

"Can you sleep?" I ask.

"Not at all."

We walk down to the lakeshore. It's still dark out,

although there's a violet hint around the edges of the sky. It'll be morning soon.

Katie and I haven't really caught each other up yet. She was too shaken to speak on the way back and I...well, I don't know if I'll ever be ready to come clean.

"Do you want to tell me what happened out there?" I ask. "It's cool if you don't, like if you're still too freaked. It looked pretty scary."

"Actually, it is scary," Katie says. "But not in the way that you think."

"What do you mean? You looked pretty terrified."

"Yeah, I was worried they were going to hurt each other."

"Wait, what? You were worried those wolves would hurt...each other?"

"Exactly, I knew they wouldn't hurt me because"—a grin creeps across Katie's face—"because they're my mates."

"WHAT?!"

I stare at Katie with my mouth hanging open codfish style.

"Okay, dish. Tell me the whole story. Now."

"It all happened really quickly. I'd just shifted when these two wolves showed up and instantly I was hit with how...amazing they both smelled, it was like I knew instantly they were my mates."

I feel a small pang in my chest knowing exactly what she's talking about.

"But what do you mean by both of them?"

"I can't really explain it. I didn't think it was possible. I kept wondering if my connection with one of them was clouding my senses or something, making me think I was feeling the same way for both of them, but..."

Katie stares out across the water, a familiar wistful look on her face, but also something else, something new, a sort of contentment I haven't seen before.

"They had two very distinct scents and they both made me feel the same way."

"Wow, so you have two mates then?"

I shake my head in wonder. I've heard about this happening. A wolf with two mates. But it's insanely rare.

I have to laugh because Katie has always been so crazy about finding her mate and now she has two! Go girl!

"But why did you shift back?"

"Well, when they realized what was happening they started acting territorial and fighting. I thought if I shifted back I could talk them down. That's when you showed up with Jasper. Hey, you never told me why you two were together."

I wrap my arms around my knees and pull them tighter to my chest.

"We weren't together," I say. "We must have just been close when we heard you, is all."

As soon as the lie comes out of my mouth my heart sinks. I rest my chin on my knees.

I don't know what's going to happen with Jasper and me. I don't know if he'll want anything to happen... I don't know if I want that either!

The only thing I know is that I'm not ready to talk about it. Maybe because I'm uncertain if it's real. Or maybe because I'm not sure how Katie will react. But lying to her doesn't feel great either.

"So, who are they?" I ask, changing the subject.

Katie looks at me with her eyebrows raised.

"You won't believe this..."

"Todd and Simon!?" I ask for the fiftieth time this morning.

Katie and I are standing on the side of a hill with a bunch of our campmates, staring down at a mud pit. My bro-y roommates are shirtless and knee-deep in the caramel-colored slop.

"Yep," Katie replies again.

"I can't believe it," I say, shaking my head. I haven't believed it any of the other forty-nine times.

No matter how much Katie repeats the news, I don't

think I'll ever believe who her double mates are. One of my beer-pong-playing, frat-boy roomies would have been crazy enough, but both of them is too wild to bear.

"Well, it's happening," she says, shrugging and smiling. "And so is this, apparently..."

Turns out it's a tradition if a female wolf discovers she has two mates that her potential suitors must compete to win her favor. And Todd and Simon, being who they are, have decided they are going to mud-wrestle.

That's one way to choose your life partner.

"Suitors, ready!" Olivia calls from the edge of the pit.

Todd and Simon assume their battle poses and Olivia blows her whistle.

They trudge forward, neither of them moving particularly quickly through the mud, grab each other's shoulders and wrestle.

Todd is the bigger of the two and has a clear advantage as far as brute strength is concerned. But Simon is fast and lean. He wraps a leg around Todd's knees and topples the giant backward. They both stumble, falling into the mud together. The small crowd cheers.

Todd and Simon slip and slide all over the place, grappling for a stronghold.

I can't help but laugh as they continue to splodge face-first into the mud, over and over.

"This is so ridiculous..." I notice Katie is wringing her hands in a tight little ball, watching eagerly, and I stop talking. Maybe this mud-wrestle is more serious than I thought.

A loud cheer erupts because Todd has managed to trap Simon in a headlock. He groans with the effort of keeping his friend from wriggling free. Olivia counts.

"One...two...three...four...five!"

Simon struggles but it's no use. Todd has him stuck. Finally, he submits, slapping the mud in forfeit.

"Todd is the winner!" Oliva calls out.

Todd releases Simon, who flops forward, face-planting in the mud. His opponent defeated, Todd lifts his hands in the air as the crowd goes wild.

I look to my right but Katie isn't there anymore. She's running down the hill.

Is she going to...? My mouth falls open as my best friend jumps straight into the mud and wades into the center. She reaches out and takes Todd's hand, linking her fingers through his. He thrusts their hands into the air.

The crowd cheers again and I can't help but smile. This whole thing is ridiculous but I'm happy for Katie. This is everything she's ever wanted.

Their hands fall back to their sides but stay entwined. All smiles, Todd leads Katie out of the pit.

The crowd begins to disperse and I hang back to watch as an exhausted Simon crawls out of the mud. He reaches the grass and collapses on his back.

This whole weekend is supposed to be a festival. A celebration. But just like everything else in life, you can't have a winner without losers. Katie and Todd have won. Simon has lost.

Oliva sits down next to Simon, but she doesn't say anything. He doesn't acknowledge her presence, he just lies there, taking deep, heaving breaths.

I can't keep my mind from running back to that clearing in the forest. To that moment when Jasper and I nearly touched.

Am I one of the winners? And if I am, then why don't I feel like I've won?

The hairs stand up on the back of my neck.

I need to speak to him.

As soon as I have that thought my legs start moving back to camp.

The site is quieter today. Everyone is either coupled up—walking hand in hand, canoodling in corners—or lying low.

I step inside the Alpha's Lodge and am about to go find Jasper when I hear something.

I spin around and spot Eleanor sitting on the carpet in the corner. She's crying, her little sobs sounding like hiccups.

"Whoa," I say. "Are you okay?"

"Do I look okay?" she asks, her mouth turning down in the corners and her face glazed with tears.

"Not really." I cross the room and slide my back down the wall until I'm sitting next to her.

"You want to talk about it?" I ask, fully aware that I'm probably the last person she wants to talk to.

"Not really."

"Okay. Well, is it okay if I sit with you for a bit?"

Eleanor looks up with a furrowed brow.

"Why are you being nice?"

"You look upset," I say, nudging her gently. "I'm not a complete prick."

"You wouldn't understand anyway."

"Try me."

"I...I ran...I ran all night and I couldn't find him."

"Who...oh." Realization dawns on me. Eleanor hasn't found her mate. She was so excited, had that whole strategy planned out...for nothing.

Man, first Simon and now Eleanor! How many casualties is the Mating Run going to take out?

"You didn't find your mate, did you?"

She shakes her head and continues her hiccup-sobs.

"Hey, look, it's not that bad, there'll be other festivals, right? And who knows, maybe you'll find someone out in the real world."

"You don't understand," Eleanor says. "You have no idea how important this is to me! I needed this!"

I don't know what else to say, so I carefully place a hand on her knee.

"How can I go home and tell my dad I didn't find anyone?" she asks, more to the empty room than to me. "My family was counting on me."

She's worried about what her family will think. She's worried that she's let them down, and suddenly I'm full of rage. I know how important this was to her, and how important mates are to our culture, but no one should feel like a failure just because fate is a bitch.

"They'll understand," I say.

Eleanor looks at me like I've just killed a puppy.

"No, they won't!" She pushes off the wall and stands, rounding on me and pointing a finger. "You don't understand anything!"

My shoulders drop as Eleanor stomps out of the hall. I wanted to help her, but I think I've only made things worse. This festival is wreaking havoc on people's emotions and there's nothing anyone can do. And it's all because our society treats finding a mate like the most important thing in the galaxy.

The sad truth is I do understand. I have no idea how my family will react when I tell them who my mate is. I have no idea if they'll be disappointed, or disgusted even. I clench my fists and slam them into the carpet.

This whole damn festival is unfair. Sure, some people might leave feeling like they're winners, but for everyone else, the long ride home is full of shame and uncertainty. It isn't right. The whole thing is just a pointless wrestle in the mud.

And I never even wanted to be part of it.

I'm being ridiculous. I must look like Eleanor when I found her.

So I decide I'm not going to speak with Jasper. In fact, right now I want to forget all about him and mates and this whole stupid thing!

I head back out into the sun and march to my cabin. I don't know what I'm going to do when I get there. My mom isn't coming to pick us up until tomorrow and we're so far away from civilization it's not as if I can just hop on a bus. All I know is I want to distract myself from this whole mess.

I don't want to think about mates and I don't want to think about Jasper. I want to get his dumb face out of my head. I want to forget about his intoxicating scent and hypnotic voice. Yesterday, he was basically my least favorite person, so forgetting all about him can't be too hard.

The sun is so bright I have to squint. Which means I don't notice the person rounding the corner of a cabin and run smack bang into them.

I rear back as if I'm about to topple over, feeling an annoyingly strong sense of déjà vu.

"Watch it," I hear him say.

Fan-freaking-tastic!

I've run into the exact person I was trying to get away from.

Jasper.

THE COLD SHOULDER

"Oh, sorry," Jasper says, panic rising in his expression.

I rub my head and take him in. My body is tingling in all the places we just made contact—my left arm, my forehead, my knee, my chest.

"Man, you're bad at not running into people, huh?" I ask.

Standing beside Jasper are Olivia and Aisha. Olivia has one eyebrow raised in a way that says, Pot—kettle—black, but Aisha is eyeing me curiously. I catch her glancing back and forth between me and Jasper.

Being in such close proximity to Jasper is making my head start to swim, and I know I need to get out of here. My knees are weak and my hands are desperate just to reach out and touch him.

He doesn't say anything else. In fact, he looks like he might be sick.

Same old Jasper.

I glance at Olivia, then to Aisha. Maybe he doesn't want to say anything in front of them.

Sure, I'm not about to flood my TikTok with posts proclaiming I've found my soulmate either. But why does he have to stare at me like I'm a piece of roadkill?

"Is there something on my face?" I ask, deadpanning.

Aisha steps forward.

"We were just at your cabin checking in on Simon. Double mates," she says, lifting her brows, "that doesn't happen every blue moon."

"Yeah," I say, not breaking eye contact with Jasper. "A lot of firsts this year."

I'm making things awkward on purpose and I'm not sorry. Olivia looks completely uninterested, while Jasper's jaw is so tense he could crack a molar. Aisha is rocking onto her toes, nodding.

"Well, we should get back, right Jasp?" Aisha says, taking him by the elbow. "There's always a bunch of paperwork the alpha needs after a Mating Run."

"Sure," I say, but I'm not moving anywhere. If Jasper wants to remain silent, if he wants to ignore the fact that we're mates, then that's up to him.

"Jasp?" Aisha says.

I keep my stare focused on his eyes as he darts his gaze to the ground.

"Yeah," he says, monotone as usual. "Let's go."

Jasper and Olivia walk straight past me and I turn to Aisha. My cheeks begin to tremble as tears well in my eyes. *What is going on with me?*

She reaches out and gently takes hold of my wrist.

"Sit with me at dinner, okay?" she says quietly.

I give her a pitiful nod.

I stomp the rest of the way to my cabin, swallowing the tears that I won't let fall.

Why am I even upset? I'd decided I didn't want anything to do with Jasper, or mating, or this dumb festival. So why when he ignored me did it feel like my heart was shrinking?

Inside the cabin I'm hit with another wave of Jasper's scent. They said they'd just been here.

Great! I roll my eyes. *I can't even get away from him in my own cabin.*

Across the room, Simon—freshly showered and in a clean set of clothes—is curled up into a ball on his bunk, facing the wall.

I'm tempted to do the same thing, but I don't want to

give Jasper the satisfaction. All I need is a distraction, that's all. I grab my trusty sketchbook and my headphones and head back out.

I spend the rest of the day down by the lake drawing, listening to music, and wishing there was better reception so I could at least doomscroll on TikTok. I do everything I can to try and keep my thoughts from wandering back to Jasper.

It's superhard.

Every time a romantic song comes on my playlist I skip it, but turns out there's a whole lot of songs about love. Every time a longing thought enters my head I flip the page of my book and start a new sketch, but I'm quickly running low on pages. I draw boring unromantic objects—a stone, a tuft of grass, my shoelace. Yet whatever I do my thoughts inevitably creep back to him.

What is he doing right now? Did he really have paperwork he needed to do? That seems like a lie. Will we get to figure everything out before we go home tomorrow?

I'm glad when the sun finally starts to dip below the horizon. It's nearly dinnertime and Aisha asked me to sit with her. At least I won't have to eat alone. And maybe, just maybe I can speak to Jasper.

As much as I hate to admit it, I want to see him again. Even though I'm still mad. Maybe he's just as confused as I am. Maybe he's just as freaked-the-fudge out as me.

Plus, my family is nothing like Jasper's. They're chill. Yes, the thought of telling them I'm mated to a guy is terrifying, but deep down I'm pretty sure they'd still love me.

From what I heard of Jasper's phone call with his dad, I don't know if he can say the same.

So, I fold up my sketchbook and head back to my cabin to change.

In the dining hall I find Katie and Todd sitting at our usual table. They're play-fighting and laughing. I think I might die from cringe overload when Todd literally picks Katie up and puts her on his lap. She seems to be enjoying herself so I'm happy for her, but still...totally, get a room.

Sitting across from them is Eleanor, slouching like a cloud of sadness. Simon is nowhere to be seen.

I think about going over but then I spot Aisha. She waves for me to join her.

It's still early and the dining hall is only starting to fill up. Aisha is alone at the alpha's table.

"Hey baby," she says when I flop into the seat next to her.

"Hi."

"Big weekend." I'm not sure if it's a question or a comment.

"For some," I huff.

The chairs around us start to fill up and I keep glancing toward the door where Jasper usually makes his entrance.

"So," she says, "how was your first Mating Run?"

I chuckle a little. "That's the big question, isn't it?"

At tables around the hall, couples are pressed tightly shoulder to shoulder.

"Are you disappointed?" she says, turning in her seat and lowering her gaze.

Has Jasper said something to her? If he was going to tell anyone, it would be Aisha. Hell, I'm this close to spilling my guts out to her myself.

I stop and think about the question.

"No," I say, and she smiles just a little. I'm kind of shocked by my own words, but they're true. I'm not disappointed and I can't keep it in any longer.

"The truth is..." Here come my guts. "I wasn't expecting much from this festival. Mostly, I just wanted to get through it. And no, things haven't turned out the way I was expecting, but there's this crackling ball of electricity in the center of my chest that wasn't there before and it feels... It feels cool."

Aisha's smile widens as little pools of tears appear along her lower eyelids. She takes my hand with both of hers. They're warmer than I was expecting.

"Oh baby," she says. "For the record, I think any wolf would be lucky to have you as their mate. I want you to know that, okay? I want you to remember how special you are, Max."

"You don't have to say that... I..."

I glance over Aisha's shoulder. People have started eating, but we're not supposed to start until Jasper is here. Two place settings away, his chair sits empty.

"He's not coming, is he?"

From the pity in her eyes, I can tell Aisha knows what's going on. She knew before I even sat down that Jasper was going to be a no-show. And she knows what that means to me.

"That jerk," I say, pushing away from the table.

"Max!" she calls out, but I don't turn back. "There's more to it than you know!"

Maybe I should listen to her, but I'm too angry. My body is vibrating again, only this time it isn't the mate bond, it's blind fury.

I can't believe he's too cowardly to even show up.

And I thought I was the one who didn't care about all of this mating bullshit.

He isn't just uncaring, he's low, a worm—a cold, unfeeling, slippery little worm.

I exit the dining hall and am immediately accosted by the moon's brightness.

All of the power she had the last few nights has fallen away. Now she just looks mean, like an empty promise. A big, cheesy, crater-faced lie.

It's too much.

I need to get away from it. So I turn and run. I run into the forest, wanting to get lost in the darkness.

My plan is to run until I can't feel the moon's presence any longer. But I quickly realize I'm choosing my path with purpose. I know where I'm going.

I'm not trying to escape.

I'm not running away.

I'm marching toward my fate. To Jasper.

I want to confront him, I want to tell him how big of a coward he is. And I have an inkling I know where I can find him.

It's easy to find this place now, like second nature. I walk out into the clearing, *our* clearing, and I'm not surprised to see he's already here.

Jasper is sitting on top of his rock, legs crossed, eyes closed, palms facing skyward.

I step into the moonlight and let it wash over my face. I thought I was coming here to give him a piece of my mind. I wanted to call him scared and pathetic. I wanted to tell him I didn't care if we were mates. That I wouldn't want to be mated to someone like him anyway. But the second I see him, all of those thoughts vanish as if I'd never thought them.

I want him to talk to me, but I'm scared of what he'll say.

I stare at him, my lip trembling, unsure of how to begin.

Jasper doesn't even open his eyes. He parts his perfect lips and speaks.

"You shouldn't have come here."

ONCE IN A BLUE MOON

"You shouldn't have come here," Jasper says. His words are an ice dagger being plunged into my heart.

A cold breeze drifts through the clearing.

"Why not?" I try to keep my voice from quivering too much.

He doesn't even respond.

"Is this the plan? Just ignore me forever?"

His eyebrows arch and a crease appears in the center of his brow.

"I'm not ignoring you..." His voice is monotone and rough, he speaks as if he's talking to himself.

"Then what do you call this? Hiding out in the forest, not coming to dinner on the last night of camp?"

"I came here to meditate—"

"To get away from me!"

The words burst out of me as if they have a will of their own. I don't want to seem hysterical in front of him, but I can't help it. The moon is a giant ghostly presence in the clearing, and clearly, she's still amping up my emotions.

Finally, Jasper looks me in the eye and I feel a bolt, like a static shock, pass between us.

"Max, whatever you think is going to happen here, you're wrong."

Jasper uncrosses his legs and hops down off the boulder gracefully.

"You can't just pretend that nothing happened," I say.

"I can," he says through gritted teeth, "because I have to."

Jasper takes a step as if he's about to leave, but he doesn't get far.

"Bullshit!"

He stops and I want to step closer—I want to take his hand. I want to turn him to face me and hold his pretty, angular face between my palms, but I'm too scared. Scared that whatever this is, it's already ended before it's begun.

"Look, I never even wanted to come to this stupid festival. I thought mates were a big, dumb joke. A fairy tale that everyone made up to make themselves feel better! But last night, when we were wolves, something happened and I knew...I knew..."

"What?" he mutters when I can't finish my sentence.

"I knew it was real. It's all real!"

Jasper doesn't move. He tenses his jaw and balls his hands into fists.

Why won't he look me in the eye?

"What happened last night was not supposed to happen," he says. "It was just a weird trick of the moon. It doesn't mean there's something between us." He swallows. "It doesn't mean that we're mates."

With every word, he sounds more and more disgusted, as if the thought of being my mate is sickening to him.

"It doesn't mean something else is going to happen now, and it definitely doesn't mean that I have to listen to you."

Jasper finally looks at me. His eyes are obsidian black, like starless galaxies, cold and empty.

"It doesn't *mean* anything."

My stomach crumples and I hunch over, as if I've been sucker punched. I wrap my arms around myself, clutching my aching belly.

I shake my head. My lips move but no sound comes out.

The moon bears down on my shoulders, like one of those machines that crush cars.

"No...no..."

Jasper's vacant look softens, and for a second I wonder if he might even approach me, might even try to comfort me, hug me, anything... But he doesn't move.

"Yes, Max," he says, finality thumping in his words like soil tossed onto a casket.

I press my lips together and suddenly feel my anger return.

Who does this jerk think he is!?

I'm not some kid he can gaslight into believing there's nothing going on. I'm a person in this as well and I was here in this clearing last night too.

I know what I felt—what I *feel*.

"I know you feel it too!" I shout. "You can pretend all you want. You can be a dick, you're freaking good at that. But I know what you're feeling."

"How could you possibly know what I'm feeling?!" Jasper roars, spinning to face me head-on.

His chest is heaving. Every muscle in his body is tense, veins are popping out on his arms and forehead.

"You have no idea what my life is like," he says. "No idea what I've been through! I am the next alpha of this pack and you're some kid from the suburbs. How could you possibly know *anything* about what I'm feeling?!"

I'm scared Jasper's head is about to blow off, but even so, I remain calm. Somehow his anger has sapped me of all of mine. I don't feel scared or sad or lonely anymore... I feel confident.

I take a step forward.

"I know what you're feeling because I'm feeling it too."

He doesn't say anything, so I take another step.

"I felt it last night. I've been feeling it ever since we met that day in the city."

Another step.

"This feeling is too big to ignore. We can't just pretend it doesn't exist."

"It doesn't," he hisses.

I freeze midstep. When he doesn't bolt, I carefully lower my foot to the ground.

"It does," I say. "I know it doesn't make any sense and, if I'm being honest, I probably wouldn't have chosen you either, but, Jasper, you're my—"

"Don't say it."

"You're—"

"Don't..."

"You're my mate."

My foot hits the ground as Jasper's mouth tears open, letting out a ragged, high-pitched roar.

Fangs sprout from his gums. His muzzle elongates and his eyes move apart. Pitch-black fur spreads across his face. His shoulders hunch and his bones look as if they're about to burst through his skin.

His legs crack backward with a spine-chilling crunch, and he tumbles forward onto his paws.

His expensive clothes explode into shreds as his muscles swell.

It takes less than a few seconds for Jasper to shift completely into his wolf form.

I stand frozen.

Jasper growls, snaps his jaws once, and then spins, darting off into the woods.

He's running away!

I can't let him. If I can face up to the truth about us, so can he.

If I don't leave now I'll never catch him, so without taking my clothes off I shift, tearing the fabric of my jeans and shredding my favorite hoodie.

I land with a thud and shake out my fur before leaping in his direction.

His scent is like a trail of tantalizing breadcrumbs—visible to my wolf eyes. I follow the bioluminescent trail leading me to him.

I can sense his determination to outrun me, which only makes me run faster.

Then all of a sudden the path is gone.

I skid to a halt at the edge of a dark pool of water. Jasper is nowhere to be seen, the trail's gone cold.

In front of me a waterfall is streaming down the side of the cliff face. Crystalline water, like falling diamonds, crashes onto the ridge and tumbles into the pool.

For a second I'm distracted by how stupidly gorgeous it is, too caught up to notice Jasper stalking up behind me.

I turn with just enough time to brace myself as he lunges, knocking me onto my back. I kick frantically and try to right myself.

The second I'm standing, Jasper lunges again, but this time I'm ready. I swipe with a paw and knock him to the side.

Even in the heat of the moment, I'm kind of amazed that I managed to land a blow on the alpha's son.

But my celebration is short-lived. Jasper runs at me again, ramming his shoulder against my side and sending me flying.

I grunt as I hit the earth and roll onto my back. Jasper crashes on top of me, pinning me to the ground.

I lie helpless beneath him.

Scared that he's lost control completely, I do the only thing I can think of: shift back into human form.

He won't tear out my jugular if I'm human, right?!

I wince and groan as my muscles shrink and suddenly the massive weight of Jasper's wolf is crushing me.

To my relief, Jasper shifts as well. He returns to human form, but he's still on top of me.

His eyes are forest green once more, his black hair hangs over his brow. Our faces are just inches apart and I notice for the first time the pale freckles speckling the bridge of his nose.

He's shaking and can't catch his breath.

I tremble as the cold from the ground seeps into my body. Suddenly, I'm extremely aware that I'm naked and so is Jasper.

But I can't move, all I can do is wait to see what he's going to do.

I'm scared I've pissed him off, pushed him too far.

Maybe I shouldn't have poked as much as I did, but I had to... I had to tell him how I feel, even if it means he's about to punch my face in.

He moves and I flinch.

Before he headbutts me I have to do something...

"Jasper, I'm sor—"

Jasper presses his lips against mine.

His kiss is hard—angry. I can feel the hair on the back of my head being mushed into the soil.

But I don't mind. My body is tingling all over and not from the cold.

I'm floating and falling all at the same time. Rocking in a sea of iridescent rainbows. Streams of color are rushing past—glitter and sparkles.

I part my lips and kiss him back.

He tastes like cherry soda.

I reach up and place a hand on the back of his head. I feel the bump on his skull where it meets his spine and think how strangely intimate that is.

My fingers dig into his soft, glossy hair.

Our faces are pressed together, our noses flattened against each other's cheeks.

Just when I'm starting to think I might pass out if I don't come up for air, Jasper pulls away.

"There," he says bitterly. "Is that what you wanted?"

Jasper stands without saying another word and walks into the forest. He's gone in an instant.

I lie on the soil, cold, alone...and naked.

HEADING HOME, ALONE

"He's not coming to breakfast is he?" I ask. I'm leaning on the door of the dining hall, not sure if I want to go in.

Not sure if I could even eat anything if I tried.

Aisha left her half-eaten bowl of fruit to come speak to me.

I don't know which is more embarrassing, having to creep back to my cabin naked last night or the look of pity on Aisha's face right now.

"He left early this morning. Before sunrise."

"Of course," I huff.

"If it's any consolation he didn't say goodbye to me either. He just left me a note saying he had to get back to meet with his father."

I roll my eyes. "Wow, a note. That's big of him."

"Look, Max. I know things haven't turned out the way you wanted—"

"I didn't even want to be here!"

"I know."

"It isn't fair. This whole stupid festival is messed up." I'm acting like a toddler who's been told he can't have ice cream, so I'm surprised when Aisha reaches out and takes my hand.

"You're right," she says. "It isn't fair. And for the record,

I'm not proud of how my friend is behaving."

There's a sharpness to her voice I haven't heard before.

"And I know you didn't ask for any of this. So I can see where you're coming from."

I sigh and rub my sneaker against the back of my leg.

"But I'm glad that you came to the festival. Even if you aren't."

"Why?" I ask, finally looking her in the eye.

"Because if you hadn't come I wouldn't have gotten to meet you. You're a cool guy, Maximilian. I'm glad we met."

A small patch of warmth, about the size of a quarter, starts to thaw my frozen heart.

Aisha reaches into her back pocket and pulls out a folded-up piece of notepaper.

"Here," she says. "I'm not the alpha's son so this might not be the phone number you were hoping for. But if you ever want to hang in the city just give me a text."

I take the paper, feeling the smoothness of it between my fingers, and grin.

"Thanks, Aisha, I'm glad we met too."

She takes a step back, raises an eyebrow, and purses her lips like she's appraising me.

"You're gonna be fine," she says. "You're a tough kid."

I drop my shoulders and exhale.

"So tough, just don't put me anywhere near a spider."

"Definitely not," she says dryly, shaking her head. "Hey, what time is it?"

I pull out my phone.

"Nearly nine."

"My ride is probably waiting," she says.

"You're leaving already?"

"Sorry, dude. I know people like to hang around, but I have to get home and sort my life out. I'm back in rehearsal tomorrow. What about Katie? Where's she?"

"I think she already has plans." She and Todd are probably off somewhere exchanging promise rings.

Aisha squeezes my arm. "Keep your chin up, okay."

"I will," I say, not so convincingly.

"Promise," she says.

"I promise."

"Good." Aisha spins to head off but looks back over her shoulder. "Hey, Max. He doesn't know what he's missing."

She waves one more time then leaves. I stand in the doorway, arms crossed, hoping the rest of the day goes quickly.

After managing to eat a whole rasher of bacon I head back to my cabin, ignoring the tearful goodbyes and lingering hugs happening all around me.

Walking through camp feels like traipsing through school on the last day of term.

The Elite Pack territory is essentially the same size as New York State, so...big. Meaning a lot of the new couples here are going to have to figure out how to do long distance for a while.

Everywhere I look, wolves are crying while exchanging phone numbers or clutching their new mates as if the world is ending.

At least I don't have to go through all that.

A day ago I wouldn't have been surprised to see Eleanor begging people to sign her yearbook. But she's nowhere to be seen. I guess not finding your mate is a real school-spirit killer.

I feel in my pocket for the scrap of paper with Aisha's cell number on it—the one good thing to come out of this festival.

Once I'm back inside my cabin I'm shocked when Simon pulls me in for a big bro hug.

"It's been a pleasure, man!" he says, ruffling my hair and acting like he wasn't the walking dead just yesterday.

He's downright chirpy. Maybe he's just as glad as me to be leaving this mosquito farm. Or maybe it's easier to move on from losing your mate than I thought. I can only hope!

I take my time packing and pop down to the lake once more before it's finally time to go. Despite never really wanting to be here, I have to admit this view is everything.

At long last my phone pings. It's Mom telling me she's waiting in the parking lot.

I shrug my bag over my shoulder and make my way through the cabins, keeping an eye out for Katie. I haven't seen her all morning but I promised her mom we'd drive her back, so I need to find her.

When I pass her cabin I walk past a couple making out against the wall and do a double take.

Katie!

Todd has my best friend pressed up against the wooden beams and is exploring her molars with his tongue.

I cough as loud as I can to get her attention. Once, twice, and finally, on my third cough, she pries herself away from Todd's octopus-sucker-lips. Her mouth is so red it looks like she's smudged lipstick all over her face.

"Mom's here," I say. "I'll give you guys a second to say goodbye."

I turn my back to give them some privacy and want to plug my ears with cotton wool at the stream of cutesy pet names that follow.

"I'm going to miss you sooooo much, schmoopsie-bear," Katie coos.

"I'm going to miss you even more, angel-cake princess. Call me the second you get home."

The cute names stop, replaced by the even more irksome wet, smacking sounds of making out. I wait as long as I can stand.

"Mom says she's leaving without us if we don't go now," I say, spinning around and taking Katie's hand. "Nice to meet you, Todd."

I literally have to pull Katie away from his grope-y sausage fingers.

"I'll text you when I get to the car!" Katie calls back.

When we're a little distance from the camp, and Katie has stopped turning to look behind her, I nudge her side.

"You happy then?" I ask.

"Oh Max," she says. "I wish you'd found your mate so

you could know what it feels like."

Katie leans her head on my shoulder and sighs contentedly.

"Yeah," I say, "same."

As we crest the hill I spot my mom in the distance and roll my eyes when she starts waving frantically.

"Somebody looks happy," she says, raising her eyebrows at the state of Katie.

"Oh, Mrs. Remus, this must be how you felt when you met Mr. Remus. Isn't it wonderful?"

Honestly, I wouldn't have been surprised if someone thought she was completely wasted. I guess that's what Beyoncé meant by "drunk in love."

"It's incredibly special," Mom says as Katie slides into the back seat. "I don't ever remember my face looking like that though."

I can't help giggling at my mom's joke. Even now that they've stopped kissing, Katie looks like she's face-planted into a bowl of strawberry frosting.

"So Katie found her mate," Mom says, raising her eyebrows in my direction.

"Uh-huh."

"What about you?"

"Can we just get going?" I say, dropping my bag in the trunk and slamming it shut.

"Sure," Mom says, looking at me sideways.

I haven't exactly lied, but I'm not about to just come out and say, "Oh yeah, I found my mate and he's going to be our next alpha, but he hates me, and did I mention he's a dude!?"

Still, I don't like the way Mom is looking at me—like she can tell there's something I'm not saying.

"What?!?"

"Nothing," she says, holding her hands up innocently. "Did you have a nice time at least?"

"It was a real howl."

I jump in the car and shut my door.

Mom turns the key, revving the engine, and my stomach feels like it's caught in the fan belt. We pull out of our parking spot and begin driving back down the path toward the highway.

I turn in my seat and glance back at the camp. It's already out of view, hidden behind the hill. I feel like I've forgotten something. Or left something important back in my cabin.

One last look then I force myself to turn around, focus on the road ahead of me.

There's no point looking back now. I attended the Blue Moon Festival and it was everything and nothing like I thought it would be.

I sigh in relief as we merge onto the highway and pick up speed. It's finally over. I never wanted to go and barely enjoyed myself the whole time we were there, and now it's done.

So why don't I feel happy?

Why do I feel like I'm leaving the party early?

I reach up and rub my shoulder where the rogue bit me. The wound has healed entirely. The scars are just white dots against my peach-tone skin. But I feel as if he's still biting me, his fangs digging deep in my flesh, holding on for dear life.

And I'm still waiting for someone, my someone, to come and save me.

As road signs zip past, I realize he was never going to come and save me. And it doesn't matter now.

I'm going home, back to my life from before. Before the festival and before *him*...

CAN'T GET YOU OUT OF MY HEAD

"You shouldn't have come here," Jasper says. *The stars are reflected in his black eyes.*

The shadows of the forest loom large across the clearing.

My body is trembling. My toes are digging into the grass. Where are my shoes?

The scent of cherry blossoms floats by on the breeze.

"Why?!" I call out, but I know he won't tell me.

"Why?!" I call again like I called last night and the night before.

Tears brim and fall, freezing in midair and becoming lost in the grass.

"You don't belong here," Jasper says. *His head is lowered, his face in shadow.*

I try to reach out but he's too far to touch.

I try to walk to him but the faster I step the farther away I become.

"Jasper!"

"Go home, Max."

He's grinding his teeth so hard I can hear it.

"Go home."

"No! I came to speak to you. Because we're mates. Because the moon said I should."

"What moon?" he asks, grinning and gesturing above.

I look up and there is no moon in the sky. Just stars and darkness.

"That's not possible!"

"We don't belong together, Max. We could never belong together."

"Stop," I say, beginning to sob. "Please, stop."

"I could never want you."

I cry out in pain, clutching my shoulder where the rogue bit me. It's like I'm being bitten all over again. I pull my hand away and look down at the blood dripping from my fingers.

"Why are you doing this?!"

"Because you don't belong here—"

I gasp and my eyes shoot open. I throw back my covers to try and cool my burning, sweat-slick skin, taking deep breaths to try and calm myself.

It takes a second until my heart stops racing.

Again? I think, huffing and flopping my head back against the pillow.

"Every damn night," I mutter to the ceiling.

It's been four weeks since the festival, and every single night I've had the same dream. Jasper, the clearing, the rogue bite. All of it, on repeat, for four weeks.

Why can't I just forget?

I've been doing my best to keep my mind off Jasper. Not that that's been an easy task.

I bought a new sketchbook but it's still sitting empty on my desk with the rest of the junk I toss there.

I've thought about drawing. But whenever I go to begin something new, nothing comes, no inspiration. Just images of *him*.

Katie's been somewhat occupied with her new mate, so it's not like we've been hanging out.

And Netflix just isn't hitting the same way.

Still, I manage to get through the days. Summer vacation is nearly over, so I've been getting organized to go back to school. Picking classes and buying stationery.

I've gotten really into mixing breakfast cereals, trying to find the optimum combination.

Some days I don't even think about him—not really.

But then night comes and I'm right back in that dumb clearing. And there he is...

I can't escape him. He's like a dream ninja, always sneaking around in the dark recesses of my subconscious until I'm asleep, and then, bam! He pounces.

I fumble around on my bedside table, looking for my phone, and knock over a half-empty glass of water in the process.

"Damn." I sit up and look around but I can't see my phone anywhere. I grab the pair of jeans I was wearing yesterday from where I left them in a pile on the floor, dipping into the pockets and pulling out my cell.

I squint at the time and groan—it's not even four yet. I fall back onto my squeaky mattress and something catches my attention. A scrap of paper sticking out from the pocket of my jeans.

I stretch out to grab it and open it up. It's Aisha's number.

I'd almost forgotten she'd given it to me. I'm not proud to say I've ignored it since I got home. Not because I don't want to be her friend. But I know seeing her would just be another reminder of him.

Staring at the number in the darkness, I start wondering if a reminder is exactly what I need.

I haven't told anyone about what happened during the Mating Run, so as far as I know, Aisha is the only person who knows the truth.

Maybe if I can just talk about it I can stop dwelling on it. Stop holding onto it.

Even though it's not light out yet I start typing a message.

"I'm glad you texted me," Aisha says, holding out her Frappuccino to bump against mine. "Even if you did wake me up."

We're sitting in Bryant Park just a hop away from the Public Library, where we met. The grass is dotted with office workers scarfing down salads on their lunch break and groups of tourists taking selfies.

"Yeah, sorry about that." I rub the back of my neck. "The thing is, I thought I lost your number and I found it this morning and I guess I got carried away."

"Why were you looking for it at four in the morning?" she asks, grinning.

"I was...cleaning!"

"Cleaning? At four in the morning?"

"I'm an early riser."

I sip on my straw, hoping she's bought my lie.

"Right..." She totally hasn't. "So, how have you been, dude? Honestly."

I sigh and pull a tuft of grass out of the soil then toss it into the wind.

Over by the roadside two guys are playing Ping-Pong. They look well practiced because the game is intense, a steady rally that doesn't look like it's going to end anytime soon.

"Max," Aisha says, pulling my attention back to her. "What are you thinking?"

I take a breath and fiddle with my shoelace.

"I guess I'm just pissed. I'm pissed because we're wolves so we have to go to that stupid festival and we have to have mates."

I take a breath and swallow and keep going.

"And I'm angry at fate or the Moon Gods or whoever for doing this to me and I'm angry because I have no one I can just talk to about all of this."

I'm starting to get worked up and my throat is constricting like I'm about to cry.

"Mostly, I'm just angry at myself."

Aisha reaches out and wraps a hand around my ankle.

"Why are you angry at yourself? None of this is your fault."

"Because I was always so certain that I wasn't like other wolves. I was different. But now I'm just as matesick as everyone else. Only the cruel twist is that my mate wants nothing to do with me."

I wipe a single tear from my cheek with the back of my hand. Aisha sits for a second without saying anything, just thinking.

"You should be angry," she says, finally. "But you shouldn't be angry at yourself for having feelings that are completely natural. The only person you should be angry at is Jasper. I know I am."

My mouth pops open. I never thought Aisha would be so openly hostile toward him. She's actually pissed though, which makes me giggle.

"I know he has a lot going on and I know his dad is constantly on his back about stuff. But that's no excuse for acting this way," she continues. "Not when it can only cause pain to you and him."

"You think he's in pain too?"

"I can't say for sure. He hasn't spoken to me since the festival either."

"Oh, sorry." I feel kind of guilty, like I might have something to do with Jasper ignoring Aisha.

She shrugs. "I know him pretty well, and I know when he's going through something his first instinct *isn't* to reach out. So that's how I know he's hurting, because if he wasn't...I'd have heard from him. Unlike you, he doesn't want to talk about it."

"Aisha, I never wanted to..."

"It's no biggie, dude. I know he'll reach out when he's ready, don't sweat it."

"How can you be so chill about it?"

"Oh I'm still gonna be angry," she says, tilting her head sassily. "He's gonna get it from me when he finally returns my texts, don't you worry."

I laugh and smile for what feels like the first time in over a month. But that easy feeling only lasts a second.

"And hey," Aisha says, "I gave you my number for a reason. If you ever need to speak with someone I'm here, and this"—she wiggles her fingers around herself like she's doing a spell—"is a place of acceptance."

I giggle again.

"Thanks," I say.

"If it isn't the sexiest she-wolf since Shakira!" I look up to see who's interrupted us and spot a guy with a bald head and a wide smile walking in our direction.

"Hey baby," he says, plopping down next to us and kissing Aisha on the cheek.

"Hey babe," Aisha replies before catching my mystified expression. "Max, this is my boyfriend, Troy."

"Nice to meet you, bud!" Troy sticks out a hand, grinning from ear to ear.

I can't help but smile back as I return the gesture. He shakes my hand until I think my wrist might be broken.

"What are you cool cats chatting about? Is it secret wolf business?"

My mouth drops open. When Aisha told me she had a human boyfriend I never guessed she would have told him the truth about what she is.

"Nah, we were just bitching about people with bad manners." Aisha winks at me.

"Some people," Troy says, shaking his head fervently, agreeing with us even though he has no idea what we were actually talking about.

"How was class?" Aisha asks.

"Man, it was major. Our professor is mad smart and he was telling us all about intercellular communication."

"Wow," Aisha says, smiling and rolling her eyes.

"Think about it though! All our cells are like talking to each other."

I make my eyes wide and nod along but actually, I have no idea what Troy is talking about.

"I can only imagine what your cells would be like," he continues. "Like do your human cells talk to your wolf cells? How do they communicate? Now that's major!"

Aisha laughs and shakes her head before shrugging at me.

"Man, I'm starving; you hungry, babe?" Troy asks Aisha.

"I could eat," she says. "Max, you want to come back to ours for a bit?"

"Yeah, if that's okay."

"Of course, man!" Troy says, hopping up excitedly. "It's major!"

We jump on the nearest subway and head out to Brooklyn. Aisha and Troy live in an apartment in Bushwick. Their building doesn't have an elevator so we climb the five stories to their floor.

Behind the rust-colored door is the coolest loft apartment I've ever seen. It feels like the set from some sitcom. Exposed brick on the walls and the polished cement floor give the place an industrial vibe, but everywhere rugs and tasseled cushions and blankets are thrown about, softening the vibe and making everything seem comfortable. A couple of houseplants dotted about the place bring in some life.

"Make yourself at home, Max," Aisha says, dropping her jacket next to the couch and flopping down.

I find a beanbag opposite her and collapse back into it.

"You guys in the mood for ramen?" Troy asks.

"That sounds amazing," Aisha says. "Troy makes amazing ramen."

"Awesome."

For the rest of the afternoon I hang out with Aisha and Troy. They're so laid back and cool, and they're constantly finishing each other's sentences. They sit next to each other with a leg or an arm draped over each other in a way that says, You're my person, without being clingy or annoying. Troy's excited-puppy vibes are offset by Aisha's chillness. They're nothing like the wolf couples back at the festival.

We put on music and I watch Troy play *Animal Crossing* while listening to Aisha tell stories about the crazy girls from her ballet school. For a second I even forget to be angry or sad.

"Whoa, when did it become night?" I ask, staring out the window, surprised to see stars. "I should get home or my parents will get weird."

I grab my bag and zip up my new hoodie.

"Sick to meet you, man," Troy says, holding up a fist for me to bump. "It's been major."

Aisha stands and walks me to the door.

"Thanks for having me, I think this is just what I needed."

"Good," she says and pulls me into a tight hug. "Call me or text anytime you want—if you need to talk or anything. Okay?"

"Thank you."

"Get home safe, dude."

I leave Aisha's apartment and head down the stairs. If my parents didn't hate me staying out past dark I don't think I would have ever wanted to leave. Maybe Aisha and Troy might want to adopt me.

Outside, the streetlights have come on and I notice a few fallen leaves on the sidewalk. Summer is coming to an end. I pull out my headphones and am just about to turn on some music when I hear Aisha's voice.

"Hey Max!" she calls, leaning out her window. "Check your phone!"

I grab my cell. Aisha's sent me a text, forwarding one of her contacts. I open the message and my heart stops.

Jasper Apollo.

She's sent me Jasper's phone number.

I stare up at her in shock.

"Don't expect too much, but I thought you should have it!"

"I..." I don't know what to say.

"Look out for yourself, Max."

Aisha disappears back in her window as a breeze begins to blow, kicking up the newly fallen leaves and whirling them around.

The entire train journey home all I can do is gawk at my phone. At *his* number. This whole time I thought there was no way of contacting him. I was sure he would have asked Aisha not to give me his number. But now I have a direct line to him.

Only, I have no idea if I should use it. He's made it pretty clear he doesn't want anything to do with me.

But has he? He kissed me.

He. Kissed. Me.

Sure, it was a mean, bitter kiss, full of spite. But there's a reason he ran from me that night in the clearing. He feels this too.

What would he say if I texted him all of a sudden? Would he ignore it? Tell me not to message him again? Maybe we'd start chatting and realize we have more in common than we think.

As the train hurtles along the track, stopping at each station to let passengers off and on, I keep my head down. I press my lips together and scrunch my brows.

I start to type...

I'LL TELL YOU MINE IF YOU TELL ME YOURS

It's official. I hate my phone.

It's been three days since Aisha gave me Jasper's number. For three days I've thought about texting him. But every time I start typing something I feel so stupid.

I type and delete, type and delete.

Everything I write feels so idiotic and pathetic. What am I going to say? "Hi, Jasper, it's Max. Remember me? The mate you rejected? Well, I'm just texting to say I haven't stopped thinking about you, even though you're a total jerk."

I'm starting to wish Aisha never gave me his stupid number.

Every night I lie awake composing texts in my head until they don't even make sense anymore. I'm the worst texter in history.

I'm lying on my bed in the afternoon, glaring at my phone which I've tossed onto a pile of dirty clothes in the corner. If I squint hard enough maybe I can destroy the damn thing with the power of my mind. I concentrate all my energy, picture it blowing up in a little puff of smoke. I squint harder...

The screen lights up, giving me a freaking heart attack!

Have I summoned Jasper with the power of my mind?

Pull yourself together, Max.

I force myself off my bed and sneak slowly to the laundry pile.

I grab my phone and sigh with relief when I see that it's just a text from Katie. She's asking if she can come round for dinner.

I shake my head and let my shoulders drop.

You're being ridiculous.

I text Katie back, glad to have a distraction for the evening.

"Sorry I've been a bit AWOL," Katie says, picking a daisy out of the grass.

We're sitting on the steps of my back deck, looking down at the forest as the sun sets.

"It's fine," I lie and shrug. "You just found your mate, I'm sure you've been getting very busy."

Katie's face turns cranberry pink.

"Max! It hasn't been like that—we haven't...we haven't done that yet."

"Hey, no judgment here," I say, leaning against her to let her know I'm only playing.

"We've talked about it and I told him I wasn't ready just yet, and he's being really understanding."

"Well, good for Todd. I didn't know he had that kind of self-control."

"Don't be mean," she says, knocking her knees into mine and pushing me off-balance.

"I'm sure Todd is a complete gentleman," I say, trying to sound earnest.

"Actually," Katie says, looking away, "I asked to come over because I wanted to tell you something."

She's acting all coy and I have no idea why. Only that she's got the same look she had when our fourth-grade teacher caught us stealing gummy bears from the jar on her desk.

"Katie, what is it? You can tell me."

"The thing is I haven't been hanging out with Todd."

"What?"

"I've actually been seeing...Simon."

"Whoa," I say, leaning back to take a good look at the stranger next to me. Katie has always been so straightlaced. Stealing candy was about as rebellious as she got. And she's always been keen on the idea of having one person in the whole world that she's meant to be with. For her, this is wild.

"The thing is he lives so much closer than Todd, who's stuck doing college prep on Long Island, and he texted me one night and asked if we could hang and it must have been the mating bond or leftover effects from the blue moon because I said yes and we started hanging out and we just clicked and it's been so nice and do you hate me?"

Katie stops ranting and takes a breath. Her cheeks have turned from cranberry to beet and her eyes are getting misty.

"Hey, of course I don't hate you! What's that about?"

"Back at the festival I chose Todd, in front of everybody, and he's such a nice guy but I haven't seen him since then and, well, Simon is super sweet and funny and a really good kisser."

"Look you don't have to explain it to me, the mate bond makes people crazy."

"But do you think I'm like a big slut or something?"

I stare into Katie's crystal-blue eyes. She looks terrified. As if I'm going to judge her for following her natural impulses. As if I haven't been driving myself crazy staring at a boy's phone number.

"Katie, I could never think that about you."

"Are you sure?"

"Of course," I say, taking her hands and squeezing. "You have two mates, that's not everyday. No one could blame you for exploring or being confused."

"I guess..." Katie sniffs back a tear. "But the thing is I kind of think that about myself."

Two tears stream down her face, leaving shiny trails behind them, and I grab Katie and pull her close to me. I let her cry on my shoulder for a moment, rubbing her back.

It seems like you can have too much of a good thing. Looks like this whole mating ordeal is messing with Katie as well.

"Listen," I say into her hair, "according to our culture, you're supposed to spend the rest of your wolfy life with this person. And unlike most wolves, you've been given options. No one could blame you for wanting to make an informed decision."

She laughs but doesn't let me go.

"It's not a science experiment," she says.

"It kind of is. Anyway, it's not slutty to be into two guys at once. Hell, we're teenagers! If we were human it would almost be a prerequisite."

Katie laughs again.

"Thank you," she says, sitting back and wiping her face with the sleeve of her cardigan. "I knew you'd understand. And sorry..."

"What are you sorry for?!"

"For crying all over you," she giggles. "And for making all this fuss about having two mates when you didn't find yours."

My heart rate increases. I still haven't told Katie the truth about what happened at the festival. About me and Jasper.

"I mean, I know you didn't want one and everything but still..."

She continues and I start to sweat because I know I can't hide it from her any longer. Not after she's been so open and honest with me. And not when my phone is still burning a hole in my pocket.

"I don't want to seem like I'm rubbing it in your face or whatever—"

"I found my mate!"

I slam my mouth shut. Those four words sit between Katie and me like a window. Will she hoist it open or shut the blinds?

"You...found your mate?" she asks.

I swallow and gulp down a ball of saliva.

"Uh-huh."

"Max, but you didn't say anything? What? How? Who?" Katie looks like a curious owl, her eyes are so big.

"Well, remember how when Todd and Simon were fighting I came to find you?"

"Yeah, of course, and you showed up with Jasper... You and he... Wait, Max...is it...no. Did you—is Jasper your mate?"

I bite my lip and wait as realization dawns.

"You're mated to Jasper!?"

If I speak right now I'll probably burst into tears—so I nod.

"But is that even possible? He's...a...a..."

"He's a boy," I say, finally finding my voice.

My jaw wobbles and I crack my knuckles.

"But..." Katie stops herself, her mouth hanging open. "Oh."

There it is. The truth. Katie is staring at me like she doesn't recognize me. Like I'm a completely different person than the boy she grew up with.

My whole body is shaking. Adrenaline is pulsing through my veins at maximum volume. There's nothing I can do now except sit and wait to see if I still have a best friend.

"Max," she says quietly. "Why didn't you tell me?"

"I didn't know if you... I didn't know what you'd think."

She does this weird half-laugh-half-sob thing and then she smiles, big and wide, and toothy.

"Max! You found your mate!"

Katie grabs me by the shoulders and pulls me in for another awesome best-friend hug.

When we pull apart Katie is crying but I know they're tears of joy.

"I'm so happy for you!" she sobs. "I think it's wonderful!"

Playfully, she punches my shoulder.

"What's that for?" I ask, laughing as well now.

"You should have told me!"

"I know, I just wasn't sure how you'd react."

Katie calms down a little and takes my hands. She gives me that big, earnest stare of hers and leans forward.

"Max, I love you. You can tell me anything."

For the first time since the festival, I feel a little bit of weight leaving my chest. Keeping this from Katie has been stressing me out more than I ever knew. But I'm so glad she knows now and that she's cool with it. I guess I shouldn't have doubted her.

"I know," I say. "I should have told you right away. The thing is I'm in uncharted territory with all this mate stuff and I never even learned how to sail."

"So, talk to me now. What's he like? Have you been hanging out? Have you met Alpha Jericho?"

I shake my head.

Katie tilts her head to the side like a confused puppy. "Why don't you seem more excited?"

"What?"

"You found your mate but you're acting like nothing happened. Wait, didn't Jasper leave the festival early?"

I glance at my shoes.

"Oh, Max. Tell me everything."

Once I start talking I can't stop.

I tell Katie all about the Mating Run, and the night after—about Jasper's kiss and run.

I tell her how he wants nothing to do with me but that I have his phone number and I don't know what to do.

"Give me your phone," she says, holding her hand out flat.

"What are you going to do?"

"Just give it to me."

I figure after three days, if I haven't been able to decide what to do with Jasper's number, I might as well put my fate in Katie's hands. At least they're the hands of someone who cares about me, who I can trust.

I hand her my phone.

Katie—who obvs knows my passcode—unlocks the phone and starts swiping about. Before I know it, she hands it back to me and I look down at what she's done.

In an otherwise empty chat screen, she's sent Jasper a message. All it says is,

Hi, Jasper. This is Max. Can we talk?

It's simple and to the point and kind of perfect. Nothing like the rambling, overshare-y, totes-emosh things I was planning on sending.

"There, now it's his problem," Katie says.

But I can't take my eyes off the screen. I keep waiting for a dialogue box to appear, for those three torturous little dots to show up. But nothing comes.

"Maybe he'll just ignore it," I say, shrugging.

"Just wait," Katie says, rubbing my knee.

"Kids! Dinnertime!" Mom calls from the back door.

Dinner is roast chicken with crispy potatoes and salad, and it smells so good. I place my phone faceup next to my plate, still tingling with anticipation that any second the screen might light up.

"No way, kiddo. No phones at the table," Mom says.

With a sigh, I slip my phone back into my pocket.

"So, Katie," Dad says from across the table, "how did you find the festival?"

"Yes! Tell us about the festival," Mom joins in. "Max hasn't told us anything."

Katie glances in my direction.

Please don't out me to my parents!

"It was great!" Katie says, turning from me to my dad with a casual smile.

"And your new mate? His name's Todd, isn't it? How's it going with him?" Mom asks.

"Actually," Katie says, looking at her plate and fiddling with a spud, "his name is Simon now."

"Oh," Mom says, sitting back to process this new information. "Well, the more the merrier!"

Mom laughs awkwardly but I can tell she's doing her best to be supportive.

"Double mates are a rarity," Dad says, sipping a glass of red wine. "I read a book about it once, tricky business. Still, it must be nice to have a bit of choice."

"Sorry you got stuck with me," Mom says sarcastically to Dad.

"I'm still figuring it out," Katie says, desperate to change the subject. "This chicken is delicious!"

After dinner, I help Mom load the dishwasher. Once it's full I flick it on and am about to head back into the dining room when she stops me.

"Are you all right, kiddo?" she says, leaning back on the kitchen counter with a tea towel draped over one shoulder.

"Huh? Yeah," I say, shrugging.

"I'm worried about you," she says. "Since the festival you've been a bit...off. I'm wondering if it has anything to do with Katie and her mates."

"Mom"—I roll my eyes—"I'm fine. I'm happy for Katie."

She squints at me as if she's trying to use X-ray vision to see into my brain.

"Okay, kiddo."

Moon Gods get me out of here. I make a dash in the direction of the living room.

"You'd tell me if something was wrong, wouldn't you?" she asks before I can zip away.

For a split second, I stand frozen in the kitchen wondering if maybe I should just come out and say it. Maybe she'd be as understanding and supportive as Katie. Maybe it would lift even more weight off my chest.

I open my mouth, unsure of what I'm about to say, when the doorbell rings.

Both Mom and I stay where we are, listening as Dad opens the door. Muffled conversation drifts in from the living room but I can't make it out.

Suddenly, Dad clears his throat loudly and calls out. "Max, there's someone here to see you."

I glance back at Mom, totally confused, but she shrugs and gestures toward the living room.

On my way to the door I lock eyes with Katie, who is

sitting on the couch. Why does she look so freaked out?

Something weird is going on.

A strange feeling creeps into my body. I'm feverish. My fingertips are sparking.

I step into the hall and stare at the open front door.

Oh...my...Moon Gods.

Jasper Apollo is standing on my front porch.

What in the Teen Wolf *is happening?* I never even imagined he would show up here. But what's even more shocking, disturbing even, is how he looks.

His hair is ruffled and unkempt, his white T-shirt is wrinkled, half tucked in and half out. There are dark circles under his eyes and a serious, stern look on his face.

He's usually so put together, so void of emotion. Something is definitely up.

I reach the doorway and I don't know what to say. Part of me wants to reach out and hug him because I can feel how stressed he is. But part of me is scared. Why is he here? What is my family going to think?

"Jasper," I finally croak. "What... What are you doing here?"

He lifts his head and I'm startled by how bloodshot his eyes are. Has he been crying?

"I need your help," he says. "Aisha is missing."

THE MISSING BALLERINA

"What do you mean missing?"

My head is spinning so fast I'm worried it's about to fly off.

Aisha can't be *missing* missing...can she? If Jasper has shown up here, looking like *this*, then something has to be crazy wrong. But people don't just go missing, at least, I didn't think they did.

"Where could she be?" I ask when Jasper doesn't say anything. He stares at the empty hall behind me.

"Is there somewhere more...private we can talk?"

"Sure," I say, stepping outside and shutting the door behind me. I get the vibe that Jasper wanting privacy is more about how uncomfortable he seems. His hands are shoved in his pockets and his shoulders are up around his ears.

"We can talk on the driveway." I walk past him, setting off the motion sensor. The lights flick on, illuminating the drive. "Is that yours?"

I'm staring wide-eyed at a black Jaguar sports car. It's so low to the ground. How does it go over speed bumps?

"Yeah," Jasper says, leaning against the side of his car.

"So what happened?" I ask.

"I haven't heard from Aisha in three days. We were

supposed to meet last night and she never showed up."

Jasper is shaking, like he's freezing even though it's super warm out.

"Okay, maybe she lost her phone. Have you tried her place?"

He shuffles his feet and sniffs, grinding his teeth.

"Jasper, what is it?"

"I don't know where she lives."

What? I thought Jasper and Aisha were best friends. I'd assumed he was over at her apartment all the time. Hell, I assumed he had a spare key. I don't understand why he doesn't even know what street it's on.

"We fought once when she moved in, and I told her I couldn't go there."

"I don't understand."

"I... I didn't approve of her situation at the time."

I've never heard Jasper mumble so much, I can barely hear him.

"What situation? Why wouldn't you want to go there?"

"Because she lives with a human."

"Oh."

I don't mean to, but I take a small step backward. My parents have drummed it into me since I was tiny that there's nothing wrong with humans and nothing wrong with interspecies mating.

I don't know why I'm surprised. Jasper comes from one of the oldest families in the pack. His father is the alpha. He is *literally* the institution. They represent tradition and the status quo. Old-fashioned values. I guess I just thought Jasper wouldn't be like that.

I'm starting to see why he may have reacted the way he did when he found out he was mated to me. If he isn't okay with his best friend dating a human, I can only imagine how he feels about people like me...him...us.

"I'm not proud," he continues.

"You don't have to explain," I say, putting up my hands. "Everyone's friendships are different."

"I know I was out of line," he says, growling a little as he forces the words out. "I was a dick to her back then and I wish I could take it back."

"Why didn't you?"

Jasper looks at me between the strands of hair that have fallen over his eye.

"I wish..." His bottom lip trembles slightly and I feel terrible. His best friend is missing and I'm giving him a hard time because he once believed something—although awful—that lots of wolves do.

"I wish things were different," Jasper says.

"Look, I'm sorry," I say, stepping forward again. "None of that matters now. If Aisha is missing we need to find her. It's just if you don't know where she lives, how do you know she isn't there having a technology detox or something?"

The idea of giving up my phone or my computer for more than fifteen minutes makes my skin crawl, but I know some people like to deny themselves in the name of self-care.

"She isn't," Jasper scowls.

"But she could be there right now and you wouldn't—"

"She's missing! I can feel it!"

I back up again, scared that the bulging vein in Jasper's forehead is about to explode.

"Whoa, whoa," I say. "Okay, sorry."

He shakes his head to calm himself down.

"Aisha and I may have our differences, but she's the closest friend I have and I can sense when something isn't right with her. And right now I know things are very bad."

"Okay," I say again, edging forward. "I want to help, if I can. But why... Why did you come to me?"

Jasper looks up once again and his eyes are darker than normal.

"You were the last person to see her."

"What?"

"You were in the city. You hung out. She...she told me she gave you my number."

"Oh." I rub the back of my neck remembering the text Katie sent Jasper just a couple of hours ago. "Yeah she did... I...wasn't sure if you'd want me to... I didn't use it..."

"Did she take you to her apartment?" he asks, ignoring my completely dorky dorkness.

"She did," I say, suddenly realizing how I can help.

"Tell me where she lives?" He's already fishing in his back pocket for his car keys.

"I..."

I can see the street in my mind, picture the steps leading up to her door. But I can't recall any details. No street name, no building number, no apartment number. "I don't remember."

"You don't..." Jasper starts taking short angry little breaths.

"I don't remember the name of the street, but I remember where it is! I remember which door it is and everything. If you take me with you I can show you."

The cogs are turning in Jasper's head. Judging by his expression he reeeeeaaally doesn't want to have me tagging along. But he doesn't have a choice. If he wants to check Aisha's apartment then I'm his best option. And as much as he hates it, he knows it too.

"Fine," he sighs. "We have to go now."

"Let me just tell my parents!"

I'm already running back to the house, my heart thumping in my chest.

I hope Aisha is just sitting at home, with her phone switched off in a bag of rice. And I hope Jasper isn't so pissed at having me in his car that he drives us off the road. But if Jasper is right and something is really wrong I need to help. Aisha has been so amazing to me. Jasper might not want me to come with him, but he can stick it.

It takes a bit of explaining and a bit of convincing to get my parents on board. They keep asking to speak with Jasper, who, I'm assuming, is waiting in his car unwilling to step inside my family home. When I eventually manage to impress on them the urgency of the situation, they let me go.

I hug Katie and she kisses my cheek before I run back out to the car.

I open the passenger-side door and step inside.

The car roars like a tiger as Jasper reverses out of my driveway and we speed through suburbia.

Jasper is driving so fast I think we might qualify for the Grand Prix. But his turns are smooth and the engine noise has sunk back down to a low purr.

Sitting in Jasper's car feels like sitting in a spaceship. A thin strip of blue light runs around the inside, giving futuristic vibes, and the dashboard looks like the control panel of Nick Fury's Helicarrier.

Jasper changes gears seamlessly and his hand drifts dangerously close to my knee. I hold my breath. Should I move away? I don't want to be too obvious about it.

Jasper changes gears again and his gaze darts, briefly, in my direction. I snap my eyes back onto the road and keep them there for the rest of the journey.

Finally, we cruise slowly down Aisha's street. I point and yelp when her steps come into view.

"That one there!" I say, and Jasper pulls into an empty parking space.

At the door we come face-to-face with a lit-up panel of apartment numbers and their corresponding buzzers.

"Crap," I say, "I don't know which one it is."

Jasper glares at me quietly, telling me with his eyes to be more useful.

"I'll just try them all until someone lets us in."

I have to speak to a grumpy old man, a stressed-out single mother, and someone who I definitely woke up, before we hear the sweet sound of the door buzzing and the lock clicking open.

We push through and I barely take three steps before Jasper puts his hand out to stop me.

"What...is there...?"

He lifts his nose into the air, a stern look of concentration furrowing his brow.

"Quickly," he says and starts leaping up the stairs two at a time.

"What is it? What did you smell?"

I'm not as out of breath as I expect to be when we reach the fifth floor.

"Jasper, what's up? What did you—"

"Shh," he says, bringing a finger to his lips. "Wolves have been here. At least three."

I try to catch a whiff of their scent but there's nothing but a musty hallway and a masala curry cooking two floors down.

"I can't..."

"Is it this way?" Jasper says, walking in the direction of Aisha's apartment.

"Uh, yeah."

I follow Jasper, who heads right to Aisha's door. I suck in a sharp breath when I see it's been kicked in. The lock is torn right out of the frame.

"Aisha!"

Jasper charges into the room, claws at the ready and fangs bared.

I stand in the hall wondering what I should do.

Beyond the door, the room looks dark and uninviting. A stark contrast to the last time I was here.

Even though I'm freaking out of my skin, I know I can't let Jasper go in there alone. So I brace myself and head inside.

My eyes take a second to adjust to the darkness. Red light from a neon sign shines through the window, casting a creepy-AF glow across the floor.

It's quiet.

Jasper is standing on the rug, blacked out by shadow. He's still but I can tell he's trying to use his scenting ability to figure out what's happened here.

Whatever it was, it's over. The place is empty. And it's a mess.

Cushions are ripped open and strewn across the floor. The curtain rail is broken, there is shattered glass on the rug. Aisha's coffee table has been upended and is lying like a turtle on its shell, unable to right itself.

I wrap my arms around my chest.

"What happened?"

Even though I know it's a futile question I can't help asking.

"She fought," Jasper says unblinkingly.

He crosses the room to the kitchen counter and bends down to inspect it.

"Blood," he says.

"Is it..." I can't bring myself to finish the question. *Is it hers?*

"Someone came in here and attacked her," Jasper says, casting his glance across the room once more, trying to piece together the story. "And they took her."

"But why—"

A low moan interrupts and my muscles seize up in terror.

There is someone else in here.

"Don't move," Jasper says, his eyes landing on a set of gym lockers. Aisha told me she'd found them on the street and brought them home to use as a cupboard. He moves swiftly, pushing an already upturned chair out of his way, and crosses the room.

Without hesitation, he readies his claws and tears the locker door off its hinges. The door flies across the room, clattering on the concrete. And I hear a man scream.

"Stop!" I yell as Jasper pulls back his hand, preparing to strike. "It's Troy!"

Aisha's boyfriend is squished into one side of the lockers, his face contorted in terror.

"What did you do to her?!" Jasper growls.

Troy shakes his head. His whole body is quivering. I get that Jasper is upset, but I also know there's no way the awesome, friendly guy I met here would have done anything to hurt Aisha.

"He's bleeding," I say, noticing the red patch on Troy's shirt and rushing to him. I take his hand and help him out of the locker.

He looks relieved to see me.

Jasper, still eyeing the human suspiciously, grabs a chair and turns it right side up. Troy is full-on quivering as we help him lower himself onto the seat.

"What happened?" Jasper demands.

Troy looks up at him as if he's replaying it in his mind.

The look of horror in his eyes is unmistakable.

"They... They...took her..."

"WHO?!" Jasper roars.

"We need to get him to a hospital," I say, interrupting the interrogation but keenly aware that Troy is beat up really badly.

"Not until we know what happened," Jasper shoots back.

"It's fine," Troy stammers, placing a hand over the bloody patch on his stomach and grunting. "You have to save her."

"Tell me what happened," Jasper says, leaning closer.

"There were three of them, big crazy-looking guys," Troy says. "They busted in here and turned into wolves. One of 'em got to me, slashed me with his claws, but Aisha, she was mad. She told me to hide, shoved me in the locker, and she changed too. She fought them, all of them. But they were too strong."

Troy's words become more and more mumbled, choked by the sobs racking his body.

"They got her. Once they had her they didn't care nothing about me. So they just left but I... I couldn't stop them. I couldn't save her. All I did was hide..."

He breaks down completely and I look at Jasper, pleading with my eyes. He gives me a subtle nod, so I pull out my phone and dial 9-1-1.

"The ambulance is on the way," I say as the call ends.

Troy has calmed down a little but he's shivering like it's below freezing.

Jasper kneels in front of him.

"Troy, I need you to tell me everything you saw. I need to know who these wolves are."

"It was all a blur, man. They took out the lights."

Jasper huffs in frustration. He stands and paces about the room.

"There must be something," he says, running a tense hand through his hair.

I grab a blanket that's draped over the back of the sofa and wrap it around Troy's shoulders. I kneel beside him.

"I couldn't save her," he says to me. "I couldn't do anything. I just hid."

"It's not your fault, there's nothing you could have done," I tell him. "Those wolves would have killed you if you tried to fight them."

Troy shakes his head. I wish he could believe me but I understand how he's feeling.

I glance behind me but Jasper is still pacing, trying to think of his next move.

Looking back to Troy, I try one more time. I ask him as calmly as I can, "Are you sure you don't remember anything? Anything at all about these guys?"

"I'm sorry, man. I'm really sorry."

"It's okay," I say, sighing, and lay a comforting hand on Troy's shoulder. His head jerks up, his eyes wide like saucers.

"Wait," he says, snagging Jasper's attention. "One of them had a tattoo on his shoulder. I caught a glimpse of it just before he changed."

"What did it look like?" Jasper asks, storming back over.

"It was like a wolf head with a bolt of lightning running through it."

Jasper takes a step backward, his nostrils flared and his fists clenched.

"Does it mean something?" Troy asks desperately.

I shake my head but look to Jasper.

Whatever the tattoo means, it's completely oblivious to me. But from the look on Jasper's face, it's obvious to him.

I stand up and step to Jasper.

"What does it mean?" I ask.

"It means I know who took her."

"What? Who?"

"Rogues..."

ON THE ROAD

The lights of the ambulance flash red and white across Jasper's face as we watch Troy being lifted inside.

I can tell from the way Jasper is clenching his jaw that he thinks we've already waited too long.

"Let's go, I'll get you home," he says when the ambulance has pulled away. He starts marching to his car and I have to jog to catch up.

"What?! No, I'm coming with you!"

Jasper stops at his door and stares across the metallic roof.

"This isn't up for discussion."

"She's my friend too," I say as sternly as I can muster.

Jasper sighs audibly, the sound becoming a growl as he rolls his head on his shoulders.

"You have no idea how dangerous rogues are."

"Yes, I do," I say. "Remember the time I had one attached to my shoulder?"

He smacks his hands on the roof of the car and I swear he makes a dent in it. "Aisha is out there and she is in real danger! I don't have time for this!"

"Exactly," I say. "If you drive me all the way home it's only going to waste more time."

Jasper huffs angrily but he knows I'm right.

"Fine," he says through his teeth. "Get in."

I don't wait a nanosecond. I open the car door and slip into my seat, fastening a seat belt before Jasper can even get the keys in the ignition.

I glance at him, hoping he's seen just how fast I'm being, how serious I'm taking things. He rolls his eyes and hits the accelerator.

"Um, where are we actually going?" I say once the city is behind us. We've merged onto the highway heading west, and I suddenly realize I have no idea what Jasper's plan is.

"Just outside of Pittsburgh, there's an abandoned industrial complex, old factories, and warehouses that went out of business in the '80s. It's basically a wasteland now, but rogues like to hang out there."

"Pittsburgh?!"

Jasper's eyes remain on the road, but I can see the fury lurking behind them.

"How do you know the rogues who took Aisha will be there?"

"After they took over the place they set up a makeshift town. They call it Rogue City. It's become a mecca for rogues from all over the country. It's like their state capital or something."

I try to swallow the tennis-ball-sized lump that has formed in my throat. One rogue was scary enough, let alone an entire city full of them.

"But I thought rogues were loners? Isn't that why they're rogues?"

"Rogues are wolves who've lost their packs. That loss makes them unstable, but they're still wolves. They still crave community the same way we do." Jasper's knuckles whiten as he grips the steering wheel harder. "Their idea of community is just more like a cage-fighting ring."

I shrink into my chair as I imagine what this criminal hive must look like and start to regret forcing Jasper to bring me along.

"And the tattoo?" I ask quietly, unsure if what I want is any more exposition.

"It's the insignia of a particularly violent sect of rogues. Wolves wear that tattoo to let others know where they stand."

"Where *do* they stand?"

"Against us. Against my father and the whole pack system."

"Right. So it's sort of like an identifier. Kind of like how all the wolves of the Elite Pack have a similar scent?" I ask.

Jasper looks at me sideways.

"No," he mutters. "They're nothing like us."

"So that's why you think Aisha is there?"

"It's how I *know*."

Jasper presses down harder on the accelerator and for a second I think the car is about to take off.

A couple of hours later we leave the highway.

"Where are we going now?" I ask.

"It's a shortcut."

We end up on a long gravel path with no streetlights. Fields of dust stretch out into the darkness on either side of us.

I'm glad that we've finally slowed down a little, but I catch Jasper yawning out of the corner of my eye.

"I think I see some lights up ahead," I say, peering past the blare of the headlights. "There might be a diner or something we can stop at for coffee."

"We don't have time to stop."

Pressing my forehead against the window, I stare longingly as a diner comes and goes. For another twenty minutes we drive in silence.

Then all of a sudden two pinpricks of light appear up ahead. Headlights!

I shudder a little as my mind starts playing tricks on me, making me imagine all sorts of scenarios in which the rogues know we're coming and have waited until we're alone out here to play a deadly game of chicken.

The lights become brighter and we start drifting across

the centerline. The vehicle ahead comes into view. It's a truck the size of Megatron and it's barreling right at us!

The blare of the horn sounds and I glance over at Jasper, whose eyes are closed. He's asleep!

"Jasper!" I shove him and put one hand on the wheel to try and steer us away.

He wakes up, blinking, and quickly realizes the immediate danger we're in. He spins the steering wheel hard to the right.

With just an inch of grace, we avoid a major collision. Megatron blasts past us, sending out shockwaves in his wake. Our tires screech, filling the cabin with the smell of burning rubber as the car spins.

We whirl off the road, careening off the tarmac.

I clutch the dashboard as Jasper holds the wheel, trying to regain control.

In a cloud of dust and dirt, we finally skid to a stop. For a moment I remain frozen, unable to catch my breath, worried I may have a heart attack at the ripe age of sixteen.

"Are you okay?" Jasper asks, breathless.

I'm too in shock to reply.

"Are you hurt?!" he asks again, firmer this time.

"Yeah, I'm—I'm fine," I stammer.

"I must have let my eyes close for just a second and..."

Jasper is still gripping the wheel; the muscles in his arms are rock solid.

"Hey, it's okay," I say, trying to calm him down. "I'm fine."

His chest is heaving up and down and there's a red flush to his face that I've never seen before.

"I'm... I'm sorry," he says, without looking at me.

"It's okay."

"No, it was too close. Too close."

Jasper's eyes glaze over as if he's replaying the incident over and over. Suddenly a distinct memory steps forward from the back of my mind.

This one day when I was a kid my dad took me skating at an ice rink. I was wearing red mittens that Mom had knitted for me for Christmas and I was out on the ice turning in circles trying to get my dad's attention. He was reading a paper and not watching my amazing moves.

Suddenly he dropped his paper and stood up with this look of horror on his face. I will always remember that look. Because then I felt it.

A shadow coming to rest on my shoulders like a coat of grief. I burst into tears in the middle of the ice.

Someone, I don't remember who, helped me off the rink and my dad took me into his arms. I looked down at the paper he had been reading and saw a black-and-white photo of a car crash.

The title read "New York Socialite and Philanthropist Mitsuha Apollo Dies in Car Accident."

That was the day the pack lost their luna and the day Jasper lost his mom. I can still feel the communal grief we experienced as a pack. I can't imagine how Jasper must have felt.

I wonder if he's thinking about that car accident now that we just avoided one of our own.

We sit in the car for a few minutes. I don't say anything and Jasper doesn't let go of the steering wheel.

Eventually, taking deep breaths, I reach out and put my hand on Jasper's arm. He flinches at my touch but doesn't pull away.

"Jasper, it's all right. I'm okay. We're okay."

Slowly, he unclenches his fists and releases the steering wheel.

I spot a single tear running down Jasper's cheek as he places his hands on his knees.

Then he turns to me and says again, "I'm sorry."

I smile back.

"No harm done," I say, shrugging, desperately uncomfortable and doing my darndest to lighten the mood. "But maybe we should think about finding somewhere to stay for the night? You're exhausted."

Jasper looks around as if he's considering his options and then straightens his jaw.

"No, we can't stop, Aisha needs us." He turns the key in the ignition and the car roars to life.

I wipe my face with my hands as he presses down on the accelerator, and then something beneath us pops.

Both of us jump out of the car and I run around to Jasper's side to find him staring at a deflated tire.

"Do you have a spare?" I ask tentatively.

"Dammit!" Jasper shouts and kicks the ground.

I'll take that as a no.

Pressing his hands to the side of his head as if he's trying to keep his brain from flying out his ears, Jasper groans and walks off across the field.

I chase after him, grab him by the arm, and spin him around.

"Jasper, it's going to be okay, look," I say, pointing toward the horizon where another small bundle of lights indicate life. "We can walk down there. Maybe there's a motel or something and we can—"

"It's not going to be okay!" Jasper says. "Don't you get it? They've taken her. They've taken Aisha."

He stares at me with fierce desperation in his eyes and I know exactly what he means. *They've taken Aisha.* She's not just the coolest person and the best ballet dancer in the world, she's also the most understanding, caring, and empathetic person I've ever met.

She's the only person Jasper told about me and him, which means she's the only person in the world who he can talk to.

She's the only person in his world.

"Jasper," I say, staring back at him, "I understand. I know how important she is. But..." I rack my brain, trying to think of anything that might help. But the truth is Jasper is right. We can't wait. Aisha is in the hands of some seriously nasty wolves, and any time we waste is more time she remains their prisoner...or worse.

But Jasper is about ready to collapse. His eyes are encircled with dark rings. His shoulders are hunched over. His hands are shaking.

We can't keep driving, let alone infiltrate a hive of rogues, not with Jasper in this state. We'll both end up dead.

We need to rest and we need to fix the car, which means I need to do something to show Jasper that a few more hours isn't going to be the difference between life and death.

"What was that you said to me back at my place?" I ask, a few pieces falling into place in my mind.

"What are you talking—"

"You said that you could tell Aisha was in trouble because you have some—some kind of connection to her? You said you could sense when something wasn't right."

"Yeah," he says, tilting his head forward.

"So, do that now. Reach out to her and see if she's okay."

"Max, it doesn't work like that, I—"

"Just shut up and do it," I say, surprising both of us with my tone. "Just...give it a shot."

"Fine," he huffs. He backs up and looks around, pacing in a little circle until he's found a good spot to sit. Crossing his legs so that his feet are resting on top of his knees, he takes a breath and closes his eyes.

I watch as he steadies his breathing. *In and out. In and out.*

I study the tranquil, focused look on his face.

For a moment I feel like I can sense the movement of the stars above me, feel them circling in a wide arch above my head.

A cool wind blows through the dry grass.

"She's alive," Jasper says. He's opened his eyes and his body is less tense than before. He sounds relieved.

"Is she..."

"I can't tell much," he says, standing. "But she's alive and she doesn't seem injured."

"Well, that's amazing," I say.

"She's still the captive of a pack of rogues."

"Yeah, of course," I say, rubbing the back of my neck.

"But if they haven't hurt her yet, they probably have a reason not to."

"What are you thinking?"

Jasper is staring ahead at the cluster of lights.

"Most likely they're using her to get to me," he says. "Maybe as a way to hurt my father. Or maybe as revenge."

"For what?"

"For their comrade whose arm I ripped off at the festival."

"Oh." I remember seeing it—the bloody hole where the rogue's arm should have been—and start to feel the chill of guilt trickle down my spine.

If they want to get back at Jasper for what he did, then I'm partly responsible for Aisha's abduction as well. If it weren't for me, Jasper might not have had to fight the rogue invader.

I think Jasper notices my face drop because he swiftly changes the subject.

"Anyway, you're right. We can't go anywhere tonight. We should see if there's somewhere we can sleep up ahead."

Jasper heads back to the car and grabs a couple of things from his glove compartment.

"Come on." He waves to me as he starts walking along the side of the road toward the lights.

I jog to catch up with him.

We walk in silence, with only the chirp of crickets for company, until we reach the little township.

It's dead quiet and my goosebumps are out of control. We might as well have wandered into a scene from some low-budget horror movie.

"There," Jasper says, pointing to a motel sign up ahead.

A bell jingles as we push through the screen door into the reception, and I feel like we're walking into a time warp. The place hasn't been updated since the '70s. Norman Bates and his mother are probably knocking about somewhere.

In a moment, an unexpectedly friendly looking woman with curly gray hair, wearing a pink-woolen sweater, enters through a door behind the desk, holding a cup of coffee and a TV remote.

"You boys okay?" she asks, giving us a suspicious but mostly concerned look.

"One of my tires exploded a little way back down the road and we were hoping you might have a room for the night."

"Oh, that's awful," she says, plunking down her coffee and the remote. She opens a drawer and I'm relieved when she fishes out a key, attached to a large green plastic triangle. "You're in luck because I've just got the one room left. But you're welcome to it."

"Thank you," Jasper says, pulling out a slim leather wallet and taking out a silver credit card.

"My husband can probably fix that tire of yours in the morning too. What kind of car was it?"

Once Jasper has explained where the car is and paid for our room, the pink-sweater lady tells us she'll get her husband on it first thing, then wishes us a good night.

Relief floods my body as we walk down the line of doors to our room. Jasper slides the key in the lock and I follow him inside.

I flick on the light and we both stop short, our mouths gaping open in terror at the sight before us.

"There's... There's only one bed."

MOTEL DREAMS

I fluff up my pillow as best as I can then drop it back onto the carpet. I stare longingly at the bed from where I've laid a spare blanket out on the floor.

What have I done?

Why did I volunteer for this?

There was no way Jasper and I were going to sleep in the same bed, no sir. And I guess I thought he needed to rest up more than me.

But despite the faded olive-colored carpet, the floor is as hard as concrete and my butt is already starting to ache.

I'm beginning to think my sacrifice was a big mistake— huge.

It's going to be a long night.

The torrential pour of the shower disappears and I glance up toward the bathroom. Jasper's left the door ajar.

There's only a Snickers-bar-sized gap through which steam is escaping, but it's enough. I can see Jasper. He's wrapped one towel around his waist and is drying his hair with another. Water droplets speckle his shoulders and back.

Oh my Moon Gods... I can't look away. Every muscle in

his back moves as he rubs at his scalp.

My stomach is full of moths, my mouth is watering...

Before I know it he's turning around, but I can't tear my eyes away from his bare torso...

Until he spots me watching and in a panic, I dart my eyes to the ceiling. I count the dead bugs collected in the light fixture.

The bathroom door slams shut.

It's going to be a *really* long night.

Up until now, I haven't noticed the weird energy between Jasper and me. We've been too distracted by rogue break-ins and oncoming traffic. But now that we are in this musty, dimly lit motel room and everything is quiet, I can feel it. *The pull.* It's stronger than ever.

I have to stop myself from thinking about him, imagining him in the shower... I squeeze my eyes tight and I flop down on my blanket. I try to bury my head in the pillow.

A minute later I hear the bathroom door open. I don't move or look up just in case I get another mind-melting look at Jasper. Everything is quiet except for his footsteps and then the sounds of covers being pulled back and the squeak of bedsprings.

"Do you need any more pillows?" he asks, breaking the silence.

"Uh, no, I'll be fine," I lie.

I decide to risk it and sit up. Jasper is wearing a black T-shirt—thank goodness—and sitting cross-legged under the covers with his back against the headboard.

I breathe a little sigh of relief.

"Thank you," he says. "For taking the floor."

"Oh, that's all right. It's pretty comfy actually."

Jasper shakes his head a little.

"You don't have to do that."

"What?"

"Make me feel better."

"I...wasn't, it really is comfy!"

He laughs a little, looking at me like he knows I'm lying.

"Okay," he says. "I'm going to meditate a little before I

sleep. Do you want the light off?"

"Ah, no, that's okay. You can leave it."

I lie back down and twist about trying to find the most comfortable position, settling finally on my back.

Jasper's breaths become long and deep.

Eventually, he flicks off the light, but a question has popped into my mind. I open my eyes and the room is dark except for a strip of orange light poking through the gap in the curtains.

"Hey, Jasper?"

He sighs quietly.

"Yes?"

"Why do you meditate so much?"

"I need to make sure my mind is attuned to the pack. But it takes practice."

"Attuned like how you can sense Aisha? What's that about anyway?"

"Every alpha has the ability to sense the members of their pack. What they're feeling, if they're in pain. It helps us know if the pack is in danger."

"So your dad can do it too?"

Jasper scoffs. "He's amazing. He can pinpoint the exact location of every Elite Pack wolf. I've got nothing on him."

"But you can sense Aisha really well?"

"That's because we're close. It's easier if I know the person...if I care about them."

He swallows.

I stare at the unfamiliar ceiling and wonder if he's doing the same.

"It takes work to be as attuned as my father," he says.

"So you can't sense everyone?"

"I'm still working on it. My dad says I don't practice hard enough."

"I find that hard to believe."

I laugh quietly and Jasper does too.

"Can you sense me?" I ask when we fall quiet again.

My heart starts thumping so hard I can hear it.

Why did I ask that? Idiot!

"Yes," he says. "I can sense you, Max."

Silence. I hold my breath and clutch my blanket between my fingers. A car whooshes past outside.

The bedsprings creak as Jasper rolls over.

"Good night," he says, ending the conversation.

"...night."

I wake up in the night to the sound of bedsprings and moaning.

"No...don't...don't..." Jasper groans.

I sit up and look around in the darkness. Nothing has changed since we went to sleep.

Only Jasper is tossing and turning like he's possessed.

"Dad...I can't...Mom..."

"Jasper?"

He won't stop mumbling and twisting so I throw off my blanket and walk to the side of the bed.

Sweat is beading on his forehead and his face is squished like he's in pain.

"Jasper," I say again, a little more forcefully.

Super slowly, I reach out and take hold of his shoulder. I say his name again and shake him lightly.

His eyes burst open as he sucks a short, fast breath in through his nose. Our eyes lock and he looks confused, as if he has no idea where he's woken up.

"It's me," I say, retracting my hand. "You were having a nightmare."

He breathes a sigh of relief and relaxes into his pillow.

"Did I wake you?" he asks.

"Not really, that floor is actually pretty difficult to sleep on." My bottom lip is trembling a little. "Are you okay?"

He runs a hand over his face. "It was just a dream."

"Okay, good night."

I turn to walk back to my spot on the floor but Jasper grabs my wrist.

I freeze.

I don't dare look back so I just stand there with Jasper holding me in place.

"Stay," he says.

"What?"

"The floor isn't comfortable just...stay."

He lets go of my wrist and moves to the other side of the mattress.

I rush to my floor bed and grab my pillow.

My pulse races faster than a Formula 1 car as I return to the bed. Jasper is already lying on his side, facing the opposite wall.

Carefully, I place my pillow against the headboard and slide in.

I lie with my eyes wide open and my arms crossed over my chest like I'm lying in a coffin.

"Night," Jasper says.

I blink once then twice. He's right there, radiating heat.

My whole body is trembling.

What would happen if I were to move my hand a couple of inches to my left?

Would he kick me out or...something else? Do I even want that?

I'm lost in my thoughts until I notice Jasper's breathing has slowed.

He's asleep.

I roll over onto my side and try to forget about the boy behind me.

Before I know it, I'm out as well.

In the morning, I roll over and squint at the sun blaring through the open curtains. It's hot, too hot. I'm sweating like a slice of ham left out of the fridge. Frantically, I push back the covers.

The bed is empty, there's a ruffle in the sheet next to me where Jasper slept.

He's not here.

For a second, I'm scared he's left me and driven on to rescue Aisha by himself. I wouldn't put it past him.

With a yawn, I sit up and take in the room. It's less

creepy in the light of day. Just a plain motel that's seen better days.

My mouth is chalky so I roll out of bed and grab a bottle of water from the minibar.

Put it on the alpha's tab.

My phone is sitting on the coffee table and I glance at the time—7:01 a.m.—then groan at the string of texts and unanswered calls from my parents. In all the excitement I never found a moment to call them and tell them I wasn't coming home.

I'll have to speak to them later, I think when I spot a note on the bedside table.

"Gone to get car," it says in a hurried scribble. *Phew.* Jasper hasn't deserted me. The wave of relief I feel is more potent than I'd like to admit.

I go to the bathroom to freshen up. I'm almost fully awake when a horn blares outside.

Stepping out into the sunlight is like walking into a literal fire. I have to shade my eyes with my hand to make out Jasper standing next to his car with his arm sticking through the open window, his hand on the horn.

"Let's go," he says.

While Jasper drops the key back at reception I grab my things and jump into the passenger seat. I send off a quick text to my parents.

I'm fine. With Jasper. We have to go get Aisha from Pittsburgh. Call you when I'm back.

I hit Send and wince, then immediately turn my phone off. I know they're going to fly right off the handle when they see that text. The latest I've ever stayed out without their permission was the night of Katie's sweet sixteenth when we snuck into a piano bar in Manhattan. We didn't even drink but my parents grounded me for a month.

I've tried to soften the blow as much as possible but they're not going to be happy when they find out I've gone on a road trip to Rogue City to rescue a girl I barely know from some properly dodgy bad guys.

It'll be worth the grounding if we can save Aisha.

With a fresh tire and a good night's sleep, we hit the road.

"How did you sleep?" I ask once we're back on a proper highway.

"Fine," Jasper says curtly.

"It looked like you were having a pretty intense dream," I say, trying to sound casual.

"I don't remember."

I turn to look at Jasper but his eyes don't leave the road.

"You have to remember. You woke up. You told me to sleep in the bed."

"Yeah, you shouldn't have done that," he says coldly.

It wasn't like I even wanted to! He's the one who asked me to stay. I don't know why I thought things this morning would go any other way. I should have expected this from Jasper.

He's back to being a jerk.

"So you're just going to pretend like you don't remember anything?" I ask.

"There's nothing to remember," he says and pushes down on the accelerator.

I guess that means the conversation is over.

A coverage of gray clouds has rolled in by the time we leave the highway and begin snaking our way along the cracked and faded roads toward Rogue City. Grass and weeds shoot up along the sides of the tarmac.

There are no houses, just the occasional shack in the middle of a field.

Plumes of smoke are rising just on the other side of the horizon. Dark, smoky towers, like columns holding up the clouds.

"What are those?" I ask.

"They keep the furnaces burning for power," Jasper replies.

"So that's it?"

Finally, Rogue City comes into view. The first thing I see are the factories and warehouses. It's an industrial graveyard. All the buildings look abandoned and tumbledown.

It's just how Jasper described it. And if the outside appearance is anything to go by I shudder to think what's going on inside those buildings.

But then I notice a change in the landscape. The dusty, weed-infested grassland drops away, replaced by crops—neatly arranged in rows and well tended. Corn and tomatoes and other vegetables grow in abundance on all sides.

"This looks like a farm," I say.

"The rogues have had to fend for themselves for a long time. They're cut off from wolf society, but they have no place in the human world either."

"That's tough," I say.

The more farmland we pass the more I start to think this doesn't look like a run-down haven for crime and more like a scene from the black-and-white bits of *The Wizard of Oz*.

It isn't exactly picturesque. But there is life here. People must take care of these crops. From what I've been told about rogues I didn't know they could trim their toenails let alone master agriculture.

"Have you been here before?" I ask Jasper, who doesn't seem as interested in the surroundings as me.

"No, but my father has told me what happens here."

"It looks like corn," I say, staring at a harvest-ready field. "Corn is what happens here."

"They're rogues," Jasper says, snarling. "They'd kill you before you even had a chance to pick an apple."

"But it doesn't look like—"

"It doesn't matter what it looks like. They're all the same and they have Aisha."

I shut my mouth. I don't think Jasper is about to change his mind about this.

"We should park up somewhere before we get too close to the city."

I nod, trying to be encouraging, but the truth is...I'm starting to get nervous. Nothing on this trip has been quite like I expected and despite the humble farmland throwing me for a loop, I know somewhere in this place Aisha is being held against her will.

Jasper parks his car behind a clump of trees, a good distance away from the warehouse graveyard.

"Wait here," he says, stepping out of the car and quietly pressing his door shut.

What?!

Quickly as I can, I push my door open and jump out.

"I'm coming with you."

"No, it's too dangerous."

I huff but I don't have a counterargument. He's right. Going in there is super dangerous. But if he's willing to do what it takes to get Aisha back, so am I. And...I don't want him going in alone.

"I can help," I say. "What if something happens?"

"Then I'll deal with it. You'll only get in the way."

I hate that my jaw tenses and my eyes cloud over with tears. I feel like a petulant kid being told he can't use the swing set.

"But—"

"No, Max. For once just do what I tell you."

I back down, letting my shoulders drop.

"Wait here," Jasper says one last time before creeping off along the tree line.

I watch him disappear between two bushes and suddenly my heart starts pounding.

Maybe it's the thought of being left behind for a rogue to stumble upon and disembowel. Or maybe it's the sight of Jasper walking off into danger. But I know I can't stay here.

As gently as possible, I close the passenger-side door and lift my nose into the air. Jasper has left a trail of lemony mint and cherry blossom for me to follow.

Rogue City here I come.

ROGUE CITY LIMITS

I follow a little ways behind Jasper, stopping when he ducks behind a graffiti-splattered wall.

For a second back there, I was starting to think the farm part of the rogues' territory was kind of cute. But now that we've crossed the line from dirt to cement, everything seems different.

The buildings are straight out of a postapocalyptic disaster film.

Where am I? District 13?

Windows are missing, with jagged, iceberg-shaped shards sticking out from their frames. The walls are dark with age, cracked by weeds spurting between the bricks, and covered in some pretty uninspired graffiti.

"What is that smell?"

There's an indistinct odor coming from inside the buildings. A mix of scents that I don't recognize. It's like mixing paints in art class. Eventually they all mingle together to create an indistinguishable shade of brown.

This must be what it smells like when wolves of different packs come together. The various scents become one pungent mess.

"Reminds me of the subway," I say, chuckling to myself.

Rounding a corner, I watch as Jasper sprints across an

open cement courtyard.

I'm about to chase after him when I hear a voice.

"Wanna play again?" They sound like a teenager. *Are there kids here?*

I turn and peek over the edge of a splintering windowsill.

Inside the warehouse, there are rows of tents, laundry hanging on strings along the walls, and a fire burning in a rusted oil barrel

The first person I see is a man wandering at the far end of the room. He's too far away to be the owner of the voice and way too old. A few tents down a woman is lying asleep on a bare mattress. Not her either.

But these people don't look like the rogues I'm familiar with. They look more like the homeless people you see around Manhattan than the crazed wolf who tried to take a chunk out of my shoulder.

Then it dawns on me. The tents are faded, the clothes on the laundry line have holes and stains. This isn't a bustling city or a den of criminal activity. It's more like a human refugee camp.

"Your turn, Cassie."

I hear the voice again.

"I dealt last time, I always deal," a girl—Cassie—replies.

I rise higher onto my toes, straining to peer over the windowsill. A guy and a girl are sitting on the floor beneath me. They're about my age with matted hair and pale, sunken cheeks. They're skinny and dirty, but they're grinning, slapping cards determinedly into a pile.

"Snap!" Cassie yells, slamming her hand on top of the pile.

My grip on the windowsill slips and I stumble backward.

"What was that?" the guy asks.

"Probably just those guys over in the grain silo, they've been holed up in there for weeks."

"Those guys are shitty," the boy says.

Breathing a quick sigh, I look around and realize I can't see Jasper anymore.

I hunt for his scent, widening my nostrils, and finally find it leading in the direction of a building in the distance. There's a tank attached to the side with a slide-like pipe connecting it to a hole in the roof. Scrawled in red spray paint on the sidewall is an image just like Troy described.

A wolf and a lightning bolt.

I hurry in the direction of Jasper's scent, trying to stay low.

I cross the open expanse of concrete and reach the building but notice a dark shape out of the corner of my eye. My curiosity takes over. I turn away from the open sliding door and press my back against the cinder-block wall, edging my way to the corner.

I peer around the corner, being careful in case someone is waiting there. Luckily, there aren't any wolves hanging around, but there is a fancy car parked next to the silo. It's a black town car, with blackout windows and shiny silver hubcaps that scream wealthy New York businessman.

What is a car like that doing in a place like this?

A metallic bang sends panic shockwaves fizzing up my spine. I turn back to see the large door, my way in, has been slammed shut. The lock thuds into place.

I don't think I've been spotted. But I have no idea how I'm going to get inside. And Jasper has just been locked in.

Behind the car is a wrought iron fire escape, climbing the side of the building to a door on the second floor.

With one last glance behind me, I tiptoe my way to the stairs.

They creak a little as I climb, but they seem sturdy enough.

It's hard to keep my legs from shaking as I reach the door. I gently turn the handle and have to lean my full weight against it to make it budge. But I exhale with relief when it swings open.

I step inside and onto a metal walkway running in a square around the outside wall of a tall open space.

Above me, there's a panel in the ceiling where grain, or

whatever, used to pour through from the silo. Now the only thing pouring in is sunlight. My eyes have to adjust to the dimness, but when they do I spot her. On the other side of the warehouse, Aisha is slumped on the floor, leaning against a beam with her hands tied behind her.

I slap a hand over my mouth so my involuntary gasp doesn't attract attention. Because Aisha isn't the only person here. Right beneath me is a man.

This guy looks like he's been in a bar fight or two. Tanned, muscular arms jut out from a denim jacket with the sleeves torn off. The Rogue City emblem is tattooed on his right shoulder. Across from him another guy in a leather jacket is sitting on a chair cracking peanuts from their shells.

I kneel so as not to be seen and I look around wondering if there are more of them.

There has to be more of them, right? And where is Jasper? It's hard to make out his scent here with the stank of rogues and the yeasty stench of the warehouse.

I turn my attention back to Aisha. She's slumped on the ground, with a bruise in the right corner of her mouth and a small bloodstain on her jeans. Her head is drooping against her chest, and her eyes are closed like she's sleeping.

As if she can sense me, she rolls her head to the side and opens one eye drowsily.

She's still alive.

"Hey boys!" a gruff voice calls out from the shadows. The other two perk up. "The boss is here."

A tower of a man lumbers into view. His legs are thick like logs, threatening to tear through the seams of his faded jeans. His white T-shirt is covered in stains, and a scar runs down the side of his face. *Scarface?* My heart jumps into my throat at the sight of the knife attached to his belt. *That thing looks more like a machete.*

"Where is he then?" the peanut-shucking guy responds.

"He's waiting in the car," Scarface says. "Wants us to bring out the girl."

"Has he got the money?" the guy with the tattoo says. I lean away from the edge of the walkway as Scarface turns to his associate.

"He wants to see the girl first."

"That wasn't the deal," Tattoo groans, rubbing his eyes. "Let me talk to him."

He crosses the room and Scarface follows as he heads outside. Whoever their "boss" is, he must be out in that town car.

Now it's just Peanut left with Aisha. Or maybe not. There's movement in the shadows behind her.

Like a total ninja-badass, Jasper emerges directly behind Aisha. He crouches down and while Peanut is distracted, Jasper elongates one of his claws and slices through the rope holding her in place.

Aisha lifts her head, opening her eyes groggily, and Jasper places a hand on her arm. Her eyes pop open and her body goes rigid. She's awake! And she knows we've come to rescue her.

Jasper leans close to Aisha and whispers in her ear. I don't know what he says but she nods, subtly enough not to draw attention to herself. Then brandishing some tool in his hand—a wrench or a spanner, I'm not sure, I never took shop class—Jasper rises and approaches Peanut from behind.

I know what he's about to do! He lifts the wrench above his head and gets ready to knock the dick out.

But, before he can strike, Tattoo and Scarface reappear.

I lean forward hoping he'll hear their footsteps but he's too focused on his target. Jasper is about to be found out! And he's crazy outnumbered!

I know I have to do something, so I jump up, my feet landing heavily on the metal walkway. "Jasper, watch out!"

Everyone's eyes shoot in my direction. I'm not sure who is more shocked to see me. Peanut, Aisha, or Jasper.

"What the...?" Scarface says.

"They stink the same as her," Tattoo says. "They're from the Elite Pack!"

Peanut growls and spins around, swiping a claw at Jasper, who jumps backward.

Scarface and Tattoo come running and I hop about, not knowing what to do. Have I just made everything worse? Jasper is down there with the three of them and I'm up here being completely useless.

"Up there!" Peanut shouts, gesturing at me, and before I know what's happening, Tattoo has me in his sights. He leaps into the air, clutches onto a beam, and scales the structure like a professional free runner.

He lands heavily a few feet away from me and grins, exposing yellowed teeth.

"I'm going to rip you in half," he says.

"Max!" Jasper yells. It looks like he's about to attempt his own Spider-Man-like feat, but he's intercepted by Scarface.

Geez, how tall is that guy? Even Jasper looks tiny next to him.

He pulls the blade from its holster and swings at Jasper. I want to keep watching to make sure he's okay but I have a big rogue problem of my own.

"I bet you bleed real nice," Tattoo says, taking a step toward me.

"Actually, I've never been very good with blood," I say, almost tripping backward.

I wish I had time to shift. As a wolf, I might stand a chance against this guy. But if I shift, he'll shift, and I have a feeling his wolf could swallow me whole.

"Oh I don't know, you look pretty ripe to me," he taunts.

I glance back to the floor below hoping Jasper might be on his way to save me. But he has his hands full taking on both Scarface and Peanut. He jumps into the air, spinning, and delivers a fly kick to Peanut's face. Scarface is on him as soon as he lands, and he has to duck and roll to avoid being sliced in half.

Aisha is on her feet too now and, much to his surprise, she leaps on Peanut's back, plunging her fangs into his neck. He screams but I have to turn my attention back to the snarling rogue advancing on me.

"You're going to feel so much pain," he says, punching a fist into his open palm. "And I'm going to enjoy every second of it."

He charges at me. I scream and slam my eyes shut, bracing for the impact. But it doesn't come. Instead, I hear a pained howl and open my eyes to find Tattoo clutching the knife lodged in his thigh.

"You little shit!"

On the ground, Jasper is standing with his arm outstretched, having just thrown Scarface's blade with pinpoint precision, leveling my attacker.

"Get away from him," Jasper yells.

Tattoo groans as he rises to his feet. I turn and run.

There's a ladder on the far side of the room and if I can just make it down I can join Jasper and Aisha and maybe we can make a run for it.

Aisha grunts as she hits the floor. Peanut has managed to throw her off his back. "Take this, bitch!" he says and delivers a swift kick to her side.

Whatever advantage Jasper had on Scarface is gone. I wince at the cracking sound that echoes off the walls as Scarface's fist smashes into Jasper's cheek.

Not the face!

At the ladder, I find my footing and I'm halfway down when a rough hand grabs my wrist. Tattoo is leaning over the ledge, holding me so tight I worry my hand might pop off.

Behind me, Aisha cries out in pain. Peanut drives his foot into her rib cage again and again. Jasper is in my periphery, trapped in a headlock.

This rescue is a disaster and it's all my fault.

My fingers are ripped from the metal bars as Tattoo lifts me into the air. He holds me above his head, bringing our faces level.

"Got you now, little mutt. Shame I'm going to have to put you down."

I'm dangling above the concrete floor, kicking my legs about frantically. In my thrashing, I notice the knife still sticking out of Tattoo's leg. A wet patch of blood has seeped into the denim of his jeans.

"Hey," I say. "The vet called. They're going to have to amputate!"

I set my jaw and kick. My foot makes contact with the knife and Tattoo screams in pain.

His grip loosens and my wrist slips free. And then I'm falling. I flail my arms about as if I can swim through the air.

I brace for impact but luckily, my fall is cushioned. I crash down on top of two bodies. Somehow Jasper, still trapped in a headlock, has managed to get himself and the rogue wrapped around his neck beneath me. The three of us tumble to the ground in a pile.

The shock of my arrival is enough for Jasper to escape the pythonlike arms of Scarface, and we scramble to our feet.

Jasper dives for Peanut, tackling him to the ground while I rush to Aisha and pull her up.

"Are you okay?"

"I can walk," she says.

There's a spine-bending crack as Jasper slams Peanut's head against the concrete, knocking him out cold.

"Whoa," I say.

"That way..." Jasper says, pointing to the open door.

Scarface is still getting to his feet, and Tattoo is only halfway down the ladder. We have less than a second until they're on top of us.

"NOW!!"

He doesn't have to tell me twice. I take Aisha's hand and we run for our lives. Jasper arrives on Aisha's free side and together the three of us burst out of the warehouse into the sun.

From inside come the spine-tingling sounds of bones cracking and muscles tearing.

"They're shifting," I say. "They can run faster as wolves."

"She's too weak to shift," Jasper says, glancing at Aisha. "We have to make it on foot!"

"Okay." I nod. "Let's go!"

Jasper slings Aisha's arm over his shoulder and in one

fluid motion lifts her into his arms.

For a split second, I look to my left and notice the black town car is no longer parked beneath the silo. *Where has it gone?*

There's no point thinking about that now, not when there are two massive, supremely pissed-off rogues chasing us.

"Hurry!" I scream and we race back toward the car, the two rogues right behind us.

Before I know it we've left the industrial bomb site behind and are sprinting between two rows of orange trees.

"We're nearly there!" I say as the clump of trees where we parked comes into view. But the rogues are gaining speed.

"We're not out of the woods just yet," Jasper says, accelerating.

I match his pace, somehow able to keep up. I thought this speedster gig was a blue-moon-specific skill but apparently, I've still got it.

"Get in!" Jasper says as soon as we reach the car. He opens the back door and places Aisha inside. I hurry to the passenger side and dive in.

We pull out and the rogues appear in the dusty path ahead of us. Jasper grips the wheel and pushes down hard on the gas.

"Hold on!" he says.

His eyes are fully black as he plows forward. I glance from him back to the rogues, who aren't backing down. It's the life-or-death game of chicken I imagined!

Jasper's muscles are tense and he's not breathing; he isn't going to stop.

An inch from collision the rogues bail out. They dive out of our way, but one of them is not quite in time. There's a bang and a crack as the front bumper makes contact with one of their back legs. I watch as he flips and lands awkwardly in a row of cabbages.

We careen off the path, throwing up a trail of dust, and glide back onto the road. I flop back in my seat, wiping the sweat from my brow.

"That was close," I say.

I turn back one last time and the rogues are gone, left back behind the horizon. Aisha is also staring out the back window, making sure we put enough distance between us and them.

When we're safe she turns to me and I take her hand.

"We made it," I say, unable to contain the burst of laughter erupting from my soul. Aisha smiles and laughs right back at me.

"You did it!" she says, beaming but still holding her most-likely broken ribs.

I leave my arm stretched out behind me so I can keep hold of Aisha—I need constant physical contact—and glance at Jasper.

He's quiet, eyes fixed on the road.

"Jasper, we did it," I say, wishing he would at least crack a smile.

"What were you thinking?" he says. "You could have gotten us all killed."

"I wanted to help."

"Well, you didn't! You put everyone in danger, including yourself. I told you to stay in the car."

"I thought—"

"No, Max. You didn't think. You never do."

I shrink back into my seat as we drive on in silence. It's going to be a long journey home.

THE ALPHA'S HOUSE

"Where are we?" I say, blinking awake as we pull up between two towering walls.

It's dark out and up ahead an enormous, ornate gate is swinging open.

Have I woken up outside Wayne Manor? Is Batman waiting inside with hot cocoa?

I must have fallen asleep somewhere on the road back to New York. Only this isn't Manhattan or Stony Point. This isn't anywhere I recognize.

While we wait for the gates to swing open I make out the dull roar of the ocean in the distance. But that can't be right. Can it?

"We're in the Hamptons," Jasper says.

I sit up, shaking my head. I must still be asleep because I'm definitely dreaming.

"The Hamptons?! What are we doing here?"

"Aisha needs to rest and this is the safest place to bring her."

Aisha is asleep in the back seat, leaning against the window.

"I can take you home once she's settled in."

"But what is this place?" I stare at a line of perfectly spherical trees as we cruise down a long gravel driveway.

"This is my house," Jasper says, swallowing.

"Oh."

We glide along until the front of Jasper's house comes into view.

The building is three stories tall and looks as if it's made entirely out of concrete and glass. Brutal and minimalist, it looms above us—alien and unwelcoming. A large entryway is lined with flower beds curated to perfection. A few palm trees wave their fronds in the breeze and a fountain bubbles in the center of the forecourt.

Was Tony Stark the previous owner?

To the left of the front door is a cherry tree— inexplicably still in blossom, despite it being well out of season. Pink and white petals are strewn about the lawn like candy.

This place is too, too wild and I've only seen the front yard!

The driveway curves around the house, leading to a garage door longer than my parents' entire house. The door slides open as we approach.

Lights ping on inside and we slip into an empty space between two other cars. I step out of Jasper's Jaguar and let my gaze drift along the line of vehicles. *It's like a damn car dealership in here!* Sports cars sit next to SUVs, jeeps, town cars, and motorcycles.

And there aren't just cars either. On the far wall, a couple of Jet Skis sit on some industrial-strength shelves. There are quad bikes and golf carts as well. It finally dawns on me... This isn't just Jasper's house. This is the alpha's house.

Without waiting for me, Jasper carries Aisha into the house, so I stop gawking and follow behind.

It's hard to take anything in at first. It all seems so big and glossy. Every surface looks pristine. I'm scared I'm going to scuff my shoes on the polished concrete floor or bump into a perfectly white wall and leave a mark.

There's sculptures in the hallway and abstract paintings that take up entire walls. The furniture looks unused. The whole house is straight out of the pages of

Architectural Digest.

Jasper leads us up some stairs which overlook a sterile living room. Four couches that could fit my entire family three times over sit facing each other between a built-in fireplace and a wall of windows.

Beyond the expansive lawn outside, I can make out the rolling slope of sand dunes, and behind them the sea.

I follow Jasper down a long hallway of doors and into a dark bedroom.

Gently, he lowers Aisha onto the bed, where she rolls over onto her side.

"Wait here," he says, turning back to me. "I'm going to get her some water and see if I can get a healer here in the morning."

He passes me, heading back in the direction of the hall.

"Wait—" He's gone before I can ask him my question. I want to know if the alpha is home.

"He doesn't mean it, you know," Aisha says, looking over her shoulder.

"Hey, you should try and sleep."

I walk to the bed and kneel beside her, taking her hand.

"He only acts like a jerk"—Aisha's voice is hoarse— "because he's scared."

"How hard did you hit your head?"

Aisha laughs, but her laughs quickly turn into coughing. She sits up to try and get more air into her lungs.

"Whoa, are you okay?"

She nods and the cough settles down.

"No more jokes," I promise. "Get some rest."

Aisha nods and lies back against the pillows, closing her eyes.

I spin around and take in the room. It's big, of course, probably about ten times the square footage of my room. The bed is a California king. There's room for a full sofa and entertainment system, complete with PS5. A large wooden desk sits in one corner and built-in shelves take up an entire wall, stuffed with books and trophies.

This is Jasper's room. I thought maybe he'd take us to a

guest room or something but no... This is his space, his inner sanctum.

My skin starts tingling. If I close my eyes I can feel him, he's everywhere around me. His scent...

I don't know how I didn't realize sooner.

I wander around the room absorbing every little detail, taking snapshots in my mind.

It's nothing like my room at home. For one thing, it's way tidier. There are no posters on the walls, no stuffed toys leaking fluff from where they got torn eight years ago. No stickers on the headboard and no pile of dirty clothes.

My eyes run over the many, many awards, golden cups, plaques, and shiny little men standing on plinths with Jasper's name engraved on them. He's won more prizes than Meryl Streep!

His desktop is bare except for a laptop and a photo in a silver frame.

Who does he care enough about to give their photo such pride of place? I head to the desk and pick up the picture. It's a black-and-white portrait of a stunningly beautiful lady. I recognize her instantly.

Mitsuha Apollo, Jasper's mom. Her black hair is pulled back beneath a straw hat and she's smiling effortlessly. She has the same light freckles across her cheeks as Jasper.

"That's my mom," a little voice behind me says.

I turn and find a young girl standing in the light of the hallway.

She's wearing light-blue pajamas with Anna and Elsa from *Frozen* printed on them. Her hair is dark like Jasper's. She looks like the kid version of the woman in the photo.

"Is it?" I fumble with the frame, trying to place it back on the desk so it doesn't fall over.

"Who are you?" the girl asks, walking straight into Jasper's room.

"Me? Uh, I'm Max. Who are—I mean, what's your name?"

"I'm Jodie."

She does this cute little shrug when she says her name.

"What are you doing in my brother's room?"

"I...I..." For some reason, this kid is intimidating the socks off me. It must be that alpha bloodline.

"Hey, stinky face," Jasper says, returning just in the nick of time. "What are you doing up?"

"I couldn't sleep because you weren't here. Where were you?" she says.

"I had to help Aisha." He crosses the room and places a glass of water on the bedside table next to her. "You remember Aisha, right?"

"Of course I do," Jodie says, swinging her arms from side to side. "She's here all the time!"

"Don't be jealous, stinky face," he taunts.

So, Jasper has a thing for lame nicknames. Although, come to think of it, he hasn't called me *bonehead* in a while.

"Come here." Jasper steps to Jodie and kneels to hug her.

I stare in astonishment. I've never seen him show this kind of affection to anyone. It's kind of baffling and kind of adorable.

"Is Dad here?" Jasper asks.

Jodie sticks a finger in her mouth and shakes her head. "Un-uh."

"Oh, is that why you couldn't sleep?"

Jodie scrunches up her face. "You both left and I got stuck here with Melissa."

Who's Melissa? And what did she do to deserve that look of hatred?

"I thought Melissa was a good babysitter," Jasper says.

"She made me carrots for dinner. Carrots! Gross."

"Carrots?" Jasper says, making a face like he just ate an out-of-date Twinkie. "We can do better than carrots. You want a snack?"

Jodie nods enthusiastically and Jasper looks up at me.

"Are you hungry?"

I haven't thought about my stomach since early this morning, but the second Jasper asks if I'm hungry it starts growling like a wolf possessed.

"I could eat."

Jodie sits on the granite kitchen counter, swinging her legs and chomping on a grilled cheese sandwich, as Jasper slices a knife diagonally through a second sandwich and slides the plate in my direction.

"Here," he says.

"Thanks!" I grab the sandwich and take a massive bite.

I moan audibly and Jodie shoots me a weird, grossed-out look. But this grilled cheese is the absolute GOAT. It tastes so good. They must have some kind of fancy-person cheese because this is the best thing I've ever put in my mouth.

Jasper goes to work grilling himself a sandwich.

"Did Dad say when he was going to be home, Jodes?" he asks, flipping the grilled cheese with professional flair.

"Nope," she says with her mouthful.

Jasper catches me looking at him.

"Sometimes Dad has to leave at short notice for business. Melissa manages the property, so she lives on-site and we pay her extra in case we need her to babysit last minute."

I nod like a madman, trying to pretend like everything he just said is totally normal.

It sounds like Jericho is away quite a bit. Not that you could blame him. He's the alpha. He has an entire pack to take care of—and a big one at that.

It's kind of obvious Jasper is used to taking care of his little sister.

"How is it?" he asks Jodie, whose face is greasy and smeared with mustard.

"It's good," she says, nodding. "One of your best."

She laughs and it's so contagious I start giggling as well. Finally, when he can no longer avoid it, Jasper starts laughing too. I can't help but stare at him. I don't think I've ever actually seen him laugh before. Of course, his smile is ridiculous and the one dimple he gets in his right cheek is so adorable my heart might burst.

I wish he'd smile more often.

"Okay, time for bed, stink face," Jasper says when we're all done eating.

"Fine," Jodie says, sighing. "But do I have to brush my teeth?"

"Yes."

"But I already did it..."

"Then you should be good at it."

He hoists her off the counter and begins to carry her out of the kitchen. I have to hand it to her, she's brave. Not many people would have the courage to stand up to Jasper like that.

"Uh, hey, I should probably call my parents," I say. Mom and Dad are probably so freaked out right now, I wouldn't be surprised if they've called the coast guard.

"Sure, the living room is through there." Jasper nods in the direction of a hallway.

"Thanks."

Jodie takes Jasper's hand and they leave on the way to Sleepytown.

"Is Max going to visit all the time now?" Jodie asks once they're out of my eyeshot.

I can't make out Jasper's answer.

That's okay though. I'm just glad to have made a good impression with one member of the Apollo family.

I wander into the room with all the couches, pulling out my phone and switching it on. Immediately I'm bombarded with text messages and missed calls.

Slouching into a sofa, I dial the house.

"Hello? Max is that you?!" Mom shrieks down the line.

"Mom, it's me. I'm fine."

"Where have you been, Max? We've been worried sick!"

There's no point hiding anything from my mom so I start at the beginning and tell her all about our adventures with the rogues. Midway through the story Dad picks up the other phone in the study and I have to start all over again.

Each twist evokes some exaggerated reaction from my parents. Either they're terrified for my life or they're angry at me for acting rashly.

Once I'm done my parents launch into a monologue about how worried they were and how much stress I've caused them. I stare at the walls of the alpha's sparse living room. There aren't any pictures of Jasper or Jodie in here. There's no sign that a family even lives here.

I think about the walls of my parents' house, covered in so many embarrassing photos of me it's ridiculous.

"Mom, Dad!" I say, interrupting them. "I'm sorry. I'm really sorry. I should have called. I shouldn't have let you worry. But I promise you I'm fine."

They're quiet on the other end.

"Are you there?"

"We're just glad you're back and you're safe, honey," Mom says, her voice tight like she's crying.

"I'll ask Jasper to drive me home in the morning, okay?"

"Okay, Max," Dad says. "We love you."

"Love you too," I say and we hang up.

This house is state of the art, it's amazing, but as I slide my phone back in my pocket, I feel buzzed knowing that my home trumps it in every single way.

I wonder if I should wait down here for Jasper or go find him. My phone is low on battery and I'd hate to miss another of my parents' calls, so I decide to head up in search of a charger.

On a landing halfway up the stairs, I stop to look at a picture on the wall. It's the only family picture I've seen in the whole place.

Alpha Jericho is standing on the beach in a loose button-up shirt, which can barely contain his broad chest, and khaki pants. An angsty-looking teenaged Jasper is standing to his left in a not-beach-appropriate black T-shirt and skinny jeans. Jodie is kneeling behind a sandcastle to Jericho's right, smiling the toothless grin of a kid in the midst of a tooth fairy invasion.

There's a fourth person in the picture who I don't recognize, although he does look strangely familiar. He's wearing a gray uniform and leather gloves. He doesn't look like part of the family—maybe an employee?—but I can't shake the feeling that I've seen him or someone who looks a lot like him before.

Other than the weirdly familiar stranger, it's a cute family portrait.

I head upstairs to try and find Jasper and hear his voice from down the hall.

I glance inside the door to Jodie's bedroom and spot Jasper sitting on a beanbag next to her bed. Jodie's tucked in with her head resting on a fluffed-up pillow while Jasper reads to her from a *Sailor Moon* graphic novel.

The girl's got taste!

Jodie's room is massive too but it's messier than Jasper's. Toys and books are scattered across a fuzzy pink rug. The walls are lit in the warm orange glow of her *Raya and the Last Dragon*-themed lamp.

Jasper reads until Jodie is asleep. When she's dozed off he pulls the cover tighter around her and kisses her forehead.

I hurry back to his room to plug in my phone.

Not wanting to wake Aisha, I go back to the living room, somehow breaking into a sweat just from walking between rooms in this mansion. Something flickering in the garden draws my attention and I peer through the glass wall.

"Whoa!"

"There you are," Jasper says, looking across the pool. He's found me, pants rolled up, legs dangling, enjoying the cool water.

"Sorry, I didn't want to interrupt," I say. "And I couldn't help myself. This pool is mega."

Of course they have a ridiculous swimming pool right in their backyard.

"Sure, but why are you sitting in the dark?" He walks to

a little shed off to the side and ducks inside.

The lights in the pool flick on, casting those trippy rectangular patterns across the tiled bottom.

"Here," Jasper says, appearing at my side and holding out a can of orange soda.

"Thanks." I crack it open and take a sip. "Jodie seems cool."

"She's a special kid."

"I can tell. How's Aisha doing?"

"A healer is coming first thing. But I don't think she's injured too badly, nothing that won't heal in a day or two. I think she's just tired and shaken up."

"Of course." I take a sip of soda and think about how terrified Aisha must have been. I'm glad we were able to rescue her.

"I want to apologize," Jasper says, clearing his throat. "For what I said in the car after we...well, you know."

His fingers are making dents in the sides of his can.

"I know you were just trying to help. It wasn't great of me to get angry the way I did."

"You were stressed," I say. "We'd just escaped a bunch of dudes with some serious anger issues. And you were right. I should have thought it through. I have a tendency to jump into things without thinking about the consequences."

"Only because you care."

I shrug. "Maybe. Or maybe I just didn't want to get left behind. But either way thanks, you know, for apologizing. I know you have a lot going on. I can see that much." I gesture toward the house with my soda. "I don't want to be another problem for you."

My head drops and I rub my pruning toes together. All this time I've been pitying myself, thinking Jasper was rude and selfish for ignoring me. But his life is wild. After just two nights with him I've had a taste of how intense it must be and I'm exhausted.

"You're not..." he says, and I look up to find him glancing in my direction. "You're not a problem, Max."

Our eyes linger on each other for just a moment before

it becomes too awkward and I have to look away. There's a leaf on the bottom of the pool. I stare at it, studying its subtle movements.

"Sometimes I wish I could be more spontaneous," Jasper says, taking a sip of his drink and kicking his legs a little in the water. "Ever since I was a kid my whole life has been scheduled and planned. Play this sport, study hard, meet this foreign dignitary. I barely had time for making friends."

"That sounds hard."

"The truth is I'd often see kids like you and Aisha running around, making noise and getting into trouble, and I'd be jealous."

I laugh. "You're jealous of me? No way."

He shakes his head. "Sometimes."

"But, like, how can you be jealous when you have this amazing pool?!"

"I didn't say it was often."

I can't believe it—Jasper is getting pouty, he's all clenched jaw and no eye contact.

"We can swap backyards anytime you like," I say, and I can tell he's trying hard not to crack a smile.

"You're such a bonehead," he says.

I gasp in feigned shock. *How dare he?!*

"I thought you'd stopped calling me that."

"Nah, why would I stop calling you a bonehead, when you're a total bonehead, bonehead?"

I knock my shoulder into his, trying to put him off-balance. "Stooop."

He shoves me back. "Bonehead!"

I turn my back on him *very* dramatically. "You're a dick."

"Hey bonehead, remember that time we went out in a canoe?"

What? Why is he asking me if I remember—

Midsentence, Jasper pushes me and I fly forward, splashing through the surface of the pool. I come up gasping, flapping my arms about, spitting water.

"Why did you do that?!"

"Payback," Jasper says, cackling.

"That's not fair." I swim to the edge of the pool and grab his dangling leg.

"Nonono, what are you doing?" he asks, still laughing.

With all my might I pull. Jasper splashes into the pool, throwing water into my face. He comes at me like a shark, grabbing my shoulders and forcing me under.

I grab his arms and we wrestle. Our legs get tangled as we both try to keep the other one down.

Eventually we both come up gasping for breath.

I try to wipe the water out of my eyes, but Japer splashes me and I turn in open-mouthed shock.

So that's how he wants to play this!

I splash him back and I keep splashing him until he finally puts his hands up in surrender.

"Okay, okay! You win!"

I smile and tread water, satisfied.

Jasper chuckles while making circular motions beneath the surface with his arms.

After all our splashing the night seems quieter than before. And Jasper... Jasper is staring at me.

Droplets are trickling from his hair. There are more dotted across his lips.

With one smooth stroke Jasper closes the distance between us. He swims right up to me.

What is he doing?

I prepare myself to be dragged under again but he doesn't strike.

We bob up and down in the water huffing, keeping our eyes locked. The stars spin overhead in quadruple time.

I let the smooth pulsations of my stroke pull me closer to Jasper, shrinking the remaining space between us.

He doesn't back away.

I run a hand through my hair, pushing it out of my eyes, and Jasper parts his lips.

Every cell in my body is longing to connect with him.

Our mouths draw nearer.

Is this really about to happen?

I tilt my head and go in for the kiss.

THE ALPHA'S SHADOW

The patio lights flick on.

Jasper and I snap apart, pushing away from each other and twisting our heads to the house to see who has interrupted our *almost* kiss.

I tread water and can't believe what was just about to happen.

Jasper and I were going to kiss—a real kiss, not like that one back at camp—until someone turned on the lights.

I don't notice Jasper getting out of the pool until I turn and find him already out and heading for the shed.

A dark shape moves inside the house, drawing my attention. A couple of men in suits are standing in the living room. They both have shaved heads and earpieces.

"Get out," Jasper says.

"What's going on?"

"My dad is home."

"What? Your dad...the alpha?!"

I hurry for the shallow end and manage to claw my dripping body out of the pool. Jasper tosses me a fresh beach towel.

My clothes are soaked through and I'm not sure whether to take them off before drying myself, so for a second I just stand there.

"What are you doing?" Jasper asks, looking at me like I haven't noticed I'm on fire.

"Sorry."

I pull the towel over my shoulders and start rubbing my hair.

"He's out here, sir." I nearly jump out of my skin at the deep, gruff voice. One of Alpha Jericho's men is leaning out the back door.

"Your father needs to see you," he says to Jasper before disappearing back inside.

Jasper stares at the doorway. He pulls his shoulders back and lifts his head. He's bracing for impact.

Once inside, Jasper and I stand shivering with our towels pulled around our shoulders. Water drips onto the floor while we wait.

Two of Jericho's security team—because I guess that's who they are—are watching us, me in particular, with unreadable expressions.

There's a small shift in their posture as a shadow appears in the hallway, and a moment later, the immense form of Alpha Jericho emerges.

Every muscle in my body becomes tense and I clamp down my jaw to try and stop my teeth from chattering.

The alpha approaches, his stature dwarfing everyone in the room. He is dressed for business in a sky-blue button-up that could explode off his muscular chest at any second. His jaw is a perfect square and his eyes are startlingly golden. Only his salt-and-pepper hair gives away his age.

Energy is pulsing off of him as he walks toward me, and a lump forms in my throat so large I'm worried I might choke.

"Where were you last night?" Jericho asks Jasper. My legs wobble at the sound of his voice. If he speaks to me I might pass out completely.

"We...I..." Jasper falters, head bowed. "Rogues took Aisha."

Jericho's brow creases with thought. He looks angry when he's thinking.

His eyes dart to me.

"Who is this?" he asks.

My mouth feels as dry as the Arizona desert.

"He's a friend of Aisha's," Jasper says as if he barely knows me.

Jericho's eyes don't leave mine. He squints and his nostrils flare. Is he scenting me? Trying to figure out if I'm a member of his pack? Or is it something else? What else can he figure out about me from my scent?

"Go wait upstairs," he commands.

My legs are moving before I can open my mouth. "Yes, sir."

The security beefcakes watch me as I head to the stairs, but Jericho keeps his gaze on his son.

Once I'm out of sight I stop and listen.

"What were you thinking running into rogue territory like that?" Jericho growls. "Not to mention taking civilians with you!"

"I'm sorry, Alpha," Jasper says.

"I thought I'd taught you better than that."

There's a pause and I can't hear anything for a moment. Then Jericho continues.

"You have no business putting people in danger."

"She's my friend; I had to—"

"Had to what?" Jericho's voice echoes through the house. "You had to be the big man, didn't you?"

"I'm not a kid anymore, Dad."

Jericho scoffs. Man, this guy is tough on Jasper. I feel bad for him. But the way his dad talks is not unfamiliar. I guess this is where Jasper gets it.

"Not a kid, hey? Then can you explain what you were doing joking around in the pool late at night?"

"He slipped... I—"

"I don't want to hear it, Jasper. It's time you start acting like the leader of this pack."

Jasper doesn't respond.

"And until then, if you have a problem with rogues you call me—"

"But you weren't here!"

Smack! The hard, flat sound of a slap throws the room into silence.

I press my head back against the wall. Did Jericho just hit Jasper?

"Hey." One of the beefcakes has appeared at the top of the stairs. "Shouldn't you be getting cleaned up?"

"Uh, yes. I was just looking for a bathroom," I say, spinning around like I'm completely lost.

"It's that way." He gestures in the direction of the bathroom.

"Right, thanks."

I start to make my way there when he speaks again. "No more snooping, all right kid?"

I shake my head like I've got no clue what he's talking about and laugh awkwardly. He isn't buying my performance, but I keep it up until the bathroom door clicks shut behind me.

Before me sit a claw-foot tub and a marble counter. Everything in this bathroom is shiny and hard. Just like everything in this house.

I go to sit on the edge of the tub and pull the towel tighter around myself. Suddenly, I feel crazy tired. It must be past midnight and it's been a mammoth couple of days.

My clothes are still wet and I'm starting to get really cold but I don't know where else I'm supposed to go. I don't want to run into Jericho or one of his goons. And I don't want Jasper to think I'm snooping around in his room. So I sit in the bathroom until I hear a knock on the door. I open it slightly, just enough for Jasper to shove a fistful of clothes through the gap.

"Get dressed," he says. "I'm taking you home."

"Oh, okay."

I shut the door and get undressed. Jasper has given me a pair of basketball shorts and a T-shirt that's at least three sizes too big. They don't look like his regular apparel. Maybe he wears them on laundry day?

I look for any sign of Jasper when I step out into the hall but find no one. The door to his room is ajar, so I head inside.

Jasper is facing a set of drawers across the room with his shirt off. He has one arm over his head and is inspecting his rib cage. He touches it lightly and flinches.

"Are you okay?" I ask.

Jasper drops his arm but doesn't turn to look at me or respond. He pulls a shirt from one of the drawers and slips it on, moving awkwardly to accommodate for his sore ribs.

Did a rogue give him that injury or...did Jericho do more than slap him?

To my left, Aisha is asleep in the bed. I don't care what Jericho says. Jasper did the right thing going after his friend. It's exactly what I would have done. I'm kind of proud of him for it.

If Jericho can't see that then he's an idiot.

"Are you ready?" Jasper asks, dressed and turning to face me.

"Yeah, I just need my phone and I'm not sure what to do with these." I hold up the ball of my sopping-wet clothes.

"Here." Jasper hands me a backpack without thinking about it, like it's a trash bag.

"Are you sure?"

"Really." He lowers his gaze. "It's nothing."

I shove my clothes in the bag and grab my cell from where I've left it plugged into the wall.

"Good to go. Are you sure you want to drive? It's pretty late."

Jasper is waiting by the door. "My father wants me to take you home."

"Yeah, but it could be dangerous."

"He's the alpha," Jasper says, whirling to face me. "He's *your* alpha. What he wants he gets."

I don't move. Jasper is being ridiculous. He nearly killed us both already by driving tired. He shouldn't have to drive me home just because his dad says so.

"Max," he mutters, and I notice his hand is shaking.

If we don't leave now I won't be the one who's in trouble. As much as I hate seeing Jasper like this, there's nothing else I can do except go with him.

"Coming."

I follow Jasper back out to his car.

In the garage, I wait for Jasper to unlock the doors before throwing my bag of clothes onto the back seat.

I step one foot into the car but freeze when I notice a car on the other side of the room that wasn't here earlier. It's a black town car, almost identical to the one I saw outside the rogue hideout. No, it *is* identical.

But why would the same car be here? Unless...

Alpha Jericho just arrived home.

Was he in this car? Does that mean he was there in Rogue City when we rescued Aisha?

None of this is making any sense.

It's late, I'm tired and maybe my eyes are playing tricks on me. I shake my head as my vision goes fuzzy.

"What are you waiting for?" Jasper asks from the driver's seat.

I must be hallucinating or putting dots together that aren't there. Because the idea that Alpha Jericho was somehow involved in Aisha's kidnapping is too wild to be true. It's insane.

"Nothing," I say and slide into the passenger side.

The entire ride home I keep picturing that car. The more I think about it the more convinced I am that it was the same. But I can't think of any reason why the alpha would have been in Rogue City. At least none that are good.

Jasper doesn't speak to me for the entire ride and I can tell that's how he wants it. He's in no mood for me to start asking questions. If I were to suggest his father had something to do with Aisha's abduction, he'd be more likely to bite my head off right now than listen. So I keep quiet.

My street is silent and empty as we pull up outside my house. Jasper puts the hand brake on but doesn't turn the engine off.

In films, this is where the cute teen couple would have an awkward but sweet first kiss. My date won't even look at me.

"Well, I..." This is it. The end of the line. I have to get out of the car and go inside and that means leaving Jasper.

I have no idea if he even wants to see me again, and this feels so rushed. After everything we've been through in the last few days, leaving now feels too abrupt, too final.

There has to be more.

But I don't know what to say.

"Jasper—"

He reaches across me and opens my door. My breath hitches at the brief moment of closeness, but when Jasper sits back in his seat, all that's left is the cool night air telling me it's time to exit the vehicle.

I thought we were making progress. We nearly kissed, didn't we?

Whoever that boy was, the one I spoke to by the pool, he's not here in the car.

In the course of one conversation with his father Jasper's changed, reverted to the emotional husk I met at camp.

I grab my bag from the back seat and step one foot out of the car.

"See you round," I say, looking back one last time.

"Goodbye, Max."

Jasper won't look at me, his eyes stay trained on the steering wheel.

I stare at the side of his head, wishing my eyes were emotional laser beams so that I could transmit everything I'm feeling straight into his brain.

Just look at me, you dumb jerk! Just one time. Look at me!

He doesn't budge.

My face tightens. There's no point even trying. I step out onto the road and slam my door shut. The engine revs and Jasper zooms away before I've even mounted the curb.

I watch Jasper's red taillights until they turn a corner and are gone.

Maybe forever.

HEY, OLD FRIENDS

The next few weeks are a blur.

Life goes back to normal—as if the entire summer was a fever dream.

I don't hear from Jasper.

Aisha messages saying she's feeling better and has even gone back into rehearsal.

I hang with Katie but she's always distracted texting with either Simon or Todd, I have trouble keeping up with which one she's into.

I keep thinking back to everything that's happened. The Mating Run, my road trip with Jasper, fighting the rogues, and meeting the alpha. But the more I try to remember the events of the last couple of months the fuzzier they become.

Before I know it I'm back at school. The corridors all look the same as they did when I left for the holidays. The gym lockers still smell the same. The conversation in the cafeteria is the same. But I'm not the same.

I try to pay attention in class but I keep catching myself staring out of windows or doodling in my notebook. No matter how hard I try to focus, my thoughts keep drifting back...to him.

My old life feels like an old sweater that doesn't quite fit anymore.

To top it all off, Katie isn't here. After their move to Queens, her mom had her transfer to a new school closer to home.

She's always been my wolfy lifeline in this human school and I need her more than ever.

Three weeks after starting back, Katie invites me to hang on the weekend and I jump at the chance.

We meet in Astoria Park, under the Robert F. Kennedy Bridge.

"I can't believe your mom still won't let you have people around," I say while hugging her.

"Oh my Moon Gods," Katie says, rolling her eyes. "She still hasn't found a wallpaper for the living room and she is determined not to show anyone her bare walls."

"She is a discerning woman, your mother."

I link my arm through Katie's and we walk along a path, green grass on one side and the East River on the other.

"How's your new school?" I ask. This is a traumatic question for both of us.

She sighs. "It's fine. Boring without you. But I've made a couple of new friends."

"No one as awesome as me, right?"

"Oh for sure. That person doesn't exist." We both laugh. "I was surprised to see a familiar face in a couple of my classes though."

"What? Who?"

"You'll see." She grins at me coyly. What's she up to? "I thought it might be fun to make this a bit of a group hang."

I groan internally. I want some quality time with Katie, not Katie and whoever it is she's invited to meet us. What if they're super lame?

"Is that all right?" she asks, reading my nonplussed expression.

I try to force a smile.

"Yeah, sounds great! Who are we meeting?"

"You'll see." She bumps her hip into mine and smiles. "Before we meet everyone else though, tell me, have you heard from Jasper?"

Every time I hear his name my little heartbeat skyrockets and my stomach jumps into my throat. It's hard to explain. I hate talking about him, it only reminds me that he's completely blanked me, but at the same time, it's all I want to talk about.

"Ugh, no." I throw my head back dramatically.

"What a dick!" Katie says, and I have to laugh.

She's never been much of a swearer so even the tamest curse words sound weird coming out of her mouth.

"You know what you should do?" she asks. "You should just rock up at his place someday unannounced, and demand to speak with him."

"Okay, sure," I say. "And what would I tell him?"

"I dunno, tell him about your undying love."

"My what?" Jasper has my emotions mixed up in a blender and turned up to eleven, but undying love is a bit much.

"You could just tell him how you feel," she says, earnestly this time. "I know that sounds corny but it's all you can do."

A cloud passes overhead, casting us in shadow for a brief moment.

"He's an idiot if he doesn't feel the same."

My cheeks become a little warm.

"Oh, there they are!" Katie points across the grass and starts waving manically.

I squint in the direction of her wave and spot two people sitting on a blanket.

"Is that...?"

"Hey, Eleanor!" I say as we approach the picnic already in progress.

"Hi Max," she says. Someone must have refilled her bean tank since the festival because right now she's full of them.

Sitting across from her is Todd, a big goofy grin on his

face and his ginger hair glinting in the sunlight.

"Hey bro," he says, putting his hand out to do some weird handshake I don't know how to reciprocate.

"Hey."

Katie gives Todd a big hug and a sloppy kiss, then she drops to the blanket.

"Hey girl," she says, reaching out to take Eleanor's hand.

"Since when are you two gal pals?" I ask, looking between them.

"It turns out Eleanor goes to my school. We have four classes together! Can you believe?"

"Math, English, Economics, and French," Eleanor says, looking pleased with herself.

"I cannot believe," I say.

"It's been amazing having a pack friend this year," Eleanor gushes. "Those humans just don't get it."

I feel a pang of jealousy that Eleanor gets Katie now. Katie is snuggling into Todd's beefy chest and I get this weird sensation, like I'm a kid and everyone is hogging my Nintendo.

Katie shoots me a big smile and starts talking with Eleanor about their classmates. Todd joins in as well and I sit quietly, a bitter taste in my mouth. Katie has this whole new life, this whole new circle of friends, and I have...what? An unanswered text? A pair of basketball shorts and a backpack?

An almost kiss in a pool?

"So Todd, how's Simon?" I ask.

That shuts everybody up. I know it's a douche move, totally unfair to Katie, but it just slipped out.

Todd clears his throat and Katie's cheeks flush bright pink. She shoots me a stabbing look.

"Crazy isn't it!" Eleanor jumps in, unaware of the tension between Katie and me. "Two mates, some people have all the luck. But Katie's made the right choice with this one." She gestures to Todd. "They're too cute. Don't you think?"

"Really cute," I mutter, grabbing a handful of chips. I shovel them into my mouth and stare at Eleanor. "How are you feeling, Eleanor?"

"Sorry, what?" she asks and looks at me like I'm crazy. But I'm not crazy, I'm on a warpath.

"The last time I saw you you were pretty upset about not finding a mate. How are you feeling now?"

Katie drops the triangle of sandwich she was about to bite down on. She's pissed. But so am I. I wanted to hang out with her, not the president of the glee club.

"I'm fine," Eleanor says, lying. The muscles around her mouth have gone tight and her pitch has jumped about twelve octaves. "Not everyone can find their mate on the first try. We can't all be like these two lovebirds here. Or the alpha's son."

My breath catches in my throat and I nearly choke on barbecue-flavored chips. What does she know about Jasper? I glance at Katie with wide, questioning eyes. Has she told Eleanor about him and me?

Katie shakes her head just enough for me to know she hasn't broken our trust. So what is Eleanor talking about?

"Jasper?" I ask. "I didn't know he found a mate."

"Oh yeah. Everyone's been talking about it."

My face is on fire. Panic is rising in my gut like floodwater. *Everyone's been talking about...me?*

"That's funny!" I say, fake laughing way too much and scratching the back of my neck. "I haven't heard anything about that."

"Oh, that's weird," Eleanor says. "I thought you and Aisha were friends."

"What?" My panic is quickly turning into complete confusion.

"Yeah, I thought she would have told you she and Jasper were mates."

"Jasper and Aisha?" I release an open-mouthed cackle as the panicked floodwaters ebb. My stomach starts to hurt, I'm laughing so hard.

"Why is that funny?" Eleanor says, completely clueless. "I'm happy for them."

"They're not mates," I say.

"That's what everyone's saying. At least that's what my dad told me and he knows the alpha, so—"

"Obviously not very well," I snap.

Eleanor shrugs like she doesn't care. "I thought that's why they both left the festival early. To be together in private."

Even though I know it isn't true, I still feel the sting of jealousy knowing people out there think Jasper is mated to someone else.

"Max?" Katie asks. "Are you okay?"

I stare at her for a beat too long.

"Yeah," I say. "I'm fine. Just thirsty."

There's an untouched can of grape soda lying on the picnic rug so I crack it open.

"I guess I was wrong," Eleanor says as I gulp down the drink. "I'll have to tell my dad."

My pulse finally settles back into a regular pace.

For the rest of the picnic I try my best to play friendly. I even find myself laughing at some of Todd's lame jokes and smile when I catch Katie grinning proudly at her mate.

I can't help glancing uneasily at Eleanor though. She's moved on from her little mistake, but I still feel shaken. It's not like I want the world to know about me and Jasper. You won't catch me shouting it from any rooftops. But knowing what people are saying makes my skin crawl.

When the sky starts turning orange, Katie says she'll walk me back to the nearest subway. She hugs Todd and tells him she'll meet him back here, then kisses him...with tongue. Grape soda swirls in my stomach, threatening to come back up.

"What was that all about?" I ask when we're finally walking back along the river.

"You mean Todd? I know I said it was over for real last time but then we started messaging again and he asked if he could see me this weekend and I couldn't say no, but I still want to see where things go with Simon and—"

"No, not that," I interrupt. "Although, hold that thought because I need more deets. I'm talking about what Eleanor said."

"You mean about Jasper and Aisha?"

I nod.

"She's mentioned it before and I just let her go on believing it. I thought you'd prefer if people assumed that rather than, well you know...the truth."

"I guess I was just surprised how much it hurt."

"Oh, Max." Katie wraps her arms around me. "I'm sorry things aren't great for you." She stops walking. "You know what? I think I was right earlier."

I laugh. She has the same look in her eye she did the time she promised she'd get us tickets for *Dear Evan Hansen*, even though it was sold out. "Right about what?"

"Maybe you *should* march up to his house and tell him how you're feeling. Who says he gets to control the conversation, right?"

Little goosebumps start to pop up along my arms. Time was I would have argued with Katie and told her she was being ridiculous. Even a month or so ago, I was terrified of sending Jasper a text message. But thinking about seeing him again is making me light-headed. After what we went through with the rogues, I'm not scared of him anymore.

And if Katie can somehow get us in to see Jordan Fisher belting out "Waving Through a Window," I can face up to Jasper.

The only problem is getting to him.

"He won't even text me back," I say.

"If he won't message you back then you need to take the fight to him. Surprise him."

"I don't know if I can just walk up to the alpha's house, security is pretty tight. They probably have land mines and trip wires in their front yard!"

"You just need a good excuse to see him. I'm sure you can think of something."

Behind Katie, some guys are shooting hoops on a fenced-in half-court. A skinny dude in a red uniform makes a shot from the three-point line and scores.

Basketball shorts and a backpack.

That's it!

Katie is right. I'm not going to sit around and pine like I

have been. Not when I know how I feel and not after what nearly happened in that pool. Jasper is feeling this as much as I am, he's just got more reasons to ignore it than I have. So it's up to me to make the first move.

And maybe I already have my excuse.

"You know what?" I say. "I think you're right. It's time I visited Jasper."

FACE THE FACTS

This is a terrible idea.

Approaching the alpha's estate feels like strolling up to a high-security prison and begging to be taken out by a sniper.

I have Jasper's backpack slung over a shoulder with his washed and ironed clothes inside.

Hopefully, they're my ticket in.

Katie said that she would cover for me and tell my parents we were hanging out, in case they call her place to check up on me. I've spent basically all of my savings on a cab out to the Hamptons.

Now that I'm here, however, I'm starting to think this whole thing has been a mistake. The gates loom over me like I'm an ant—easy to squash.

There's a keypad and a speaker on a column to the right. I pull my shoulders back and march to it. This may be a mistake but I've come all this way. There's no chickening out now.

I press the call button and wait for a response. Nothing happens. What if I've shown up and nobody is home? I wait for a long moment before pressing the buzzer again. Still nothing. I'm about to turn around and head home when I hear a click and some static and then a woman's voice.

"Hello, can I help you?"

I freeze. I can't do this. I don't even know who the woman on the other end is.

Maybe if I don't say anything she'll think it's a prank and forget I ever rang.

"I can see you," she says. I glance up to the top of the fence where a security camera is pointing in my direction. *Of course.*

"H-hi," I say, leaning into the speaker.

"Can I help?"

"Yeah, I was just wondering if...if..." I'm still freaking out. This is never going to work. Why did I think Jasper would answer the door at his own house?

I remember something—something Jasper said about the house having a manager.

"Is that Melissa?" I ask, crossing my fingers.

"Yes, who is this?"

I breathe a sigh of relief. Maybe this is my in.

"I'm a friend of Jasper's. I was here the other night and borrowed some clothes." I twist my shoulder so the backpack is in full view of the camera. "I just came to bring them back."

There's a long crackly pause and then a beep and the gates swing open.

"Come in."

It worked!

My collar is damp with sweat by the time I arrive at the end of the driveway. The house looks the same in the daylight. Cold and hard. To my left the black town car is sitting in front of the garage doors. The hairs on my arms stand to attention.

I'd almost forgotten about the car, chalking it up to coincidence. But seeing it sitting there, dark and low to the ground, my stomach is suddenly full of dread.

Somewhere deep in my soul I know I have to do this. But as I ring the doorbell I glance back to the car.

Something doesn't feel right.

Melissa pulls the door open and I'm refreshed by how

normal she looks. Softly curled brown hair falls over the shoulders of her blue woolen sweater. She stands on one pink-sock-covered foot, leaning against the doorframe, perfectly at home.

"Hi," she says, smiling broadly. "You must be Max."

I shake my head in disbelief. "You know my name?"

"Jodie told me. She's great at remembering names, especially when she gets to stay up past bedtime and eat unhealthy snacks with unexpected visitors."

I feel my face flush and glance at the ground. One of my shoes is untied, it must have come undone on the walk up.

So Jasper didn't tell her about me then.

I rub the back of my neck. "Yeah, sorry about that."

"It's not your fault," she says, waving a hand dismissively. "It's your friend Jasper who should know better. Speaking of..."

She narrows her eyes at me.

"Jasper doesn't usually ask his friends over to the house. Is he expecting you?"

"Uh, not really," I say. "He just lent me this stuff after I fell in the pool and I wanted to return it."

"Right." She nods but continues to stare at me with a suspicious pout. "So, he'll probably be surprised to see you then?"

"Probably." My voice catches in my throat, making me sound like I've just hit puberty.

"Good, Jasper's been in a real mood lately. Maybe a surprise is just what the doctor ordered. That or a kick in the ass. Come on through."

Melissa opens the door wide and ushers me inside.

"Do you know the way to his room?"

Even if I didn't remember my way there it wouldn't matter. The second I walk into the house I can feel Jasper's presence.

"I can find it," I say, heading toward the stairs.

"Do me a favor," Melissa says. "Don't tell him I let you in?"

I laugh. "Sure."

234

Jasper's door is closed when I arrive, so I knock, but there's no answer.

I turn the handle. It's dark inside and Jasper's usually all-too-appealing scent is mixed with a stale, musty odor.

"What are you doing here?"

I jump. I hadn't spotted him in the dimness. Jasper is on his bed, sitting cross-legged. Probably meditating.

He opens one eye as I walk in. His room looks different. Dirty plates and half-empty water glasses are scattered across the desktop. Books are strewn around the floor. Laundry is overflowing from the hamper like a designer-label landslide. It's almost as messy as my room.

"Are you okay?" I ask. I want to open the curtains and let some sunlight in but Jasper might kill me if I do.

"I'm fine," he responds. "How did you get in?"

"I'm not supposed to say."

"Melissa." He shakes his head in frustrated disbelief.

"Yeah, but it wasn't her fault. I told her we were...friends."

"What do you want?"

What do I want? I want him to get off that stupid bed and talk to me like a person. I want him to acknowledge that there's something between us whether he likes it or not. I want him to act like he feels something, *anything*!

"I brought your clothes and your bag back."

"You didn't need to."

Neither of us speaks for a second, I shift my weight from one foot to the other, then finally, I drop the bag at the foot of his bed.

Well, I did. And here it is.

"Is that all?" he asks.

I don't know why I bothered coming here. I should have known this is how it would go.

"Yeah," I say, running a hand down the side of my face. "That's it."

I turn to go but stop myself at the door. If I leave this room right now I'm going to regret it. I'm going to walk outside and be filled with the same unresolved sick feeling I've had since I last saw him. The one that sapped me of my appetite and turned me into a zombie at school.

I swing around and face him. "Actually no, that's not it."

He groans and rolls his head back.

"Jasper, we need to talk about this. We can't just ignore it."

He swings his legs off the side of the bed and stands in one fluid gesture. "There's nothing to talk about."

"How can you say that? Whatever this is, it's eating me up inside. I can't think, I can't eat, I can barely function."

"You're going to have to learn."

"I can't do that!"

Jasper rushes at me. "You don't have a choice!"

My chin starts wobbling. I feel like my chest is collapsing.

"Why not?" I try to get the words out without sobbing but it's too late. Tears are already falling onto Jasper's very expensive carpet.

"My father has told me to choose a mate. A woman who is fit to become the luna of this pack."

"What?"

"In two weeks at the Harvest Moon Celebration, I'm going to announce my chosen mate in front of the whole pack. I don't have a choice."

My vision blurs. My head throbs. My heart...is torn apart.

How is this happening? He's going to sacrifice our connection just because his father told him to.

The pain in my chest is so intense, I can only imagine what it will be like when Jasper breaks our mate bond for good.

"Max, are you—"

"What is wrong with you?!" I yell. "How can you just stand there and pretend it's not real?"

Spit flies from my mouth as I continue to break down.

"Don't you feel empty? I do! I feel like nothing matters, like life is meaningless. But maybe if we just accepted each other, if we—"

Jasper scoffs and turns his face away.

"Don't you feel *anything*?" I ask.

"I..." His jaw clenches and unclenches. "I do feel things,"

he grits out. "But what you're not getting is it doesn't matter."

"I don't believe you."

"Face the facts, Max! Whatever exists between us is irrelevant. The pack needs a strong alpha, and a strong alpha has a luna by his side. That's all there is to it."

I don't know what else to say.

Jasper straightens his spine, regaining his composure.

"The alpha has given his command and in two weeks I will have chosen new mate. A female."

I scrunch my hands into fists and my body judders with sobs. We stand in the dark—me crying and Jasper doing nothing to comfort me.

"You should leave now," he says, finally.

"But you're... You're my..." I meet Jasper's gaze. My eyes sting but I keep them locked with his. "You're my..."

He narrows his eyes. "There's no version of this that ends the way you want it to."

"I can't believe that," I say.

"Believe it! Someone like me could never end up with a person like you."

I fold over as if I've been punched in the gut.

Jasper doesn't move.

His words are cold—empty and final. There's nothing more to say. Any shred of hope I was clinging onto is gone.

I bite down, set my jaw, and turn to go. I hate him for hurting me this much and I wish there was a way I could hurt him back.

In the hall I stop and look back over my shoulder. I have one last question for Jasper.

"Whose car is that out front?"

"What?"

"The black town car out front, whose is it?"

"My dad's," he says.

I run my hand down Jasper's doorframe.

"I saw it—outside the warehouse when we rescued Aisha."

He narrows his eyes. "What are you saying?"

"Your dad was there, Jasper. He was part of it."

"That's impossible," he spits. "You have no proof."

"You can sense what I'm feeling, right? Does it feel like I'm lying?"

Silence.

Before he can say anything else I leave. I hurry out of Jasper's house, down his stupidly long drive, and out the ridiculous gate. I don't breathe until I'm out by the road with the gate swinging shut behind me.

I think I might break down and cry but I don't. A wave of exhaustion crashes over me and I drop to my knees.

I stay like this for a while, letting the ocean breeze cool my stinging cheeks.

Then finally, when I'm ready to stand again, I pull out my phone and order a cab.

Screw the cost, I've already lost everything that matters.

OVER IT

"That's it," I say. "I'm done."

"Max, are you sure?" Katie asks down the phone line.

I dig my feet into my blanket and press my head back against my bedroom wall. It may be Monday but I've managed to convince my parents I'm not feeling well, so they've let me stay home from school.

The truth is I'm not sick but I'm not well either. I haven't left my room since I came home yesterday and, right now, I'm not sure if I'll ever want to again. All I want to do is sit on my bed and pretend like nothing exists.

I texted Katie something along those lines and she called as soon as possible. Right now she's in a toilet stall when she should be in Biology.

"Yes. I'm sure. Jasper's made it pretty clear he doesn't care so why should I?"

"He's your mate. Isn't that worth fighting for?"

"You know me, Katie. Since when do I care about mates?" There's a long pause. I think I hear a flushing sound in the background.

"Well...since you met Jasper," Katie says in a quiet voice.

She's right. Mates always seemed like such a basic thing to go wild over until I found mine. And that feeling, the one we had in the woods that night, it's hard to forget.

Hard to move on from.

If Jasper can do it so easily, though, so can I.

"Whatever. He's going to choose someone else. He doesn't want me."

"Are you sure? What if his dad is forcing him to? You said the alpha was tough on him."

I scoff. Tough is an understatement. Bordering on abuse is closer to the truth.

"Even so, you're asking me to fight for something when he's already given up."

"I just think it's worth one last shot," Katie says and then pauses. I can vaguely hear a door swing open.

"Are you there?"

"Yes, sorry. I just thought someone was coming in. All I'm saying is—you've seen how hard it's been for me with Todd and Simon. I'm so hopeless I can't even choose which one of them I want to be with."

"Yeah, you're gonna be in trouble when they find out you're still seeing them both."

"I know, don't remind me. But that's not the point. The point is Jasper's in the same situation, only he has to choose between his mate and the life he's been born into. He'd be sacrificing everything. Sounds hard, right?"

"Maybe," I mutter.

"I just think if you want something—and I know you do—you should fight for it."

"I'm just not sure—"

"Oh no, Max I have to go..."

I hear an adult voice—a teacher?—asking Katie what she's doing and then the line goes dead.

I grunt and toss my phone across the bed. Then I slide sideways down the wall until I'm lying with my knees pulled up to my chest.

Even with the curtains closed, it isn't dark enough. I want the world to disappear. I want to sink into my mattress and never get up again.

Katie may be right. Maybe Jasper is in a tricky situation, but why does that mean I'm the one who has to do all the heavy lifting? Why is it my fight and not his?

I hate that I want this so bad. I hate that I've been reduced to this ball of anxiety. I never even cared about all of this stuff and now it's the only thing occupying my mind. Why is that?

So much for thinking I was different.

I close my eyes and am trying to fall asleep when the doorbell rings. It's louder than normal, like the world is calling me back to it—unable to let me escape. I jam my eyes shut and wait, hoping whoever it is will go away. But it keeps ringing and ringing. *Damn, the world is persistent.* Finally, I groan and roll out of bed.

"I'm coming!" I moan as I run down the stairs.

The bell is still ringing as I open the door.

Aisha is standing on the doormat, her finger hovering over the button. "You look like shit."

"What are you doing here?" I ask.

"Thought you could use some fresh air."

"Aisha, I'm not in the moo—"

"Go put on some pants, I'm taking you for a walk."

"I never had a chance to say a proper thank-you," Aisha says once we're a good distance from the house. "For saving me."

I'm taking Aisha down to the river. Sunshine is glowing through the emerald canopy, and the birdsong of the forest is chirpy as hell. If I wasn't in such a foul mood it would be a beautiful day.

But Aisha is right—the fresh air is making me feel marginally better. At least I don't feel like crying right this second.

"Don't worry about it."

"No Max, don't do that. Don't minimize the amazing thing you did. You went running into a rogue nest, even though it was dangerous, just to save me. What you did was amazing."

"Okay." I blush. "You're welcome."

"You and Jasper made quite the team." She smirks and

glances at me.

"Tell *him* that," I scoff. "I bet you're invited to the Harvest Moon party or whatever."

"I am." She nods. "My family attends every year."

"Then you're in for a real show."

"Tell me about it," she says. "I nearly had a lead role."

"What?"

Aisha sighs and stops walking, she tugs at a branch nearby and pulls off a leaf.

"Jasper asked me," she says, tearing the leaf in half, "to be his mate."

I'm instantly dizzy.

"Don't worry," she says, dropping the fragments of leaf and reaching out to steady me. "I said no. Of course I said no."

"Oh, okay." My center of gravity stabilizes a little.

"Gave him a piece of my mind too."

We start walking again.

"You did?"

"Hell yeah. He had no business asking me to be his mate when I know full well he already has one. And he knows I'm in love with Troy. I chewed him out for a good half hour."

"So, he hasn't found a new mate yet?"

"I don't know. There are other people he can ask."

Suddenly, this beautiful day feels like an insult. I sneer at the ethereal beams of yellow light cascading through the leaves. The bubbling sound of flowing water from the nearby river sets my teeth on edge. How dare the world be this uplifting when there's nothing to feel good about.

"But Max, you should know this wasn't his decision. His dad is forcing him to make a choice."

"That's the thing I don't get," I say as we reach the river. I head to my usual spot and sit, clearing away some fallen leaves as I do. "Why does his dad want him to be mated so badly?"

"Alpha Jericho has high standards for Jasper." Aisha comes to sit next to me and we look down at the water passing by. "In his mind, a future alpha should be mated by now. He was sixteen when his pairing was arranged."

"Wait, Jericho's mating was arranged?"

"That's the other thing. Arranged mates are pretty common in high-ranking families. They like to keep the bloodlines as pure as possible. So for Jericho, allowing Jasper to choose someone is progressive."

"It's barbaric."

"Maybe. But we're talking centuries, hell, thousands of years of tradition here. The alpha needs a mate to continue his family's bloodline. And Jasper's whole existence is about preparing him to take over that role. This is just the next step."

"That sucks."

"I know." She rests a comforting hand on my knee. "I'm sorry."

A plump little robin lands on a branch nearby. For a second I feel bad for the little guy, all by himself out here. Until a second robin swoops in, landing next to the first. *Dumb birds.*

"How well do you know the alpha?" I ask.

"I've known him all my life," Aisha says. "But he's not much of a talker. Why?"

"I saw his car outside the warehouse where the rogues had you."

"You saw his...what?"

"I recognized it when I was at Jasper's house. The same car, with the same blackout windows. It was parked outside the warehouse. I was wondering... Do you think the alpha could have had something to do with your kidnapping?"

Aisha wraps her arms tightly around her legs and stares at a mossy patch by her feet.

"The whole time they had me they kept talking about how much they were getting paid. Debating whether I was worth the money. Lucky for me, I guess I was. Otherwise, I'm sure they would have killed me or...worse."

"I'm sorry you had to go through all that."

"There was one thing that stood out. The way they were talking about whoever had hired them, it didn't sound like they fully trusted them. I just thought they were paranoid because they were dealing with criminals. But maybe it was because whoever their boss was, he doesn't run in their usual circles."

"Not a rogue, you mean?"

"Exactly. Which would mean it was someone from a pack."

"Do you think Jericho would..."

I stop when I see the tear trickling down Aisha's cheek.

"We don't have to talk about this if you don't want to."

"No, it's fine," she says, wiping her face. "I knew there was more to it than just a random rogue attack. They didn't care about me, they were just doing it for the money. But I still don't know why someone would want to kidnap me. Especially the alpha."

Aisha unwraps her legs and stretches them out in front of her.

"I told Jericho all this. He promised he'd look into it but so far—"

"Nothing?"

"Nada."

"He could be covering it up?"

"It's possible." She shrugs.

I know she doesn't want to believe that her alpha—the man who's supposed to protect her and look out for her—could be the one who paid to have her kidnapped. But as far as I can see there are no other suspects.

"Why though?" she asks.

"Maybe..." I start but then pause, and swallow.

"It's okay, Max. Just say it."

"Maybe he didn't like that you were dating a human."

"Maybe, but why kidnap me? Why not just kill Troy?"

We both turn our gazes to the river. It swims by but we've reached a dead end in our thinking. Why would the alpha kidnap his son's best friend? It doesn't make sense. But his car places him at the warehouse.

Unfortunately, there isn't anyone we can take this information to. The pack's security forces all answer to the alpha. Human detectives would be completely out of their depth. Jasper will side with his father no matter what we say.

"Why don't you come with me?" Aisha asks finally. "To the Harvest Moon Celebration? I can bring a plus-one."

"I don't think that's a good idea."

"We could ask around, maybe speak to Jericho."

"Are you serious? Have you forgotten? Jasper is going to announce his new mate."

"I haven't forgotten, Max. I was going to see if you wanted to come anyway."

I almost laugh. "Why would I want to see that?"

Aisha turns so her body is facing mine.

"Once Jasper announces his new mate, he'll mark her in front of everybody."

"Mark her? You mean like..."

"Bite her neck, basically. And when he does, the bond you two have will be broken. And once it's broken, there's no repairing it."

"So what? I'd be going to say goodbye."

"Maybe. Or maybe you could go and fight, like you fought the rogues for me—but do it for him."

I roll my eyes. "I don't think he wants saving."

"Then do it for yourself." She slaps my arm with the back of her hand. "Do you want to live the rest of your life wondering what might have happened if you just showed up?"

The last time I showed up, Jasper told me what he really thought.

"I get it, okay? But Jasper has made it brilliantly clear he wants nothing to do with me. Going would just be some messed-up form of self-harm."

"You've got some time," Aisha says. "Just think about it, okay?"

I sigh. "Okay."

"I should probably be getting back."

We walk to the house quietly. The ground feels more unsteady underfoot than usual, as if the whole country has tilted. Nothing in the world is how people say it is. Alphas are untrustworthy and mates let you down. I wonder if Aisha is feeling the same way.

"Come on in," I say, leading Aisha through the back door. "Do you want a drink or something before you go? I think Mom stocked up on La Croix."

"I'm good, dude. Thanks."

We wander into the hall and Aisha turns to me.

"Don't assume you can't make a difference, okay, Max? You've already made such a difference for me."

We hug and while Aisha's head is resting on my shoulder she says, "What's that letter?"

On the floor in front of the door is a familiar-looking envelope.

"It looks like..."

The last time I saw an envelope like this it was from the royal secretary. My invitation to the Blue Moon Festival. I grab the letter and tear through the familiar red seal on the back.

"It's an invitation," I say, reading the swirling cursive. "To the Harvest Moon Celebration at the alpha's house. But my family never gets invited to important pack events..."

Aisha is staring at me, her eyes wide and beaming with hope.

"What?" I ask.

"He must have invited you," she says, turning things over in her mind. "He wants you there."

"He wants me...but why?"

Aisha steps forward and takes hold of both of my hands; the invitation crumples between my fingers.

"Maybe it's a sign that he's ready to fight as well."

"Maybe it's a mistake."

"Max, Jasper doesn't reach out often. This is an olive branch. Don't overlook it."

I stare at the invitation. Did Jasper invite me? Is this the sign I've been waiting for? Should I just ignore it like he's ignored me so many times?

"I don't know what to do," I say.

Aisha shakes her head like she can't believe what I'm saying.

"It's simple," she says. "You have to go."

THE HARVEST MOON

"I'm not going."

"Why not?!" Katie glares at me over a sales rack in Forever 21.

"I've been thinking about it all week," I say as she goes back to dress hunting.

Last Monday, Aisha wouldn't leave my house until I promised to at least think about going to the Harvest Moon Celebration. But no matter how much I think about it it doesn't feel right.

"Why would I put myself through that?!"

"Because Aisha might be right. Maybe Jasper wants you to go so that he can choose you in front of everybody. Wouldn't that be romantic?"

She pulls out some fuzzy neon-orange thing, scrunches up her face, and puts it back where she found it.

"There's a better chance he'll spontaneously combust in front of everyone," I say.

"You're being so pessimistic." She holds up a shiny silver number, considers it, then hangs it back on the rack.

"Am I? He's been a jerk the entire time I've known him, and when he isn't being a dick he ignores me completely."

"The stakes are higher now. What if he's realized what he's about to give up and wants a way out?" She runs her hands down the sleeve of a blue velvet dress. "If you don't go you're basically saying you don't care."

"Maybe I don't."

She stops moving and looks at me with her eyebrows raised.

I crumble under her stare. "Fine, I do care. But that's why I can't go. It'll be too hard."

"No one ever said love was supposed to be easy. Ah!" She pulls out a pink dress from the rack with a bow on the waist. "This is perfect!"

"What are we doing here, again?" I ask. "Why do you need the dress?"

"Because I need something to wear when you take me to the Harvest Moon Celebration as your plus-one."

She spins on her heel and heads for the register.

"Katie, wait up, I'm not going."

She stops and faces me. "Max, love is like shopping. You search and search for the perfect outfit. The one that matches your skin tone and fits like a glove. And it's hard work. Sometimes it's all-out war. But you never give up. And when you find the outfit you've been looking for"— she holds up the dress—"you never let it go. You fight for it."

I turn my face away. Everyone is so intent on making me go to this stupid party. And for what? So I can watch as Jasper pulls out my heart and stamps on it in front of a bunch of stuffy, judgmental wolves.

"I know it's hard for you to admit," Katie says, softening her tone. "But you love Jasper, don't you?"

I glance back at her, a deer in headlights.

I don't even have to say anything for Katie to know she's right.

"So let me go and pay for this amazing dress," she says with a knowing smile. "And then we'll go find you something to wear."

"My shirt won't stay tucked in," I say, squirming in the

passenger seat of Mom's car.

"It won't if you don't sit still," Katie says, trying to calm me down before my mother notices something's up.

Mom volunteered to drive us out to the Hamptons, so at least I haven't had to pay for a cab this time. Not that there hasn't been a trade-off. Sitting next to her in the car for two hours pretending I'm not completely freaking out is worth ten times the price of cab fare.

Luckily, she's so excited for the chance to sneak a look at the alpha's house she hasn't been paying close attention.

Her and Dad were pretty impressed that I'd been invited to the Harvest Moon Celebration. They've never been. The guest list is usually pretty exclusive. Military leaders, wolves in the top political circles, and big players in wolf society. I roll my eyes thinking of all the stuff-crusts that'll be there tonight. And how much I'm going to stick out in my on-sale blazer and scuffed sneakers.

"Uh, is this the right house?" I ask as we pull up outside the gates.

"You tell me, honey. You've been here before," Mom says.

The house looks completely different than the last time I was here. Strings of lights have been hung up all along the fence and across the open gate. Colorful balloons have been arranged in an arch over the driveway.

It almost looks welcoming.

A line of fancy cars are snaking their way up the drive. Mom lifts her chin as she joins the parade in her humble Prius.

The closer we get to the door the more I start to squirm. My well-starched collar and the burgundy bow tie Katie picked out are cutting off my airway.

"Are you all right?" Mom asks, glancing over.

"Uh, yeah. Totally fine."

We drive so slowly we might miss Jasper's announcement and have to turn straight back around.

The cherry tree on the front lawn is still in full bloom despite it being very much autumn. It's been wrapped in fairy lights and is glowing like some mystical tree from *Lord of the Rings*. Nearby a valet station is set up.

"You kids can hop out if you like," Mom says. "This could take awhile."

"Okay, thanks for driving us, Mrs. Remus," Katie says, jumping out the back door.

"Thanks, Mom," I say, pulling on the door handle.

"Max?"

"Yeah."

"Everything is okay, isn't it?"

I've got one leg hanging out of the car but I can't turn away. Not with Mom looking at me like it's my first day of school and she's scared I won't make any friends.

"Yeah, I'm fine."

"You've just been quiet lately. Ever since you came back from the camp."

Does she know something she's not telling me? Can she sense that something's up?

"Nothing's wrong, Mom." *Why can't I just tell her?!*

"Well, you know you can always, *always* talk to me and your father about anything, don't you?"

I don't reply because if I talk I might cry and then she'd *know* something was up.

"I mean it. Anything."

I nod.

"Okay, sweetie. Have a good night."

"Thanks, Mom." I slide out of the car.

"And Max!" Mom calls from her open window as I join Katie. "You look gorgeous!"

Warmth spreads in my cheeks. I wanted to slip in undetected but all of the Elite Pack's finest are shooting me weird looks.

A man at the door checks our invitation before waving us inside.

The house is glowing with candlelight. Balloons and streamers are hanging from the ceiling. They've done well to bring some party vibes to this usually cold and vacant space.

"It's packed," I say, shouting to be heard over the music

and chatter. We're surrounded by a sea of suits and super chic dresses.

"Which way?" Katie asks as we pass an ice sculpture.

We elbow our way from the entrance hall into the living room.

Wait staff are slipping between guests with trays of drinks and bite-sized snacks. I grab a few as a server passes and shove them into my mouth, hoping to eat away my nerves.

The glass-paneled wall has been rolled back, making it impossible to tell where the house stops and the garden begins.

"Let's go outside, this is too much." I wave Katie along.

The fresh air is a welcome relief, but glancing across the yard I soon realize *this* is where the party really ramps up.

Fires rage on plinths set up around the expansive back garden, casting dancing shadows onto the palms. Lights dangle overhead. White plastic flooring has been laid down to protect the grass, with tables and chairs arranged in a crescent formation around the outside. Several well-stocked bars are set up in the corners, a DJ is spinning tracks to my right, and at the far end of the garden a stage—framed by an over-the-top wildflower arrangement—has been erected.

"It looks like a wedding," Katie says open-mouthed.

She's right. The alpha's estate has been made up as if they're hosting the most extravagant wedding ever. And that's coming from someone who's watched every season of *The Bachelor*.

I gaze across the milling socialites and political powerhouses. Everyone looks so smart and tall.

My shoulders hunch and I shrink into myself, until Katie links her arm through mine.

"Let's walk."

We take the paved footpath toward the pool, which is lit up and glowing turquoise. It's the same as the last time I was here. Only that night it was just Jasper and me. Now there are people everywhere in ball gowns and suits, sipping bubbly drinks and cocktails.

"Can you see Jasper anywhere?" Katie asks.

"No sign of him."

I can't sense him either. There's too much perfume and wolf pheromone in the air.

A bro-y voice behind us breaks through the chatter. "Whoa, babe!"

We spin around to find Todd and Simon coming up the path, waving.

"Oh my Moon Gods," I say.

"Oh no," Katie says.

My friend's complexion has turned instantly blotchy, panicked red patches rising from her chest.

"What are they doing here?" she mutters.

"Hey babe," Todd says, taking Katie in his arms. His attempt to kiss her right on the mouth is thwarted when she turns her head to the side. His lips smack against her cheek.

"What's up, gorgeous?" Simon tries to do the same but his kiss lands on Katie's forehead.

"Hi, both of you," Katie says, like she just inhaled New York's entire supply of helium. "What are you both doing here?"

"My dad's an officer with the pack's army," Todd says, too proudly.

"And my mom works in the alpha's PR department," Simon says. "When you told me you were coming I asked if I could be her plus-one."

"Wow, that's so great," Katie says.

"Wait a minute," Todd says, turning to his bro. "I asked my dad if he'd bring me because Katie told *me* she was coming."

Katie's mouth is flapping about like she wants to speak, but nothing is coming out.

"Why would Katie have told you she was coming, dude?" Todd asks, then turning to Katie, "I thought you were done speaking to him?"

"I... I..." Katie stammers.

"I thought you'd given up speaking to *him*!" Simon says.

"What's going on, Katie?" Todd says, and they both turn

to look at her.

Katie knew this day was going to come eventually. I guess she just wasn't expecting it tonight.

"I might leave you guys to it," I say, awkwardly excusing myself. I wish I could stay and help but I feel like they could use some privacy. And besides, I have a mission of my own.

Katie nods, distracted by her current dilemma.

I squeeze her hand. "Good luck. Nice to see you both again."

I wave at Todd and Simon but I don't think they register me; they're both staring at Katie, waiting for an explanation.

"So what's going on?" Simon asks as I wander away.

Poor Katie. Being mated isn't easy for anyone.

I wander back out into the midst of the party keeping my eyes open for Jasper. He's nowhere to be found.

I pull out my phone and text Aisha.

Where are you???!!!

Sorry, rehearsal ran late. Be there soon. xxx

In desperate need of a breather, I head toward the side of the house where I think I can find a quiet spot to regroup. As soon as I turn the corner I dart backward.

Jasper is standing in the shadows talking to someone. He's pacing back and forth, rubbing his temple while his other hand rests on his hip. I have to peer further to see who he's talking to.

Olivia is leaning against the wall with her head bowed.

Jasper approaches and reaches out to take her hand but she pulls away.

He breaks. He drops his face into his palms, then runs his fingers through his hair. He's majorly stressed.

Olivia takes a deep breath and then says something. *Man, I wish I could read lips.* Jasper looks instantly relieved. He takes both of Olivia's hands and then pulls her into a hug.

I wish I could pretend I had no idea what just

happened.

But I do have an idea. And it makes me nauseous.

When Jasper steps back, Olivia doesn't meet his eye, she leaves him standing there. The relief I saw on his face a moment ago vanishes. He leans forward, places one hand on the wall to keep himself upright, and forces himself to take deep breaths.

Before I know it, I'm stepping toward him.

"Jasper."

He snaps to attention, running a hand over his head to smooth out his messy hair.

"Jasper, you don't have to do this—"

"I don't have time for this," he says and pushes past me.

"Jasper, you have to listen to me. I know why you invited me here."

He freezes.

"And why is that?"

"Because you wanted me to stop you. You wanted me to be here so you wouldn't have to go through with it. And, well, I'm here."

I wait with my palms open to Jasper, my arms lifted a little as if they're waiting to welcome him in.

Jasper laughs—a coldhearted, heart-stopping chuckle.

"I didn't invite you so that you could save me."

"Then why?"

"I invited you so that you would be here when I reject you. So that you could see it for yourself."

I take a step back, feeling like I've been shot point-blank in the chest. I'm an idiot. How could I have been so stupid?

Of course Jasper wasn't sending me an encrypted cry for help. He was doing what he always does—being the biggest jerk I've ever met. Only *jerk* feels too generous for what he's done this time. No, Jasper has officially graduated from jerk to complete and utter asshole!

Not wanting to give him the satisfaction of seeing me cry, I run.

"Stick around, Max," Jasper calls. "You don't want to miss the show!"

JASPER'S CHOICE

I slam the kitchen door behind me. *What is wrong with him?!*

No, what's wrong with me? I should have known better. I should have known he'd...

I lean my back on the door and bang my head against the pigeon-gray wood.

The kitchen is empty, thank goodness. I need somewhere to process what's just happened.

The black granite countertops shine like they're brand new. The last time I was in here I was with Jasper and his little sister eating a sandwich. The counters were covered in grated cheddar and Monterey Jack.

We were able to talk then. It was almost friendly.

Until his father intervened. And then something snapped.

But I don't care how tough his dad is and I don't care how hard his life is. Nothing gives him an excuse to hurt people. Not like he's hurt me.

I splay my fingers out and press my hands against the cool surface behind me.

Every wolf who's anyone is at this stink of a party. I need to calm down.

I should find Katie and tell her we need to go. From the

way Todd and Simon were looking at her I'm sure she'll be happy for an escape plan.

That's what I'm going to do.

Screw Jasper, let him choose another mate.

And screw mates! I knew this whole mating bullshit was more trouble than it's worth.

I sigh and run a hand over my face.

"Rough night?"

Who said that?

I scan the room again. I could have sworn there was no one here.

I spot a breakfast nook in the corner; Eleanor is poking her head around the corner of a booth seat.

Gosh, was anyone NOT invited to this dumb party?

"What are you doing here?" I ask.

"I told you, my dad works for the alpha," Eleanor says. "We're always invited. You look like you're having a nice time."

Was that sarcasm from the treasurer of the yearbook committee?

I wander over and slide into the booth opposite her. "Let's just say this isn't my night."

"Tell me about it," she scoffs.

"Wait a minute, why are you in here and not out there?"

Eleanor sighs and for the first time I notice how bloodshot her eyes are.

"Have you... Have you been crying?"

Her eyes dart up, locking with mine. She glares at me for a second and then looks at the phone in her hands.

"It's so unfair," she says. "Some people have it so easy."

Obsessively, she turns the phone over and over. Her hands are shaking.

"Some people even get to choose who they're mated to."

"Eleanor, what's going on? You want to talk about it?"

"Why does it have to be my responsibility to find someone? Why do I..."

"Are you okay?"

"I'm fine, Max," she snaps. She glares at me for another

second, her lip twitches, but then she softens. "I just majorly embarrassed myself."

"I know the feeling." I slope down in my seat. "What did you do?"

Maybe I shouldn't pry, but Eleanor is pretty embarrassing at the best of times; I can't imagine what she could have done to make her feel like this.

"I...asked Jasper if he wanted to be my mate."

A shiver runs down my spine and a growl rumbles in the pit of my stomach. I know Jasper is going to reject me but my wolfy side can't help being territorial.

I lean forward. "How did that go?"

"Horribly." Eleanor crosses her arms. "He looked at me like he'd never seen me before. Do you know what that feels like?" She starts to tear up, twisting the corners of her mouth. "To be rejected?"

"I have some idea," I mutter.

"He just shrugged me off like our families haven't worked together for generations."

"You never told me what your dad does for the alpha," I say, trying to change the subject.

Happy Eleanor is enough of a handful, I'm not sure I can cope with emotionally distraught Eleanor.

"When you told me he wasn't mated to Aisha I thought I still had a chance," she continues, ignoring me completely.

"I figured maybe we just never got close enough at the festival—maybe I could... I could...be his true mate."

I grind my teeth. The territorial part of me is starting to get worked up.

She's acting like Jasper is completely unspoken for, as if he isn't already mine!

"If I was his mate that would show everyone," Eleanor goes on, wiping a glob of snot from her nose. "Maybe then I wouldn't be ignored. And my family would finally be proud of me."

She doesn't even know him, she's just interested because of his status. I don't give a crap about his status.

"That's why it's unfair," she says. "All of us have to suffer by ourselves. He gets to choose a mate and he doesn't even have one!"

"Yes, he does!"

My hands are gripping the edge of the table. I have to fight the urge to pounce out of my seat and tackle Eleanor to the ground.

I didn't mean to spill the beans. But after the way Jasper's treated me, and hearing Eleanor talk about him like he's some prize in a funfair—like he's up for grabs—I lost control.

Comprehension washes over Eleanor's face. She lifts her head and stares at me.

"Is it...?" she asks, then suddenly sure of herself. "It's you."

I force myself to let go of the table, shaking my head.

"No, that's not what I meant, I'm not—"

"*You're* Jasper's mate."

I slip my legs out from under the table and stand.

"You're crazy, that's not possible." I back away. "It's like you said. He doesn't have a mate."

"Max, wait—"

"I need to use the bathroom, sorry." I turn and scamper.

The second I'm out of there I realize what an idiot I've been. Why couldn't I control myself?

If it gets out that Jasper and I are mates it's over for him...and me.

Society would never accept an alpha who is... Who doesn't have a luna.

I need a minute alone, so I sneak past the overdressed crowds, creeping along the edges of the room, until I find the stairs.

The upstairs hallway is empty. With a sigh, I slump down against the wall, letting my butt sink into the plush carpet.

Of course Jasper can't choose me. As much as it hurts, as much as I wish it could be any other way—I know that he's only doing what he has to.

It's what's best for the pack. In the grand scheme of things, I don't matter.

Suddenly, I'm not angry anymore. I feel sorry for him. This whole time he's known how this was going to end. Maybe that's why he's tried so hard to push me away.

I let my head drop.

Maybe I need to let him go as well.

"Why do you look sad?" Down the hall, Jodie is leaning out of her bedroom door.

I try to give her my best grown-up smile but my jaw starts quivering.

She wanders over and plonks herself down next to me, slipping her little hand into mine.

"I like your dress," I say, sniffing back tears.

Jodie is wearing a yellow gown—it's totally Belle, from *Beauty and the Beast*, inspired.

"Thanks, Melissa chose it for me."

"I like the color."

She shrugs. "I asked for green."

I guess no one in this house is getting the thing they want tonight.

"How come you're up here and not down at the party?"

"Everyone is boring," she says, and I laugh. She's hit the stuffy nail on the head.

"Are you sad because Jasper has to choose a mate?"

"What?" I feel my face flush. "Why would you say that?"

Jodie rests her head on my arm.

"Because Jasper is sad too. He's been boring and mopey for weeks and not fun."

"Jasper...has been sad?"

"Yeah." She sighs, a cute little exhale. "He's sad because he doesn't want to choose a mate."

I swallow. I hope I'm not about to overstep with a ten-year-old.

"Do you... Do you know why he doesn't want to choose a mate?"

"You're silly." Jodie gives my leg a gentle slap. "It's because he likes you."

"He—what? Did he say—"

"There you are," Melissa says, appearing at the end of the hall. "I've been looking for you." Then spotting me, "Oh, hi again."

"Hey." I nod. Melissa squints at me then Jodie, putting her hands on her hips.

"What are you doing up here, sweetie?"

"I was in my room playing Raya," Jodie says.

Melissa looks at me and rolls her eyes.

"Well, your brother is about to make his big announcement. Would you like to come back downstairs?"

"Not really."

I can't help but chuckle.

"Max doesn't want to either."

"Is that right?" Melissa asks, shooting me a quizzical look. "Well, he can stay up here if he likes. You, little miss, need to come with me, now."

Melissa puts out a hand and Jodie sighs; she stands reluctantly.

"You okay?" Melissa asks.

I scrunch up my mouth and give her a little nod.

"Don't be sad, Max," Jodie says, swishing her hips from side to side. "My brother is a big dummy sometimes."

Melissa does an exacerbated head roll and then ushers Jodie down the hall. "Why would you say that? Come on, you." Then turning back one last time, "Enjoy the party, Max. Don't stay up here too long."

As soon as they're gone, I press my hands into the wall behind me and stand. The announcement is happening now. If I'm going to be rejected in front of the pack's best and brightest I should at least be there when it happens.

Downstairs the house is empty. The living room has been vacated and a crowd has formed outside, facing the stage.

Feeling numb and empty and suddenly hopeful and completely sad and wrecked and tired and more awake than ever, I make my way to the garden.

I stand on my toes to peer over the tops of people's heads. Jericho is on the stage behind a microphone. Melissa is standing off to the side, holding hands with Jodie.

Jasper is standing behind his father, his head hanging low.

Jericho is talking but I can't hear anything. Sounds are muffled like I'm underwater.

To my left, Katie is standing between Todd and Simon with her arms crossed. They all look miserable.

Suddenly, everyone is applauding and Jasper steps up to the microphone. The world comes rushing back, too loud and too real.

"Hello, everyone," Jasper begins. Reverb from the sound system echoes across the crowd. He takes a moment to clear his throat. "Thank you all for coming this evening. The Harvest Moon is a special time in our society."

He's fiddling anxiously with a ring on his left index finger. He looks nervous. But even now I have to admit he looks handsome in his suit.

He's still my prince...for a couple minutes more.

"For me this time of year is particularly special," he continues. "This was my mother's favorite season. She loved to see the leaves changing color."

I picture Jasper as a kid and can't help but grin. I bet he was adorably moody.

"Every year on the eve of the Harvest Moon, we would light lanterns, make a wish, and send them into the sky. When I think back on those nights, they're some of my happiest memories."

The firelight sparkles in his eyes as he takes a breath. I know what's coming and I'm still not ready for it.

"It gives me great"—he coughs—"great pleasure to announce that this Harvest Moon all my wishes are coming true."

For the first time I notice Olivia waiting at the edge of the stage. She's whispering to herself, as if she's amping herself up for a big game.

"Ladies and Gentlemen, this year I have found my mate. The person who will become the future luna of our pack."

The crowd is silent, eagerly leaning forward.

They have no idea what's really going on.

"Please give a round of applause for my mate, Olivia Castillo!"

The future Mrs. Apollo takes a breath and walks up the few steps to the stage. Jasper holds out a hand for her as she joins him.

Everything begins to tilt. I feel as if the floor has gone out from under me. My knees buckle and I feel like I'm about to pass out.

"Olivia and I have been friends for many years. But it was only recently, at this year's Blue Moon Festival, that we—"

Jasper is cut off by a scream—a brainsplitting, bloodcurdling wail. Before I know what's happening a wolf has leaped into the center of the crowd.

The snarling beast is massive, thick saliva hangs from his curled-back lip. His fangs are yellow but sharp.

The party erupts into chaos.

People run past me screaming, flailing their arms. Women hitch up their dresses and struggle to flee in their heels.

I stand frozen as the wolf spins, snapping his jaws at the dispersing crowd. What is he doing here? Who is he?

Jericho's security forces are already shifting, approaching the intruder, when another scream tears through the commotion.

A second wolf comes hurtling out of the darkness, knocking over a table as it enters the fray.

"Rogues!" someone yells as they run past.

ROGUES?! What are rogues doing here? Why now?

A third rogue howls and barges into one of the fires. His shoulder collides with the brazier, toppling it over and sending sparks flying.

I don't know where to look when another two rogues come stalking out of the shadows. There are at least five of them, but who knows how many are still out there, waiting for their moment to strike.

Guests begin to shift, reducing their tuxedos and gowns to scraps, and join the security team who are already engaged with the invaders.

The party has become a war zone. Fire is spreading to the tablecloths, sending thick black smoke into the air. Everywhere I look, wolves are fighting, snapping, and barking like mad.

I can't move. I'm in shock. One second I'm about to be rejected by my mate and the next the alpha's house has been overrun with rogues.

What is going on?

Up ahead, Jericho is shouting at Melissa, telling her to get Jodie somewhere safe. Olivia is pulling a knife from her heeled boot, ready to fight. Jasper is nowhere to be seen.

Where is he?

I can't move until I know where he is.

A table goes up in flames to my right and smoke blocks out the light of the moon.

Todd and Simon have shifted and are protecting Katie.

All around me fire and fighting rage. Wolves collide, tearing at each other's flesh. Blood spurts across the white flooring.

Am I dreaming? This was supposed to be a party, now it's an apocalyptic nightmare.

I stare at the frenzy, knowing I should shift or run or do something...and then...

"Max!"

I hear my name and spot Jasper running toward me.

What is he doing? Another fire topples, collateral damage, as two wolves grapple in my periphery. The explosion is too hot and too close.

"Maaaaax!" Jasper cries again.

Is he coming for me...?

Behind Jasper, the wildflower arch explodes into flames. It splits in two and collapses.

The alpha's garden is in complete chaos, but all I can focus on is Jasper, running in my direction.

He calls my name again.

I take a step toward him but rear back, crying out as a sharp pain stabs at the back of my skull. I've been hit. I clutch my head and stumble forward.

The world turns sideways as I crumble to the ground, hitting the dirt hard. Everything blurs and I begin to slip out of consciousness. Shadows close in around the edges of my vision.

I try to stay awake. I try to focus on Jasper. He's nearly here—running with his hand outstretched and his mouth open, calling my name.

I try to lift my hand and reach for his but the shadows close in.

I take one last look at him...and plunge into darkness.

ROGUE SURPRISE

The first thing I notice when I wake up is the smell of salt water. I lift my head as it wafts under my nose. The familiar scent helps pull me back in the direction of consciousness.

The very next thing I notice is the pounding ache on the back of my head.

I groan and move my neck, checking to make sure I still can.

I open my eyes but it takes a minute for things to come into focus. There are no lights on, except a single dim bulb to my right.

Shadows cloud my vision but I'm keenly aware of a strange rocking sensation. *Am I on a boat?*

Beyond the throbbing in my skull is a gentle lapping sound, as if waves are breaking nearby. *I'm definitely on a boat.*

I squint to see better as my eyes adjust. Decking runs under my feet toward a pair of sliding glass doors.

Between the door and me sits a dining table and chairs, enough to seat a party of twelve.

Surrounding the deck are shiny white waist-high walls and beyond them blackness, the night sky and the midnight ocean merging to become one ominous void.

I am on a boat. And not just any boat, a luxury yacht. Not that I've ever been on one before, but I've watched enough reality TV to know one when I see it.

My pulse quickens.

Have I been kidnapped?

Why me? Why would anyone take me?

I lurch forward and am immediately flung back against the waterproof cushions. My hands are strapped to a pole with cable ties.

What is going on?

My lip quivers, even though I tell myself to keep it together. I need to stay calm. But panic is rising in my throat like bile.

A light flicks on inside the cabin, spilling its glow onto the deck—I freeze. My fuzzy eyes have just spotted a dark shape at one end of the dining table.

I squint into the light... It's Alpha Jericho! He's strapped to a chair at the head of the table, as if he's about to have dinner. Except his large head is hanging against his chest. He's out cold.

He's been kidnapped as well. Does this mean he wasn't behind Aisha's abduction?

"Where is she?" a familiar gruff voice asks somewhere behind me. It sounds like one of the rogues from Rogue City. Scarface?

"Said she'd be here by midnight," another scarily familiar voice responds. That's *definitely* Tattoo.

Two of the rogues who kidnapped Aisha are here on the boat!

"He's heavier than he looks," Scarface says, grunting.

Their footsteps thump up some steps behind me and then a body lands with a clump on the deck.

Jasper!

His unconscious form is sprawled over the decking, his hair swept messily across his face, his hands tied behind his back.

They threw him on his face, those assholes!

Scarface and Tattoo stomp onto the deck, grabbing Jasper by the arms and dragging him along. They drop him down against a wall, where he slumps over himself.

First, they abducted Aisha, now Jasper, Jericho, and me. Who are they working for?

"Look out," Peanut—the third rogue musketeer—says, emerging from the cabin with a carving knife in hand. "Here she comes."

She?

The rev of an engine roars into my periphery—a smaller boat maybe? I lean back, trying to hear better. The engine is switched off and a splash of water hits the back of the boat.

Tattoo rushes down the stairs. I hear murmurs and then footsteps. Tattoo lumbers back on deck, moving to stand behind the alpha with Peanut. Scarface lingers at Jasper's side. And finally, their boss, the person they've been waiting for, appears.

"Eleanor?!"

What the *actual* is she doing here?!

And, oops, did I say that out loud?

Suddenly, all the conscious people on the boat are staring at me.

"Oh," she says. "You're awake. I thought you'd be the last to come to."

"Did you know he was awake?" Tattoo asks Scarface and Peanut, who shake their heads.

Eleanor grins and saunters over. She's wearing the same black dress from the party. We can't be too far from the Hamptons if she hasn't had time to change.

She looks like the same old Eleanor, only something is different.

There's a wild sort of excitement in her eyes that makes my legs go wobbly.

"Eleanor, let me go," I say.

She laughs. "But then you'll miss all the fun."

"What are you doing?" I ask.

"Taking what I deserve." She spins to address the rogues. "Wake them up!"

Scarface and Tattoo slap Jericho and Jasper across their faces until they start to wake.

Jericho is the first to open his eyes and immediately begins to struggle.

"Settle down, pet," Eleanor says, leaning over the table. "We gave you a sedative." She turns to me and shrugs. "Never know when the big guy is going to go berserk."

Jericho is trying to speak but his mouth isn't working properly.

"What's the matter?" Eleanor asks Jericho teasingly. "Cat got your tongue? I hope you don't mind us borrowing your yacht, it was just sitting here all empty."

"Dad!" Jasper calls out. He's awake, so apparently he and I didn't warrant a sedative. I don't know whether to be relieved or insulted.

"Jasper," I say.

He turns to face me, his expression completely broken. He pulls at his restraints, grinding his teeth and grunting, but it's no use.

"Those bindings are wolf proof," Eleanor says. "And don't think about shifting or we'll shoot you."

Tattoo pulls out a gun and hands it to her. Jasper stops struggling.

"What do you want?" he asks.

"Me?" Eleanor points at herself. "I just want the same thing as everybody else. Someone to bring home to Daddy."

"You're doing all this for a *mate*?" I ask.

She spins to look at me, barely resembling herself.

"We can't all be as lucky as you, Max. Fate didn't want me to have nice things. They wanted *you* to have them." She points the gun right at my face and I flinch.

Who is this person? I always thought Eleanor was a bit unhinged, but in a type A, high-achiever sort of way, not in a psychopathic killer sort of way.

"I don't understand," I say.

"Of course you don't. The Moon Gods have given you everything."

"What are you talking about, Eleanor?"

"You two know each other?" Jasper asks. His desperate eyes find mine—they're frantic and questioning.

"That's right, pretty boy," Eleanor says. "Max and I became acquainted recently."

She approaches him, pointing the gun at his chest. "You and I, on the other hand, we've known each other our entire lives. And yet somehow Max is the one who can remember my name!"

I catch Peanut snickering behind Eleanor's back, but he stops quickly when she glares in his direction.

"Who am I, Jasper?" she screams in his face. "Who am I?"

He glances at me before turning to Eleanor with an icy glare.

"I don't know."

Eleanor presses her shaking hands against her temples and screams.

"My father works for your father, you asshole!"

At the table, Jericho is studying Eleanor. His face is ketchup red and a vein in the side of his neck looks about ready to blow.

Is his finger twitching?

In my mind I run through all the times Eleanor mentioned her father's proximity to the alpha. She was always quick to drop into conversation how close they were. But I never found out exactly what her father does.

"God! You're so self-involved," she continues. "My father is a good man. He's been driving your father around since before you were born and you can't even recognize his daughter."

"My dad's driver?" Jasper asks, trying to join the dots. "You're his...daughter?"

Eleanor's dad is Jericho's driver? His chauffeur? She made it sound like they were business partners or college chums.

Something clicks into place in my mind. The town car in Rogue City.

"You abducted Aisha," I say.

If I wasn't tied up at gunpoint I might feel a little guilty for having suspected Jericho, but we have more pressing matters to attend to right now.

Eleanor spins around once again. She smiles at me and drags the tip of the gun along her bottom lip.

"I was going to kill her too," she says. "If you hadn't intervened before Daddy could make the trade."

"Why didn't you just have the rogues kill her?" I ask.

Eleanor's shifty eyes dart from side to side. "We couldn't afford it."

I glance at the rogues, Eleanor's goons for hire. How much is she paying them to abduct the alpha and his son?

I feel like I'm taking an algebra test I haven't studied for. So much of this still doesn't make sense. Eleanor's dad paid the rogues to abduct Aisha so that Eleanor could take her out, but why?

"Anyway, your little interruption in Pittsburgh didn't matter in the end. Killing Aisha wouldn't have done much good." Eleanor takes a step closer to me as lightning strikes out over the ocean.

"Why?" I ask.

"Because I kidnapped the wrong wolf. Whoopsie."

A cold chill of recognition runs down my spine.

Eleanor thought Aisha was Jasper's mate. She wants to *kill* Jasper's mate...but that means...me.

"I'm glad we had our little heart-to-heart earlier," she says. "Cleared up a few things."

My voice catches in my throat but I force myself to ask the question, "Why do you want to kill Jasper's mate?"

"Isn't it obvious? To take your place."

What?! SHE wants to be with Jasper?

God, I wish she would stop flailing that gun around.

"That's not how it works," Jasper says.

"Isn't it?" Eleanor asks. "You were going to reject poor little Max and choose someone else anyway. Gosh, what privilege! Some people get to choose whoever they want to be their mate! Must be nice."

"What I mean is," Jasper sneers, "you can't just replace him. I have to mark you. And that will never happen."

"You'll choose me," she says, then levels the gun at me. "Or I'll kill him."

My eyes lock with Jasper's and I can feel the energy flickering between us. I know he's trying to think of a way to save me without sacrificing the mate bond. I can feel it. But Eleanor's gun isn't giving him too many options.

"So make your choice," Eleanor says.

Jasper glances at me, his face stricken with panic and confusion. I shake my head just enough for Jasper to see. At this point I'd rather be shot than lose our bond.

"Choose!" Eleanor yells. Her finger hovers over the trigger; she moves to pull it...but has to dive out of the way as the dining table flies across the room, crashing against the wall and smashing into a million shards.

Eleanor jumps back and Alpha Jericho, torn free from his restraints, steps in her direction. His fists are clenched and his muscles are bulging like nothing I've ever seen.

"That's enough!" his voice thunders.

In an instant, Eleanor has her gun trained on him, and her three rogue henchmen step forward, pulling knives from their belts.

"Eleanor," Jericho says, trying to speak calmly. "My son may not know you, but I do. Your father is a good man; he has worked for me for a very long time and he wouldn't want you to do this."

She scoffs. "Who do you think paid for the rogue entourage?"

Jericho scans the faces of the rogues. All three are staring at him like they're hungry and he's the Thanksgiving turkey.

"We had to save for a long time on my dad's pitiful salary," Eleanor says. "Lucky for us you've pissed these rogue creeps off so much they were willing to cut us a deal second time round."

"We can work this out," he says. "You're obviously confused."

"Confused about what?"

"My son doesn't have a mate."

It begins as a scoff, then becomes a giggle, and then finally Eleanor erupts into a full-on cartoon-villain-style cackle. Jasper and I glance at each other.

Is she about to spill our secret?

"You don't know?!" she asks.

Jasper turns to his father looking more afraid than he did when wild Eleanor had a gun pointed at him.

"Jasper and Max are mates," she says. "That's why we're all here! Unorthodox, I know, but they make a cute couple if you think about it."

Jericho doesn't look my way, but he stares at his son with more intensity than a supernova.

Eleanor chuckles. "It's a shame I have to split them up."

Jericho growls, his top lip curling upward.

"It's not possible," he says.

"Dad"—Jasper has tears in his eyes—"it is."

Jericho finally glances in my direction, his eyes darting between me and Jasper. Something registers in his expression, some kind of awareness, then confusion, as if he should have known all along, and then disappointment.

"Dad, it's true," Jasper confirms once more before turning to me.

I want to cry, I want to bust out of my restraints and hug him so stupidly hard.

"Max...is my mate."

Despite the gun, and the knife-wielding rogues, and his father's silence...Jasper keeps his eyes locked with mine. He even does this lopsided grin that makes my heart explode.

"You're my mate," he says to me. "The person I'm meant to be with."

I can't wipe my tears away because my hands are still tied, but I feel like I've been freed from some other intangible prison.

I bite my bottom lip and smile back at him.

"I think I'm going to be sick," Eleanor says, destroying the moment. Our attention snaps back to her. "So you see, Jericho, unless you want your whole pack to know what a disappointment Jasper is. You'll let Jasper reject Max and choose me."

"Dad..." Jasper says, shaking his head. Eleanor spins,

pointing the gun in his direction, shutting his mouth.

But his pleading eyes stay locked on his father.

Jericho's expression is unreadable. Disbelief is furrowing his brow, as if he doesn't recognize his own son. As if the person he's raised, the son he's molded to follow in his footsteps and lead the pack, the son who was to become the next alpha, has vanished.

And it's all because of me.

My hands ball into fists. He's going to let Eleanor win.

Why would he choose me when there's so much more at stake?

Letting Jasper mark Eleanor is the only way he can save face with the pack. The only way he can claw back any shred of his ideal future.

"Enough stalling, big guy," Eleanor says. "Make the call."

"You want me to welcome you into my family?" Jericho asks Eleanor. "After you point a gun at my son and his mate."

His...wait... What did he just say?

Jericho takes a step forward. "Not a chance in hell."

Bam!

Jericho folds over clutching the gunshot wound in his stomach. Smoke rises from the barrel of Eleanor's gun. The alpha collapses onto the deck, blood pouring out of him and pooling on the polished floor.

"No!" Jasper cries, struggling to free himself. Scarface slams him back to the floor and Eleanor moves her aim back in my direction.

"What a letdown," she says with a sigh. "Now, Jaspy, you can either make the same mistake as your daddy and let the big guy bleed out while I shoot Max here in the head, or you can reject Max and choose me."

Jasper glances at me. His whole body is slouched in defeat—we both know there's only one choice he can make.

I nod to let him know it's okay, even though nothing is okay right now.

"Fine," he says breathlessly. "You win. I'll do it, just don't kill anyone."

Jericho groans in pain, trying to stand, but he can't. The deck is covered in alpha's blood.

Unable to move, I watch in disbelief as Eleanor signals for Scarface to stand Jasper up and free him of his restraints.

Scarface's knife rips through the cable ties. Jasper rubs his wrists and takes a step forward. There's no point fighting now. Eleanor's gun remains pointed in my direction and her finger never leaves the trigger. Scarface keeps his blade pressed between Jasper's shoulders.

He's led behind Eleanor where he places his hands on her arms.

My face is on fire and I keep trying to shake the tears out of my eyes.

My heart is thumping in my ears, my stomach is in my throat. The boat is rocking like we're in the middle of a maelstrom.

I grind my chattering teeth as Eleanor pulls back the collar of her dress, exposing her neck. She lifts her chin and steels herself for the sting of Jasper's bite.

This is really happening. It's all about to end and there's nothing I can do.

Jasper glances at me one last time, tears dripping down his cheeks, and he mouths the words *I'm sorry*.

I hold my breath as he elongates his fangs, opens his jaw, and bites down...

THE SPIDER IN THE CANOE

A pink light ignites over the water.

Jasper pulls back, retracting his fangs. He hasn't broken the skin on Eleanor's neck. He hasn't marked her.

I breathe a sigh of relief. We all stare across the water where the distracting light is rocketing into the sky.

Is it a firework?

No, it must be a flare. But who shot it?

The flare reaches its peak and explodes, sending shivering trails of pink sparks fizzing amongst the stars.

It's the distraction Jasper needs.

He swiftly elbows Scarface in the head and spins, landing a punch against his jaw with a solid thwack.

Then he turns and knocks the gun from Eleanor's hand, sending it sliding across the deck.

The weapon comes to a stop about a foot away from me.

Scarface is still recovering but his rogue compadres, Tattoo and Peanut—I have to learn these guys' names—are already lurching toward Jasper.

Eleanor is knocked to the ground as the rogues land on

Jasper. He fights them off as best as he can but there are three of them and one of him.

He punches and blocks but they quickly overpower him, forcing him to his knees with their barrage of blows.

Eleanor's eyes catch mine as she searches for her discarded weapon.

I stretch my feet as far as I can, trying to get hold of the gun, while she clambers toward me.

The gun is just out of reach and no amount of stretching is going to bring it closer. Eleanor arrives and wraps her hand around the barrel, but just as she does, a wolf comes flying over the side of the boat!

Eleanor is knocked off her feet and once again the gun is flung from her grasp. Her head hits the decking hard and she drops—knocked out cold.

The wolf huffs and spins to face me.

Is that...? I've never seen this wolf before but there's something familiar about her posture and the way her feet are turned out.

"Aisha?"

She lifts her head before spinning and leaping into the air—as graceful in her wolf form as she is in her human—and lands on Peanut's back.

With her fangs bared, she tears into his shoulder. He rears back, crying out in pain.

Just then another wolf flies over the side of the boat. This one is big, with ginger-colored fur.

Right behind is another, sleeker and darker.

Todd and Simon!

Another follows, this time a female, with a familiar scent. *Olivia!*

Finally, a fifth wolf appears beside me at the top of the stairs—this one petite and blonde.

"Katie?!"

As Simon, Todd, and Olivia join Aisha battling with the rogues, Katie rushes to me and slices through my restraints.

Finally free, I rub my wrists where the cable tie has torn into the skin.

"Thanks," I say, and Katie nods.

I know it's not the right time but it's kind of funny seeing Katie's wolf. It's been awhile since I've seen her shift. I'm sure as hell glad to see her now.

We don't have time for a big reunion because across the deck our friends are doing their best to bring down the rogues. They're not giving the men enough time to shift between dodging attacks, but even in human form, these guys are strong.

Plus, they have knives.

Jasper is slumped in a heap in the middle of the fight and to his right Jericho is lying motionless. Blood is seeping out of him at an alarming rate.

"We need to get them out of here," I say, to which Katie nods. "How did you all get here?"

She lifts her head, gesturing to the back of the boat.

I peer over the back of the seat. A set of steps leads down to a smaller deck just above the lapping water. Tied to the back of the yacht are a speedboat, a tender, and a couple of the Jet Skis from Jasper's garage!

But I can't fit Jasper and Jericho on one Jet Ski.

Then I spot something crucial. The keys to the speedboat are still in the ignition.

"I can get them back to shore in that," I say to Katie. She barks in agreement.

Without needing to confer we both leap into action.

I rush to Jasper while Katie heads for Jericho.

"Jasper!" I shout, rolling him over and shaking him lightly. "Can you walk?"

The fight continues around me. The rogues have seen me but my friends are keeping them from getting too close.

"Jasper!"

"Ungh—yes, I can walk," he says with a grunt, wincing as he sits up.

Katie is tugging at the corner of Alpha Jericho's shirt but he's so large she can't move him.

"Come on," I say, draping Jasper's arm over my shoulder and helping him to his feet. We stagger to

Jericho and it takes all three of us to move the freaking giant.

Jericho is conscious enough and, I guess, strong enough to be able to get down the stairs and into the speedboat. He collapses in the back the second he's on board.

Jasper jumps in after him and as he does a pained howl comes from the top deck.

"Aisha!" Jasper says.

Katie barks and nudges me toward the boat. She's telling us to go. She spins around and leaps up the stairs to help the others take on the rogues.

"I need to help her," Jasper says, taking one step forward and nearly collapsing. I catch him by the shoulders before he falls overboard.

"No, you're too beat up. It's five against three up there and we need to get your dad to a hospital!"

We both turn to look at Jericho, whose eyes are scrunched shut; he's clutching his side. Dark bloodstains drench his clothes.

"Okay," Jasper says.

I jump in and turn the key in the ignition as Jasper takes a seat next to his father in the back. The boat roars to life. I grab the rope connecting us to the yacht, unlooping it and throwing it into the bottom of the boat.

We're free.

The second I'm back at the wheel, I realize...I have no idea how to drive a speedboat.

"It's that one," Jasper says weakly, pointing to a lever.

"Great." I wrap my fingers around the metal bar and push.

The engine whirs louder and we begin to move. There are lights in the distance, which I assume are strung up at the dock near Jasper's house.

I spin the wheel.

We pull away from the yacht, speeding up, but as we do I feel a weight land behind me.

What was that?

I freeze but continue speeding out into the open ocean,

away from the yacht, cutting through the waves like a samurai sword. Slowly, I risk a glance behind.

"Turn the boat around, Max," Eleanor says, struggling to find her balance, but gripping the gun tightly.

Man, she's determined!

Eleanor is standing in the middle of the boat, separating me from Jasper and Jericho. She must have leaped on board just as we were leaving.

"We have to get the alpha to shore," I say.

Despite the gun and the wild, angry look on Eleanor's face, I push the accelerator forward.

She stumbles slightly but keeps her footing.

"Turn this boat around now!" she screams, bringing the gun to eye level and pulling the trigger.

The gunshot sounds like a pirate's cannon. The bullet whooshes past my ear, missing me by less than a foot.

I can't help Jericho if my head's been blown off, so I stop the boat. The engine goes silent and we drift softly in the water. Waves lap calmly at our sides.

"Good boy," she says. "Now take us back to the yacht."

"Why are you doing this, Eleanor?" I ask. "The alpha is dying! I get that you want a mate but why go to all this trouble?"

"You think I care if the alpha dies?" she asks, waving the gun about. "He's not exactly a great guy. Do you know why my dad works for him? Because his father did and his father before him. Because that's what he was born to do. Not because he chose to."

From this distance, I can't hear the fighting on the yacht anymore. The night is calm, only Eleanor is raging into the wind.

"We're wolves, which means we're born into a hierarchy. Some people"—she spins and points the gun at Jasper—"are born into privilege!"

Jasper leans forward, glaring in her direction.

"While some of us are born into nothing. Told that our only purpose is to serve, like we don't even matter. Unless"—she smiles maniacally—"unless we find a mate. Someone who can elevate us from our station. That was my job, that's what my father expected me to do for him and our family."

"Look, I get it. Your dad was putting a lot of pressure on you but—"

"Do you know what my dad told me?" Eleanor asks, although I'm pretty sure she's going to tell me anyway. "He told me not to come home from the festival without a mate, someone with status, who could lift us out of our pathetic lives. When that didn't happen, the only way I could get him to calm the eff down was by coming up with this insane plan."

"Look, Eleanor," I say, "the whole mates thing is messed up, I understand, but you can't—"

"How could you possibly understand?" she snaps. "You lucked out."

"Is that what you think?" I ask. "You think me being mated to another guy, let alone the son of the alpha, is easy?"

I glance at Jasper, who is watching the gun like a hawk.

"It's better than having no mate at all," Eleanor says. "My dad will disown me if I don't come home with Jasper's teeth imprinted on my neck."

"I'm sorry. I'm so sorry your dad is like that. But the truth is we're all under pressure. I haven't even told my family that Jasper and I are mates. You saw the way Jericho reacted. You don't think that's hard?"

"It's not the same!"

I shoot another glance at Jasper. I need to calm Eleanor down. I need to keep her distracted.

"I'm not saying our families are going to disown us," I continue, trying to speak as calmly as possible, which considering the situation is not very. "But if there's one thing I learned at the Blue Moon Festival, it's that fate is tricky."

Finally, Jasper begins to move slowly.

"We're always praying for the Moon Gods to light the path between souls, but what no one tells us is that the road between souls is freaking dangerous. It's like trekking through a damn jungle. It's hard and it hurts..." I catch Jasper watching me. "Sometimes you want to turn and run in the other direction. But the thing is you can't fight it. Because if you do you'll never know how amazing and electric it can be."

Jasper smiles, his brow furrowed apologetically.

"And maybe your path isn't the one you expected," I say, turning my attention back to Eleanor. "But it's your path and it's valid."

Eleanor lets the gun drop to her side.

"I used to think I was different from everybody else, but the truth is we're all the same. We're all just trying to figure things out and do our best despite the pressure we're under."

"I *need* this," Eleanor says through clenched teeth.

"Sure," I say. "I get that. We all do. But there's one other thing I learned at the festival."

"What?" she asks.

"It doesn't matter who I'm in the canoe with. If a spider crawls on my leg we're both going overboard."

"Huh?"

Jasper catches my signal and lunges at Eleanor, knocking the gun from her hand. He tackles her sideways and the gun flies into the air, plopping into the ocean with a splash. It disappears under the surface.

Jasper has Eleanor pinned in the bottom of the boat, despite her kicking and screaming.

I grab a rope and, with Jasper's help, tie her arms behind her back.

"Let me go!" she yells. "You don't understand. This isn't fair!"

"Got anything we can use to muzzle her?" Jasper asks.

In the back, Jericho moans, and Jasper rushes to his side. The alpha is ghostly pale, his forehead is slick with sweat.

"He doesn't look so good," Jasper says with fear in his eyes. "Dad? Dad, can you hear me? Stay with me."

The alpha isn't responding.

"Let's get back to shore," I say and return to the wheel.

"Max," Jasper cries. "Hurry!"

JUST CALL HIM

A week after the Harvest Moon fiasco, Katie comes to visit me.

"Have you heard from Jasper?" she asks, chewing on a steak sandwich my dad made. I stare at her.

She's sitting in my desk chair, swiveling from side to side. Behind her, my phone sits lifeless on the desk.

I haven't heard from Jasper since he disappeared into an ambulance with his father.

Maybe I should have been the bigger wolf and sent the first text. But somehow I haven't been able to bring myself to do it.

Something still stings about the way he was ready to reject me. Why should I be the first to reach out? Why did I expect he might bother to text and see if I'm all right?

"No," I huff and lean back against my bed.

My sandwich sits on a plate on the rug between my feet—untouched.

Am I being a baby? His dad was shot. He's probably been too busy worrying about Jericho's life to check on the guy he met at summer camp.

"Aisha texted me," I say. "Jericho is doing fine. The bullet missed the important organs, and with his wolf-speed healing he'll be back at work in a week or two."

"That's good news," Katie says, chomping.

"She also said that Eleanor is locked up in the pack's holding facility but her dad hasn't been seen since the attack."

"Less good news. Still, great that Jericho is going to be fine."

"Totally." I remember the pain the pack felt when Jasper's mom died. I can't imagine what it would be like if Jericho was to go the same way.

"If his dad is in the clear, why don't you call Jasper then?"

"Has nobody ever told you not to talk with your mouth full?" I laugh but just for a second.

"Don't you think Jasper would want to hear from you after you basically saved his dad's life and stopped Eleanor from forcing him to be her mate?"

I jerk my head up.

"Did I?" I ask. "All I did was drive the speedboat. If you guys hadn't shown up... And that flare, that was a stroke of genius. How did you all manage to get out to the boat anyway?"

"When the rogues attacked the party, Simon, Todd, and I went around the side of the house to hide. We noticed Aisha arriving late and told her what was going on."

"But how did you know where we were?"

"That was all Olivia. She saw the rogues capture you guys, so she followed them to the speedboat. She found the rest of us hiding in the garage and told us what had happened to you. She'd come inside to get a Jet Ski for herself but when Aisha and I heard what had happened we weren't about to let her go alone."

"And Todd and Simon?"

"They weren't about to let me sail off into a rogue's nest."

"What about the other rogues? It looked like there was a whole pack of them."

Katie snorts. "A whole pack of rogues. Isn't that a contradiction?"

I shrug. "There were more than just the three on the

yacht."

"I guess once you guys were captured their part of the mission was complete. The party was pretty quiet by the time we left the garage. I think security probably arrested some of them."

"Well, I'm thankful to all of you. How are things with the boys? Last time I saw you three together it looked a little tense—and that was before the rogue invasion."

Katie rolls her head back and smiles.

"Tense is an understatement."

I wait a beat for her to continue but she's more interested in her sandwich than being forthcoming.

"Okay, a bit stingy with the details."

Katie's face turns Pepto Bismol pink. "Promise you won't judge?"

"After everything that's happened? Cross my heart. Of course not."

She places her plate on the desk.

"Well, they weren't happy that I'd been seeing both of them, so I asked them if they felt like they could give me up and they both said no."

I nod my approval. "Clever boys."

"And then I told them that's kind of how I feel about both of them."

"Did they accept that?"

"Not at first. They were both pretty grumpy, but we've all been hanging out together this last week and, well, they've sort of agreed to let me keep seeing both of them."

My mouth drops to the floor.

"Just until I'm 100 percent sure which is the right one."

"So you're dating two guys at once? *And* they're fine with it?"

Katie bites her lip and nods. "We're kids, right? Why should we have to make decisions that are going to affect the rest of our lives? We're supposed to be reckless."

"You lucky woman!" I can't help laughing, I'm totally happy for my best friend.

"You don't think we're crazy?" she asks.

"No way. It's super modern. Very progressive."

She sighs and picks up her plate again.

"It's just until we all know what's best," she says, bringing the sandwich to her mouth and taking another huge bite. "We'll have to see how things go."

Crumbs trickle from her mouth and onto her lap. I can't believe this girl is my mate-obsessed, Disney-princess-idolizing bestie.

But I'm super proud and crazy happy for her.

"I think you should call Jasper," she says once she's done eating. "I know things weren't great, but after everything that's happened you're still mates."

I let my head drop between my knees.

"Maybe."

"Didn't you say he admitted it on the yacht, in front of Jericho?"

"Yeah, but only because there was a literal gun to my head."

"Still," Katie says, pushing herself toward me and placing her hands on my legs. "That took guts. Who knows how his father will react now that he's back on his feet."

"True."

I hadn't thought about that. Jericho may not have wanted Jasper to wind up mated to a psychotic girl with a gun. But he also didn't look too pleased about his son being mated to another guy.

With Eleanor out of the way, who knows what Jericho is thinking. He could be arranging another lunaworthy mate for Jasper as we speak.

"Jasper could be going through it right now," Katie says.

"I guess I'm so used to Jasper pulling away. How do I know he just doesn't want to hear from me?"

"Trust the Moon Gods," she says with a twinkle in her eye. "Or if not, trust me. It's harder than you'd imagine to give up a mate."

I sigh. Maybe Katie is right. But the thought of having Jasper reject me all over again is too much to bear.

"You going to finish that?" Katie asks, pointing at my sandwich.

I snort-laugh. "It's all yours."

An hour later, Katie has to get home. Her mother—who finally decided on wallpaper for the living room—texts to say the decorators are done. She wants Katie to see the finished product.

"You can come round now," she says, hugging me at the door.

"I can't wait!"

"What about tomorrow? Come for dinner?"

"Sure," I say.

Katie steps outside but glances back. "Call him, Max. You won't regret it."

Once she's gone, I head back up to my room. My phone is still sitting on my desk.

Just call him!

I march to my desk and pick up the phone. The screen is black and I stare at it, willing myself to unlock it.

"Ah!" I scream as it buzzes and lights up. I fumble and nearly drop it. Once the initial shock has passed, I hold it in a shaky hand and stare wide-eyed at the screen.

There's a text from Jasper. I unlock the phone and there, under my one text, he's finally sent a response.

We should talk. Can you come to the house?

"I've been to this house more times in the last few weeks than I ever have in my life," Mom says. The gates to Jasper's mansion swing open gracefully.

I'm sad I won't get to see Katie's new house today. But she was totally understanding when she heard that Jasper had asked me to come around.

"Why did you say Jasper asked you to visit?" Mom inquires.

I chew on the inside of my cheek and try to think of a

good reason. I should have come up with one by now. *Stupid.*

"I think he just wants to say sorry about what happened at the party."

Outside my window the manicured trees whoosh by.

"You haven't told me much about that night."

"It was all kind of a blur," I say. "One second we were at a party and the next the rogues were attacking."

Mom sighs and slows the car a little as we approach the house. I'm sure she'd be a lot more worked up if she knew what had really happened. But I want to spare her and Dad the worry. At least, that's what I'm telling myself.

"I'm just glad you were safe. What did they want, do you think?"

Again, I should have come up with better lies by now. I've managed to get away with a vague explanation so far, but Mom is starting to get suspicious.

"I'm not sure."

We pull up out front and I unbuckle my seat belt, reaching for the door handle.

"Why does he want to apologize to you in particular, sweetie?" Mom asks, and I freeze.

"What?"

"Is he asking everyone to visit in person? Seems like that would take a really long time."

"I don't know, Mom," I moan.

"And you were hiding in the garage the whole time, right?"

I roll my eyes, but inside I'm panicking.

"Maybe he just feels bad because he invited me."

"In that case, it's a very nice gesture. He must be an extremely caring young man."

I scoff. Why didn't I take a taxi?

"I guess it's because we're..." I don't know how to finish this sentence.

"You're what, sweetie?"

I may be having a heart attack, or at least this is what I imagine one feels like.

"We're friends," I say, shrugging. "Me and Jasper

are...friends."

It's not exactly the truth, but it's closer than I've come before.

"I didn't know that," she says.

"He didn't just want my help with the Aisha thing because I was *her* friend. Jasper and I... We hung out a bit, at the festival."

"Oh."

My fingers clasp tightly on the door handle. Heat rises in my cheeks.

Mom is staring at me. Her eyes have gone all glossy like they do during the soppy part of her rom-coms.

Why is she looking at me like that?

Finally, she smiles.

"Well, he's very lucky to have a friend like you."

"Uh—thanks," I say. "Can I go now?"

Mom nods and I finally open the door.

"Mom," I say, glancing back, "love you."

"Love you too, sweetie. Always."

I think Mom might be on the verge of shedding a tear, so as quickly as possible, I shut the door and head for the house.

With my shoulders hunched and my hands in my pockets, I wait for Melissa to answer the doorbell.

"This is becoming a habit," she says, grinning as she ushers me inside.

She's right. This house is weirdly familiar to me now, in a way I never thought it would be. I don't even look twice at the oversized abstract art on the walls, or the fireplace encased in a glass box.

"Is Jasper in his room?" I ask.

"Yes, but there's someone else who'd like to speak to you first."

"There is?" *Gulp.*

Melissa guides me through the house to a stairway I've never been up before. She walks a step ahead of me onto the second floor.

I walk down a corridor, with a glass wall on one side looking out toward the ocean, and a row of doors on the other.

We come to a stop at a dark-green door. Melissa knocks—two sharp taps with her knuckles—before turning the handle and leading me inside.

Instantly, my shoulders pull back and my spine straightens. Alpha Jericho rises from his chair and places his hands flat on his desk.

"Alpha...Jericho," I stammer, bowing my head instinctively.

"Hello, Max."

THE PATH BETWEEN SOULS

"I'll leave you to it," Melissa says, touching my shoulder, then heading back out into the hall, closing the door behind her.

Once she's gone the room feels giant. The silence has weight.

"Thank you for coming to see me, Max," Jericho says, the deep bass tone of his voice vibrating in my chest like a subwoofer.

Does he think I came here just to speak with him? *Sorry, sir, I actually came to see if your son wants to date me.*

He lowers his eyes and lifts a brow knowingly as if he just read my mind.

"I'm sure you have other business to attend to," he says. "So I won't keep you long."

Can he read my mind?!

I glance around the room. Three of the walls are made entirely out of glass. Perfect blue skies surround us. With all these windows it almost feels like we're floating.

The decor is minimal, which only adds to the immense

openness of the space. The colors are muted—grays and deep olive greens. A monochrome rug lies in the middle of the room, with the square footage of a small country.

Jericho's desk is backlit by the sun streaming in through the glass. The shadows make it appear like a stone altar. The kind they tie sacrificial lambs to.

"Please," he says, gesturing to one of the uncomfortable-looking chairs in front of him. "Sit."

On his order, my feet move. He watches me with a keen, discerning eye.

Is he judging me by my walk? Am I swinging my arms too much?

Slumping down into one of his chairs, I wrap my arms around myself and look up at my alpha.

He grins and whispers conspiratorially, "Don't worry. I won't bite."

"Oh," I laugh awkwardly and force my arms to uncross themselves.

Jericho chuckles and I start to feel a little calmer. He sits, placing his gargantuan arms on the desk and linking his fingers so they make the shape of a chapel.

"I wanted to say thank you, Max. For what you did the other night."

I shuffle awkwardly in my seat.

"It was nothing really."

"Not at all," he says. "You were very brave. I might not be here right now if it weren't for you."

"Well," I say, grinning like a weirdo, "I only did what anyone would do. I'm glad you're feeling better."

Jericho turns his head ever so slightly and stares at me from the corner of his eye.

I grip the arms of the chair. My palms have become more clammy than clam chowder.

"I also want to apologize," he says.

This statement hits me for six. What could the alpha possibly have to apologize for?

"What...why?" I stammer.

"For weeks now I've sensed that something has changed in Jasper's life. Something important. And I think—no, I know I had an inkling of what that change might be."

Oh Moon Gods, he's talking about me!

"But I couldn't bring myself to face the truth, so I ignored it. I even tried to force his hand."

A shadow crosses Jericho's face and for a second his shave looks a little less close, the lines around his eyes are a little more ingrained.

"You're a good man. Your parents have raised you well."

"Yeah, they're great."

"Indeed." He nods.

"You...know my parents?"

Jericho leans forward slightly, the seams of his dress shirt strain as his muscles bulge.

"I know every wolf in my pack. Some more intimately than others. But I care for all of them, without discriminating."

His brow rises when he says the word *discriminating*, like he wants me to catch his drift. I was never very good at baseball, so I just stare at him blankly.

Suddenly, Jericho leans back, erupting into a hearty chuckle.

"We wolves are not as prehistoric as you may think," he says mid laugh. "I should have seen what was right under my nose. No, you aren't what I pictured when I imagined the person my son would wind up with for a mate."

There it is, the cards on the table.

"But you've proven to me that you have what it takes to support my son."

The heat in my cheeks could incinerate solid steel. I haven't even told my parents about Jasper and me, and here is the alpha of the pack giving me his blessing—wait, is he giving his blessing?

"Thank you, sir."

Wait, is this why Jasper asked me to come here? Because we have the go-ahead from his dad?

Suddenly, I *reeeaaaally* want to have that talk with Jasper.

"You're a good kid, Max."

"Thanks...?"

"You probably think I'm overly tough on my son."

"I...I..." I splutter and throw my hands about. If he can read my mind then he already knows what I think of his tough-love approach to parenting.

"But I want you to know," he continues, "I'm hard on Jasper because I need to be. Because one day he will be the one sitting behind this desk. Leading this pack. Last week we came closer to that eventuality than I'd like."

Jericho locks his eyes on mine and I feel like a statue, frozen by his stare.

"Being an alpha isn't easy," he says, not breaking eye contact. "And neither is being mated to one."

I hold my breath and nod my head like a stunned guppy. "Uh-huh."

Then a grin creeps into the corners of Jericho's lips. "But I have a feeling you might be up to the task."

I guffaw. Is he serious?

"I know you'll take good care of him, Max. I've seen what you're capable of." He leans forward one last time. "Don't let me down."

I shake my head from side to side. "No way, sir. I... I won't, I promise."

Alpha Jericho nods and smiles. "Good. Now go and find him."

"Yes, sir," I say, nearly tripping as I stand and back out of the room. "And thanks, again!"

The second I'm out of the alpha's office I start running. I'm already puffed by the time I get back to the entrance hall, heading for Jasper's room.

Why is this house so freaking big?!

I arrive at his doorway, bent over and out of breath.

"Max!" Jodie yells excitedly and rushes toward me. She grabs me around the waist and hugs me tightly. "I'm so glad you're okay!"

After a second of hesitation, I hug her back. Apparently, we're best friends now, which is fine with me.

"I'm glad to see you're okay," I say. I look into Jasper's room, hoping to find him watching my interaction with

Jodie, smiling. But instead my heart sinks.

Jasper isn't here.

"Hey, dude," Aisha says. She's sitting on Jasper's bed with a stack of UNO cards in front of her.

"What are you doing here?" I ask, prying Jodie off and heading inside.

"I came to visit Jasper and this little monster. I wanted to make sure everyone was doing fine after the whole—" She mouths the words, *rogue thing*.

"We're doing fine," Jodie chimes in. "My daddy got hurt but Max saved him."

I put my hands up in surrender. "Whoa, I didn't do that much."

"Jasper says you drove the boat and helped him stop that crazy girl."

"Did he say that?" I ask.

"Uh-huh!"

"You're a real hero," Aisha says, grinning at me.

"Well then so are you," I say. "You rode in to save our butts like the fudging coast guard!"

Jodie hops back on the bed and Aisha takes my hand.

"It's really nice to see you," she says.

"You too," I say, then nudging Jodie's shoulder, "and you."

"How is everything?" I ask Aisha as Jodie picks up her cards and starts rearranging them.

"Fine," she says. "Rehearsals are in full swing, although my left ankle is a little sore from where one of those guys kicked it."

"At least they're locked up now, right?"

"Amen to that."

"And Troy? How's he doing?"

"You can't keep him down for long." She throws her hair over her shoulder casually. "He's back to his normal self, chatting about biomolecular chemistry or biomes or echolocation something or other."

"Still making ramen?" I ask, remembering how delicious Aisha's boyfriend's cooking is.

"Always." She smiles and tilts her head, glancing at me

sideways. "But we're not the ones you came to visit, are we?"

I shove my hands in my pockets, suddenly bashful.

"Not that it isn't a mega happy surprise," I say. "But I was hoping to chat with Jasper."

"Thought as much." Aisha winks at me. "He's down at the beach."

"That's weird. He knew I was coming."

"Melissa told him you'd been summoned to his dad's office and he—"

"He freaked out, didn't he?"

She holds up a finger and a thumb with a gap between them the size of a grain of rice. "Little bit."

We both laugh as we share a knowing look. Then Aisha rubs my arm and says, "Go get him, baby."

I smile and head for the ocean.

The wind is rustling across the grass-topped dunes. I follow the path between them, letting my shoes sink into the sand.

The smell of salt is fresh and the roar of the waves is constant. The sun is beginning to set, casting hues of pastel orange, pink, and violet across the sky.

Jasper is standing halfway down the shore, facing the horizon—his hair ruffled by the ocean breeze.

"Jasper!"

He looks back over his shoulder and spots me.

"You're here," he says, as if he's surprised I've stuck around. His eyes are glinting like the sea, catching flecks of sunlight.

"Yeah." I rub the back of my neck.

"I thought maybe my dad would—"

"You thought he'd scare me off," I say. Jasper nods subtly. "Nah. The only thing I'm scared of is spiders."

He smiles lightly but doesn't say anything. For a moment we stand silently as the waves lap at the shore. I eye him questioningly.

"You wanted to talk."

"Yes," Jasper says. "I wanted to apologize, Max."

Okay, not what I was expecting.

"For what?"

"I haven't been—good to you."

He isn't wrong, but hearing him say it like that makes me feel awkward. I shrug as if to say it's fine.

"No, Max, I haven't," he says, more emphatically. "The truth is I knew who you were to me—or who you would be—the day we met. When you ran into me in the city. I could sense it from the very beginning...that we would be mates."

Jasper's throat moves as he gulps between sentences.

"But I couldn't bring myself to admit it, because I was too scared. I was scared of disappointing my father, but mostly I was scared that I would get hurt."

Jasper's eyes are staring into mine and I start to feel the beach drifting away into my periphery. The sound of the waves dies down and all that's left is him and me and the sand beneath my sneakers.

"When my mother died I didn't know if I would ever be able to feel good again," Jasper says, his eyes darting to the ground. "It took years until I finally felt even the slightest bit okay. Then you showed up in my life and I saw a glimpse of how...good things could be. But then I remembered what it felt like to have that taken away. And I wanted to avoid feeling that again at all costs. So I pushed you away instead."

"You had a lot on your plate," I say quietly.

"That's no excuse," he states firmly. "I've been mean and condescending. I've done everything that I can to try and make you see that I'm not someone worth hanging around for."

Jasper keeps balling his hands into fists, opening and closing them.

"I've been an asshole," he says, which I can't help but laugh at. Jasper chuckles back at me.

Then he takes a step forward.

"But what I've come to learn—what you've shown me,

Max—is that I can't pretend this doesn't exist. I can't pretend that you don't exist, and I can't ignore these feelings. Hurting you, I was only hurting myself."

My fingertips are tingling, my arms are longing to reach out and hold him. My heart is racing and my breaths are so shallow I'm light-headed.

Jasper bows his head a little and stares into my eyes.

"You are my mate, Max. You're—"

Before he can finish I kiss him. I press my lips against his.

I've caught him off guard and his lips squash awkwardly against mine. But then he relaxes, parting his lips and welcoming me in.

One of my hands finds the side of his face and the other his hip.

We find our rhythm quickly, despite never having kissed before, as if we were made for kissing each other.

His hair is soft and luscious under my fingers and I crumple slightly as his hands wrap around me—one around my waist and the other over my shoulder. He pulls me closer.

Our mouths move in unison, his lips soft like marshmallows. The sweet, cherry flavor on his tongue floods my senses. Stars erupt behind my eyes, fireworks explode and crackle in my stomach, like I've eaten a whole bag of popping candy.

My body is burning but it feels good—no, it feels freaking amazing!

This kiss is better than any roller coaster I've ever been on, more satisfying than any slice of pepperoni pizza, more thrilling than any video game, or song, or movie.

No wonder people are obsessed with mates. They get to do this whenever they want!

Jasper's hand digs into the small of my back and a happy little moan escapes my mouth. I could get lost in this kiss. I could drown in it. And then...just when I'm starting to think I *might* drown, Jasper pulls back.

The taste of him lingers on my tongue. His hand remains on the side of my face, his thumb stroking my cheek.

"Max," he says.

I grin. "Hi."

We both chuckle, and I take the collar of his white button-down between my thumb and forefinger and pull on it gently.

This moment is more perfect than I could have imagined.

Then a cloud crosses Jasper's face and his expression turns dark. He drops his hands and turns away from me.

"What's wrong?" I ask.

"You are my mate, I can admit that now," he says gravely. "But you have to know we can't be together."

I start shaking my head; my body starts trembling.

"No," I say. "No, Jasper. You always do this. Whenever we get close you pull away. Don't do that now."

"I know," he says without turning around. "I'm sorry."

"I won't let you this time. Not after everything that's— not after that kiss!"

He takes a step away and I panic. I reach out and grab his arm, spinning him violently so that he has to face me. There are tears in his eyes as he stares at the sand.

"I won't let you, Jasper! Do you hear me!? We're mates!"

"I know!" he says, pulling his arm back.

"Then what?" I ask. "What's your problem?"

"It's because we're mates that we can't be together."

The beach is swirling around me, I feel like I've been on a high-speed Ferris wheel and I'm going to be sick.

"That doesn't make any sense."

"It does, Max. You saw what happened to you, to my father, to Aisha! All that happened because people were using my mate to get to me."

Jasper won't stop staring at the ground. *Coward.*

"And they won't stop. People will always want what I have. They'll always come for me."

"So?!"

"Isn't it obvious, Max? Being with me is dangerous. Too dangerous. I can't put you in that kind of danger."

I take a step back. He can't be serious, can he?

"Isn't that my decision?" I ask, as my heart is swallowed by a black hole.

"No," he says, finally looking me in the eye. "It's mine. And I've already made my mind up. There's no use arguing."

"Is this because you're afraid to let people know that you're into guys? Because you're afraid to let people down? Because—"

"The only person I'm afraid to let down is you. And I will. I know I will."

"How can you know that?"

"Because that's what I do! Life with me will only lead to disappointment for you."

"No..."

My legs turn to jelly beneath me and it takes all of my strength not to crumple in the sand.

"Max." Jasper steps forward, reaching out as if he knows I could collapse at any second. I knock his hand away.

"How can you do this?" I ask.

He pauses.

"Because I don't know what I'd do if anything bad ever happened to you."

He takes two steps forward until his face is an inch away. He places one hand on either side of my head and rests his forehead against mine.

"I don't want to lose you," I say.

"I don't want to lose you either," he says. "That's why this is the only option. It's better if our connection remains a secret."

I sniff back more tears, wishing he would reconsider, wishing he would just kiss me again.

"I'm sorry, Max," he says, and a tear streaks a silvery trail down his cheek. "This is the only way to keep you safe."

Gently, he places a kiss on my forehead—a kiss full of the words he wants to say but can't, all the promises he wishes he could make but won't.

"See you around," he says, then turns to leave.

I watch him walk back up the shore.

"So that's it?" I call out over the noise of the wind.

Jasper stops and looks back.

"This is the way it has to be," he says.

I look away and bite my lip to stop it from trembling.

"Hey Max, will you do me a favor?"

Jasper is staring at me keenly, but he's crazy if he thinks I owe him anything.

"Stay safe, okay?"

I huff and look away.

"Hey, don't be a bonehead."

I roll my eyes.

"Promise me," he says. "You'll be careful?"

Knowing he cares is little consolation, but there's no use fighting him any longer.

"Okay," I say. "I promise."

"Good."

His expression softens and he nods once before he continues walking. In a second, Jasper disappears behind the dunes. My stare lingers on his footprints in the sand.

I turn to face the ocean and sit. I pull my knees up to my chest and watch as the waves come and go. I scoop up the sand and let it trickle through my fingers.

The sky is halfway between day and night. A deep-navy shadow is swallowing up the pastel light. On the horizon, the moon is peeking above the water, casting its glow across the waves, lighting a path out to sea—a yellow flickering trail, dancing on the water's surface.

The path between souls.

I feel as if I could walk across it, all the way to the moon's craggy surface. Away from here.

But I won't.

Because the moon has already shown me my path.

My fate is behind me, on the way back to his bedroom—his mind already moving on from thoughts of *us*.

Even though Jasper has pushed me away time and again, sitting here, I know I can't give up.

Some other wolves might move on, go home and forget they've had the craziest summer of their lives. Chalk it up to experience. Who cares about mates anyway, right?!

Not me. I can't do that. Not when my path is laid out before me.

I'll follow that path with blind persistence. I'll chase him to the ends of the world if I have to.

Jasper may think our story is over.

But he's never met a wolf like me.

Max and Jasper will return in *Chasing...The Alpha's Son.*

ABOUT THE AUTHOR

Penny Jessup has been writing from an early age. Whether it's *Riverdale* fan fiction or werewolf romances, she's cut her teeth online and now works as a freelance copywriter. She has a bachelor's in creative writing and lives in upstate New York with her partner and their dog, Taco. She loves anime, baking while listening to her favorite podcasts, and hiking in the woods near her house. This is her first novel and, hopefully, the first in a long-running series.